SUNBURN

A NOVEL

LAURA LIPPMAN

FABER & FABER

First published in the UK in 2018
by Faber & Faber Limited
Bloomsbury House, 74–77 Great Russell Street
London WC1B 3DA
This paperback edition first published in 2018

First published in the United States in 2018
by William Morrow, an imprint of
Harper Collins Publishers, 195 Broadway
New York, NY 10007

Printed and bound by CPI Group (UK) Ltd, Croydon, CR0 4YY

Designed by Fritz Metsch

The right of Laura Lippman to be identified as author
of this work has been asserted in accordance with Section 77
of the Copyright, Designs and Patents Act 1988

A CIP record for this book
is available from the British Library

ISBN 978–0–571–33567–1

2 4 6 8 10 9 7 5 3 1

Laura Lippman has been awarded every major prize in crime fiction. Since the publication of *What the Dead Know*, each of her hardbacks has hit the *New York Times* bestseller list. A recent recipient of the first ever Mayor's Prize, she lives in Baltimore, New Orleans and New York City with her family. To find out more about Laura, visit www.lauralippman.com

Further praise for *Sunburn*:

'When you reach for one of Lippman's books, you know you will be lost to your world for a bit, and totally immersed in hers.' *Daily Mail*

'A pacy, pithy modern take on the noir tradition – and influenced by the old movies that the heroine loves – this is terrific entertainment.' *Sunday Mirror*

'What, as a certain Dr Freud asked, do women want? . . . Rich philosophy for a noir tale to sustain, but Lippman handles it with masterly flair, delivering a thrilling succession of revelations and perfectly weighted twists in a fluent prose liberally salted with side-of-the-mouth wit and wisdom.' *Irish Times*

'Cool and twisty.' *New York Times Book Review*

'Laura Lippman continues to push the envelope of modern crime-writing. *Sunburn*, her take on noir, may be her nerviest novel yet, an unsparing look at how lovers can betray one another.' Harlan Coben

'Spellbinding . . . This corkscrew of a book, with its psychological insights and sensual charisma, proves once again that Ms. Lippman, as a writer, is *sui generis*.' *Wall Street Journal*

'Fast-paced and unpredictable, *Sunburn* is a smart, sly riff on love in a world of trouble that's puzzling until the very last piece falls into place.' *O Oprah Magazine*, Best Books to Read This Month

'*Sunburn* oozes with domestic unease, with women all around upending the natural order of things . . . In a novel this good, it's unfair to reveal too much of the plot or its twists, but suffice it to say *Sunburn* has more than a few, all of them satisfying.' *Los Angeles Times*

'Modern noir at its best, it will delight old-movie lovers, satisfy suspense readers, and reward Lippman's legion of fans.' *Library Journal*

'You can tell how much fun the author had updating the classic noir tropes, and it's contagious. Plotty, page-turning pleasure.' *Kirkus Reviews*

'This is Lippman at her observant, fiercest best, a force to be reckoned with in crime fiction.' *Publishers Weekly*

'Ingeniously constructed and extremely suspenseful, the novel keeps us guessing right up to its final moments. Lippman is a popular and dependable writer, and this homage to classic noir showcases a writer at the height of her powers.' *Booklist*

'A joy to read . . . A classic noir transplanted to the 1990s

with a beguiling femme fatale at the centre of the action.'
Bookseller, Editor's Choice

'Steamy, twisty and dripping with psychological suspense, it's no wonder that *Sunburn* is one of 2018's most-wanted crime novels.' *Saga*

PART ONE

SMOKE

1

It's the sunburned shoulders that get him. Pink, peeling. The burn is two days old, he gauges. Earned on Friday, painful to the touch yesterday, today an itchy soreness that's hard not to keep fingering, probing, as she's doing right now in an absentminded way. The skin has started sloughing off, soon those narrow shoulders won't be so tender. Why would a redhead well into her thirties make such a rookie mistake?

And why is she *here*, sitting on a barstool, forty-five miles inland, in a town where strangers seldom stop on a Sunday evening? Belleville is the kind of place where people are supposed to pass through and soon they won't even do that. They're building a big bypass so the beach traffic won't have to slow for the speed trap on the old Main Street. He saw the construction vehicles, idle on Sunday, on his way in. Places like this bar-slash-restaurant, the High-Ho, are probably going to lose what little business they have.

High-Ho. A misprint? Was it supposed to be Heigh-Ho? And if so, was it for the seven dwarfs, heading home from the mines at day's end, or for the Lone Ranger, riding off into the sunset? Neither one makes much sense for this place.

Nothing about this makes sense.

Her shoulders are thin, pointy, hunched up so close to her ears that they make him think of wings. The front of her pink-and-yellow sundress is quite a contrast, full and round. She carries herself as if she doesn't want to attract any male attention, at least not tonight. On the front, he can't help noticing as he slides on a barstool, she's not so pink. The little strip of skin showing above the relatively high-necked dress has only the faintest hint of color. Ditto, her cheeks. It is early June, with a breeze that makes it easy to forget how strong the sun is already. Clearly a modest type, she wears a one-piece, so there's probably a deep U of red to go with those shoulders. Yesterday, fingerprints pressed there would have left white marks.

He wonders if she's meeting someone here, someone who will rub cream into the places she can't reach. He would be surprised if she is. More surprised if she's up for leaving with a stranger, not shocked by either scenario. Sure, she gives off a prim vibe, but those are the ones you have to watch out for.

One thing's for sure: she's up to *something*. His instincts for this stuff can't be denied.

He doesn't go in hard. He's not that way. Doesn't have to be, if that doesn't sound too vain. It's just a fact: he's a Ken doll kind of guy, if Ken had a great year-round tan. Tall and muscular with even features, pale eyes, dark hair. Women always assume that Ken wants a Barbie, but he prefers his women thin and a little skittish. In his downtime, he likes to hunt deer. Bow and arrow. He goes to the woods of western Maryland, where he can spend an entire day sitting in a tree, waiting, and he loves it. Tom Petty was wrong about that. The waiting's not the hardest part. Waiting can be beautiful, lush, full of possibility. When he was a kid, growing up in the Bay Area, his ahead-of-the-curve beat parents put him in this study at

4

Stanford where he was asked to sit in a room with a marshmallow for fifteen minutes. He would get two if he didn't eat the one while he waited. He had asked, *How long do I have to sit here for three?* They laughed.

He didn't learn until he was in his twenties that he was part of some study that was trying to determine if there's a correlation between success and a kid's ability to manage the desire for instant gratification. He still thinks it was unfair that the experiment wasn't organized in a way that allowed a kid to get three marshmallows for sitting twice as long as anyone else.

He has left two stools between them, not wanting to crowd her, but he makes sure she hears when he orders a glass of wine. That catches her attention, asking for wine instead of beer in a place like this. That was the idea, catching her attention. She doesn't speak, but glances sideways when he asks the blonde behind the bar what kind of wine they serve. He doesn't break balls over the selection, which is red and white. Literally: "We have red and we have white." He doesn't bat an eyelash when they serve him the red cold. Not a sommelier-ordained-sixty-degree cold, but straight-from-the-fridge cold. He takes a sip, summons the barmaid back, and says, oh so politely, "You know what? I'm happy to pay for this, but it's not to my taste. May I have a beer?" He glances at the taps. "Goose Island?"

Another quick sideways flick of her eyes, then back to her own drink—amber, rocks. Wherever she's going tonight, it's not far from here. He looks into his own drink and says out loud, as if to himself: "What kind of an asshole orders red wine in a tavern in Belleville, Delaware?"

"I don't know," she says, not looking at him. "What kind of an asshole are you?"

"Garden variety." Or so his exes—one wife for a span of five

5

years, maybe seven, eight girlfriends, which strikes him as a respectable number for a thirty-eight-year-old man—always told him. "You from around here?"

"Define *from*." She's not playing, she's retreating.

"Do you live here?"

"I do now."

"That sunburn—I just assumed you were someone who got a day or two of beach, was headed back to Baltimore or D.C."

"No. I'm living here."

He sees a flicker of surprise on the barmaid's face.

"As of when?"

"Now."

A joke, he thinks. A person doesn't just stop for a drink in a strange town and decide to live there. Not this town. It's not like she's rolled into Tuscany or Oaxaca, two places he knows well and can imagine a person saying, *Yes, here, this is where I'm going to plant myself.* She's in Belleville, Delaware, with its saggy, sad Main Street, a town of not even two thousand people surrounded by cornfields and chicken farms. Does she have connections here? The barmaid sure doesn't treat her like a local, even a potential one. To the barmaid, blond and busty with a carefully nurtured tan, the redhead is furniture. The barmaid is interested in him, however, trying to figure out whether he's passing through tonight or hanging around.

Which has not yet been determined.

"Let me know if you want someone to give you the skinny on this place," the barmaid says to him with a wink. "It would take all of five minutes."

Barmaids and waitresses who flirt this overtly make him a little nervous. Bringing a man food or beer is intimate enough.

He lets both women alone, drinks his beer, watches the inevita-

6

ble Orioles games on the inevitable TV with the inevitable shimmy in its reception. The team is good again, or, at least, better. As the redhead's third drink reaches its last quarter inch, he settles up, leaves without saying good-bye to anyone, goes to his truck in the gravel parking lot, and sits in the dark. Not hiding because there's no better way to be found than to try to hide.

Ten minutes later, the redhead comes out. She crosses the highway, heads to the old-fashioned motel on the other side, the kind they call a motor court. This one is named Valley View, although there's no valley and no view. The High-Ho, the Valley View, Main Street—it's like this whole town was put together from some other town's leftovers.

He waits fifteen minutes, then enters the little office at the end, and inquires if there's a room, despite the big red VACANCY sign filling the window.

"How many nights?" the clerk, a pencil-necked guy in his thirties, asks.

"Open-ended. I can give you a credit card, if you like."

"Funny. You're the second person today to ask for an open-ended stay."

He doesn't have to ask who the first one was. He makes a note to himself that the chatty clerk will be chatty about him, too.

"You need my credit card?"

"Cash is fine, too. If you commit to a week, we can give you the room for two hundred fifty. We don't get many people Monday through Friday. But, you know, there's no kitchenette, no refrigerator. You gotta eat your meals out or bring stuff in that won't spoil." He adds, "If the maid sees stuff sitting out, she'll tell me. I don't want ants or roaches."

"Can I keep a cooler in the room?"

"As long as it doesn't leak."

He hands the credit card over.

"I can give you a better rate if you pay cash," the guy says, clearing his throat. "Two hundred twenty dollars."

Guy's got some sort of scam going, must be skimming the cash payments, but what does he care? He can last a long time in a place that's $220 a week, even if there's no refrigerator or stove.

He wonders how long she can last.

2

She steps out of room 5 into a bright, hot morning, unseasonably hot, just as the weekend at the beach had been, but at least there the breeze from the ocean took the edge off. People said how lucky it was, getting such a hot day in early June, when the water is too cold for anyone but the kids. School not even out yet, lines at the most popular restaurants were manageable. *Lucky,* people kept saying, as if to convince themselves. *Lucky. So lucky.*

Is there anything sadder than losers telling themselves that they're fortunate? She used to be that way, but not anymore. She calls things the way they are, starting with herself.

When Gregg had started talking about a week at the beach, she had assumed a rental house in Rehoboth or Dewey. Maybe not on the beach proper, but at least on the east side of the highway.

Well, they had been close to the beach. But it was Fenwick, on the bayside, and it was a two-story cinder block with four small apartments that were basically studios. One big rectangular room for them and Jani, a galley kitchen, a bathroom with only a shower, no tub. And ants. Wavy black lines of ants everywhere.

"It's what was available, last minute," Gregg said. She amended in her head. *It's what was available, last minute, if you're cheap.* There had to be a better place to stay along the Delaware shore, even last minute.

Jani couldn't sleep unless the room was in complete blackout. So they kept her up late, to nine or ten, because the alternative was to go to bed together at eight, and lie there in the dark without touching. The first night, about 2 A.M., Gregg made a move. Maybe a year or two ago, it would have been sexy, trying to go at it silently in the dark. But it had been a long time since she found anything about Gregg sexy.

"No, no, no, she'll wake up."

"We could give her a little Benadryl."

That had given her pause, made her wonder if she should change her plans, but no, she had to go ahead. The next day, she did ask him if he would really do that, give Jani a Benadryl. He insisted he was joking. She decided to believe him. If she didn't believe him, she would have to stay. And there was no way she could stay.

That was Saturday. She put a gauzy white shirt over her bathing suit, but even that irritated her shoulders. She huddled under the umbrella, shivering as if cold. A bad sunburn can do that, give you chills. Gregg played in the surf with Jani. He was good with her. She wasn't just telling herself that. He was good, good enough, as good as she needed him to be.

They went to the boardwalk, the smaller one up at Rehoboth, which was better for little kids like Jani than the one in Ocean City. Gregg tried to win Jani the biggest stuffed panda he could, but he never got above the second-tier prize. *Do the math,* she wanted to tell him. For the $20 he was spending, shooting water guns at little targets, tossing rings, he could buy Jani something much better.

On Sunday, she watched them build a sand castle. About 11 A.M., she said she had had too much sun, she was going back to the house. House, huh. *Place*. The highway was busy, it seemed to take forever to get across. She changed into her sundress, packed a bag, the duffel, which had wheels, and wrote a note to go with the one she had brought with her. She worried what would happen if she didn't leave a note. The notes were more for Jani than Gregg, anyway.

She bounced the duffel down the steps and onto the shoulder of the highway, followed it almost a quarter mile to the state line, where she planned to take the local bus to the Greyhound station in Ocean City. She would then head to Baltimore, although she couldn't stay long. She was too easy to find there, she would fall back into certain routines.

An older man in a Cadillac offered her a ride to D.C., and she figured why not. Then he got pervy, his sad old fingers sneaking toward her knees like some arthritic spider, and she said, "Put me out here." It was Belleville. ONE OF THE TEN BEST SMALL TOWNS IN AMERICA, according to a shiny, newish sign.

Now, seeing Belleville in the bright morning light, she wonders what the other nine are.

She doesn't have much of a head start. Gregg would have seen the note at noon or so, when they came back for lunch. He was probably more upset that she hadn't made them any sandwiches or set the table. He didn't love her and she didn't love him. He had one foot out the door. He'd leave her, get an apartment. He'd never pay child support, not without endless nagging. She might even have to get a job. So why not go ahead and get a job, but let him have Jani, see what it's like to be a full-time parent? He wasn't going to trap her.

When you've been in jail even a short time, you don't like feeling confined.

What next? She's thought a lot of things out, but she hasn't thought everything out. She has to earn some money, enough to head west by fall. She had assumed she'd do that in D.C., but maybe it's easier to do it here.

Certainly, she'll be harder to find.

She walks into the town proper, down the main street. Which is called Main Street. There is a deli, a grocery store called Langley's, a Purple Heart thrift store, a florist. But a lot of the shops are empty, long vacant by the looks of them.

She doubles back to the motel, the bar she had chosen last night when she made her ride pull over. The High-Ho. Certainly it should be Heigh-Ho?

The guy in the bar last night was awfully good-looking, kind of her type, not that she was interested. Still, she was surprised, even a little insulted, that he gave up so easy.

A car seems to come out of nowhere and she jumps, skittish. But it's too early for anyone to be looking for her and, anyway, it isn't against the law, leaving your family at the beach. She's surprised more women don't do it. She got the idea from a book she read two months ago. Well, she didn't actually read it and she had been planning her own escape for a while. But everybody was talking about it, like it was a fantasy. *If only you knew,* she wanted to tell her neighbors along Kentucky Avenue. *If only you knew what it means to walk away from something, what it takes.*

Money. She has some. She needs more.

The guy last night—he liked her, she was sure. But she doesn't want to make that mistake anymore. She has enough money to go two, three weeks. Summer is coming, there are probably some seasonal jobs still open. She wonders when Gregg will check the accounts, see how much money she moved out of their joint savings in that final week before their "vacation." Half, which is what she was entitled to.

The money will make him even madder than the fact that she left. *At least Jani is a pretty easy kid,* she wants to tell him. Imagine it otherwise. He can't. Gregg can't imagine anything. Life unspools as Gregg expects. Even the surprises—Jani, their marriage—don't surprise him. She used to be that kind of person. But she's not going to be, not anymore.

Back at the motel, she sees the guy from the bar leaning against the doorjamb of room 3. Could be a coincidence. Everyone has a life, everyone has something going on. Don't make the mistake of thinking everything is all about you, all the time.

"Hi," he says. He's the kind of guy who can get away with just that one word. *Hi.* He's good-looking in a bland way, and he probably thinks that's enough. Probably has been enough with most women. She wiggles her fingers in a kind of greeting, but keeps her hand by her side, like he's not worth the effort of bending an elbow.

He says, "How long you staying over?"

"Who wants to know?"

"Every man in town, I'm guessing."

So predictable. And not even true. She has a version of herself that catches men's eyes, but she's turned that off for now, maybe forever. The only thing it ever got her was trouble.

"I'm Adam Bosk," he says. "Like the pear, only with a 'k' instead of a 'c.'"

"I'm the Pink Lady," she says. "Like the apple."

"Think we can still be friends, me a pear, you an apple?"

"I thought it was apples and oranges that can't be compared."

She walks past him and into her room.

She doesn't come out again until the sun goes down, which means it's almost 8:30 before she emerges. Maybe some people would go crazy, sitting in a motel room, nothing to eat but a pack of peanut butter and cheese crackers she found in her purse. Mom food. Gregg is going to have to learn tricks like that now. Jani's an easy kid until she gets hungry, then all bets are off. She enjoys the silence, the novelty of no one needing her, no voices calling, nothing to be cleaned or cooked or washed. She doesn't even put the television on, just lies back on the bed, steeping herself in silence.

When she crosses the street, the sun huge and red as it sinks over the cornfields, she has a hunch he'll be there, Mr. Pear. He is. She makes sure there's a stool between them.

"What are you having?" he asks.

"How much money do you have?"

He laughs. They always think she's joking. Gregg did, that's for sure. She wishes she could say, *Pay attention. I haven't even told you my name yet, but I'm telling you who I am, what I care about.*

As if privy to her thoughts, he asks, "What's your name, Pink Lady? Not that you'll be pink for long. There's a nice shade of brown under that burn. I didn't know redheads could tan like that."

What *is* her name? Which one should she use?

"Polly Costello," she says.

3

Jani wakes up crying for her mother. She's only three years old. She can't understand what's happening. Gregg barely understands. She asks Gregg to read the note again, as if it might change since he read it last night and yesterday at lunch and yesterday morning and the night before that. The note *does* change. He adds a little to it with each reading. An additional, "I love you, Jani." Then, the next time: "I love you more than anything, Jani." Later, he thinks it might be a good idea to include: "Be good to Daddy. This is going to be even harder on him."

Pauline's been gone only two days, and the note is already creased and worn. Jani holds it against her face, pressed between her cheek and her stuffed cat, when she goes to sleep. She goes to sleep crying, she wakes up crying. In between, she has nightmares that make her cry and mutter and moan, yet don't wake her. They wake Gregg, though.

What kind of woman walks out on her family? Gregg knows. The kind of woman he picked up in a bar four years ago precisely because she had that kind of wildcat energy. Pauline was supposed to be a good time, nothing more. She scratched, she bit, she was up for anything, anywhere, anytime.

Then, in the middle of their summer fling, she peed on a stick and a plus sign formed in the circle, but it might as well have been a cross and he was up on it. Because it turned out she was a good girl all along. Good enough that she wouldn't think of having an abortion. Did not see that one coming. Plus, she was thirty-one and she figured this might be her last chance to have a kid. Maybe it was a sign? A destiny thing?

They got married fast. It wasn't so bad at first. So much was happening. She said she didn't want a wedding because she had no people, it would just make her sad, her side of the church empty, so they got married at the courthouse and used the money that would have gone to a wedding to honeymoon in Jamaica, one of those resorts where everything was included. It was cheap because it was the last week of October, the tail end of hurricane season.

They had to find a house big enough for what was going to be the three of them and they lucked out on a bargain up near Herring Run Park, a snug little brick place, very respectable, all the old woodwork and leaded windows still intact. Jani arrived. A first for both of them, but Pauline was calm while he was a mess. Now that he thinks about it, maybe that was the first sign that she wasn't right. Should any woman be that calm, taking care of her first baby? At the time, he thought it meant she was a natural mom, but maybe this was proof that she was the opposite. She is detached, removed, a caretaker, not a parent.

The sex slowed after Jani was born and it was still good enough that it made him angry that they didn't have more of it. She said that if he wanted more attention from her, he needed to help around the house. He wasn't raised to be that way. Gregg had grown up without a father, and his mother had worked overtime, in and out of the house, to make sure he knew what was his due as a man. Pauline didn't even have a job. Why was *she* so tired?

By the time Jani turned two, Pauline was still tired and the newness had worn off everything—marriage, house, baby, her. There was nothing left to distract them from the fact that they just didn't *like* each other that much. Yet the sex was still good. Looking back, he thinks she treated the sex like *that* was her job, a job she enjoyed. Listening to his friends at work, he felt smug at first because it wasn't that way with them. But now he knew, that was another sign that she was unnatural. Once a woman became a mother, she wasn't supposed to be like that. Pauline was a dirty, dirty girl. She wasn't cut out to be a mother, a wife. How had he missed it?

Then, Pauline had—it was hard to admit, even to himself—Pauline had started hitting him. *During.* It had started with him spanking her a little, not hard, just for fun, a way to spice things up. She had howled all out of proportion to the pain, tried to scratch him with her nails.

But when she calmed down, she asked if he wanted to see what it felt like. He didn't, but he didn't want to look as if he wasn't as bold as she was. She slapped his cheek. It hurt, but he didn't want to say how much because he couldn't let her be tougher than he was. Of course, he had reined himself in, didn't use his full strength because that would be wrong, whereas she wasn't holding anything back. It stung. It was painful. It was exciting.

Then, somehow, about two months ago, the acrid fights of their day-to-day life spilled over into the sex and even sex wasn't fun anymore. He had a coworker, Mandy, who went to lunch with him, listened and sympathized. He started staying out late, claiming he was working overtime. They were doing a lot of refi's at work, so it was credible. Then he went home to Pauline, overflowing with this mysterious anger.

He started dropping by the bar where he met Pauline and, yes, sometimes, he took another girl out to the parking lot. The sex was never quite as good as what he had with Pauline, in their early days, but it was better than what he had now, which was pretty much nothing.

He had proposed this beach vacation as one last family get-together, to see if they could find their way back. He spun the one-room studio rental as a part of the plan—real togetherness, one big happy. But, in the back of his mind, he was already thinking about moving out. His mom would take him in, he could always count on his mom.

Now *she's* moved out, leaving him with the kid. There had been a separate note just to him, one that he had hidden from Jani. This note was cool and businesslike. A typed note at that, which means she had written it before they ever got here. Probably pecked it out at the library, where they had word processors.

I will let you know of my plans as soon as possible. I know you want a divorce, so let's make it quick and painless. For now, it's best if Jani remains with you, in the house and routine she knows. I will call after I'm settled.

And now it's Tuesday, their last day of "vacation." He has trudged through the past forty-eight hours as if the end of this getaway was some sort of finish line. He cannot believe how hard it is to care for a child 24/7, although he told himself that's because they're not at their house, with all their stuff. Now, packing up to return home, he sees that life is just going to keep going, that he will have even more problems once he gets home. What will he do for child care? He loves Jani, but, Christ, he cannot be a single dad.

There's a $125 penalty if you stay one minute past 11 A.M. on the last day of your rental, even on a Tuesday. Jani wanted one more morning at the beach, but Gregg can't get them packed up and have the place clean enough to get his deposit back if they do that. Jani whines every second of the morning and shows a real talent for creating a mess wherever he has just cleaned—stepping in dust piles, leaving sticky prints on appliances, tables, walls. They get away with only minutes to spare, 10:57 on the dashboard clock.

When he turns to check his sights as he backs the car out of the driveway, he sees Jani in her car seat, clutching that damn note to her cheek. Those dark curls, olive skin, light eyes—she looks nothing like her mother. If he hadn't been at the hospital when Jani was born, if he hadn't been there for the pregnancy, he'd wonder if a woman could somehow fake having a kid. Jani has looked exactly like him since Day One. "That's evolution at work," Pauline told him. "If babies didn't look like their fathers, they'd reject them. She'll look more like both of us as time goes on." Well, it's three years later and the little girl in the car seat still looks like a female version of him. Put their childhood photos next to each other and you'd think they were fraternal twins. There's not a trace of her mother in her face.

Pauline's not going to dump this kid on him. He'll find her, make her do right. He's the one who's supposed to be moving out, moving on.

"Whore," he mutters.

"What, Daddy?"

"Nothing."

Two miles up the highway, he takes the left turn onto State Highway 26 too fast and the boogie board he roped to the roof goes sliding off. Horns honk around him, as if he planned this fiasco.

He'd leave the board on the roadside if he could, but that would make him no better than *her*. He pulls over and puts everything to rights, then fights for his way back into the westbound traffic, surprisingly thick for a Tuesday in June. Oh God, there's a funeral, apparently for the most popular guy in Bethany Beach, the line of cars twenty, thirty deep. He adds this mishap to the growing list of everything that's her fault. She has ruined his life. Or tried to. He'll find her, make her fulfill her obligations, make her pay.

He remembers the first slap, after he gave her permission, so hard it almost brought tears to his eyes. It was as if she had been waiting to hit him for a very long time.

4

Early in her first marriage—the less said about that, the better—Polly would get so upset at her husband that she would throw herself out of the car. At first, only at stop signs or traffic lights. Eventually she started jumping out during a slow roll. Never more than 5 or 10 mph, usually in a parking lot, but there was a heady danger to it, especially if one chose, as she did, to leap and try to land two-footed on the pavement. She never tucked and rolled, never scraped her hands. She wanted him to see her leap, turn, and head in the other direction, knowing he couldn't follow as nimbly.

Then again, they both knew she had to come home eventually.

Why couldn't she leave that marriage as easily as she jumped from his car? Part of it was money, of course. Walking home cost her nothing, except a beating. To leave, she would have needed money. Leaving required planning. The jump from the car was the opposite of a plan. It was a moment of possibility. *I'm not trapped. I come back to you voluntarily.* A lie, one she told only to herself, but an essential one in those days. A lie that she finally made true, but it took a long time. Time and money. Everything worth having requires time and money.

Speaking of—she crosses the highway, and enters the High-Ho slightly after four. Early enough so it's quiet, not so early that she seems unreliable. A lot of drunks like to work in bars. A man she once knew, a guy who fancied himself a real sage, liked to say, *If you have a thing for elephants, you work in the circus. If you like little kids, you get jobs that give you access to them. Teaching, Cub Scouts, day care. Drunks like to work in bars.* Polly has been chatting up the barmaid three nights running now, getting a rapport going, all the while ignoring the guy who's staying at the motel same as her. Mr. #3, as she thinks of him, despite knowing his name. She overheard him telling the barmaid that his truck threw a rod, but he'll be gone once they find the part.

"Any chance you can use someone else here?" Polly asks the barmaid.

"Maybe part-time," she says. "On weekends and evenings, we need a waitress to help with the kitchen orders. But if you want work, you'll do better going east to the beaches. No matter how much they load up on staff down the ocean in summertime, it's never enough, and there's always someone who can't deal with the pace, the tourists. You'll make better money, too."

"Why don't you work down there, then?" Polly takes out her pack of cigarettes, pushes it toward the woman, who helps herself to one. The barmaid has an apple-cheek prettiness, but she always smells of cigarettes, takes frequent breaks in the parking lot. Whereas Polly is that odd person who can take them or leave them.

"That hour drive is just that much too far. If I lived in Seaford or Dagsboro, maybe—but not from here. I hate driving these two-lane roads at night. Kids going too fast on the curves, old people going too slow, speed traps. Rather make just enough every week of the year, stay away from the tourists. They don't tip well, anyway. Everyone's passing through."

Polly decides not to point out that she just said the money was better down the ocean.

"What would I make here, part-time?"

"Four nights a week, including one of the big weekend nights? Maybe two hundred dollars, mostly cash. But that's if you're good. Are you good?"

"I think so."

"I wouldn't mind having a deeper bench, that's for sure. I'd like to take a weeknight off here and there. But it's the boss's decision."

"What if I need to work off the books?"

The barmaid's eyes narrow. "Why would you want to do that?"

"Not a matter of want. *Need.*"

"Someone looking for you?"

"Not for anything I did wrong. But—if I were to be found, yeah, it could be bad." She smiles. "I'm not the first woman to make a mistake, you know?"

Don't say too much and people will fill in the gaps, usually to your advantage. Polly has shown up out of nowhere, lives in a motel that rents by the week. She has a fading bruise on her jaw. That was actually from Jani's head jerking up, head-butting her by accident, but all anyone knows is that there is a purple-green shadow on the right side of her face. She touches it now, absentmindedly, then snatches her hand away as if she doesn't want to draw attention to it. Funny, touching the bruise is almost like touching Jani, smelling all those toddler smells. *This is for the best,* she reminds herself. *Jani's going to be better off in the long run.*

"Let me talk to the boss. His name is Cosimo, but we call him Casper behind his back, Mr. C to his face."

"Casper?"

"He's white as a ghost. I'm Cath, by the way."

"Nice to meet you, Cath."

Cath goes into the kitchen, doesn't come back. Time passes. Five minutes, ten. Two men come in, older guys. Polly's seen them here before, drinking the cheapest draft beers. She walks behind the counter, pulls their drafts, writes down the transaction on a napkin. These guys always run a tab, she's pretty sure.

When the barmaid returns with the boss, they find Polly still behind the bar. They don't like her presumption, but they don't mind it as much as they might. She has shown initiative.

"So you're ready to start?" Cosimo/Casper asks. Mr. C. He is really white, blue white; his skin almost glows, although he's not an albino. Maybe the closest thing you can be to one without being one. "Like right now?"

"I was just trying to help out. I know these guys don't like to wait."

"Yeah? What else you know about them?" That's Cath.

"He's Max and he's Ernest." Polly indicates which is which with her chin. "On weekends, they came in about five, but on weekdays they like to get started before the five o'clock news. They drink Natty Boh. They talk a lot about politics. And Agent Orange and DDT. They say food tasted better when they were allowed to use DDT, so I think one of them might be a retired crop duster, although maybe he just worked at DuPont. They also warned me that there's a gun in your desk drawer, so I better not think of lifting so much as a dollar out of the till, Mr. C."

The barflies cackle, nod, and Mr. C seems charmed by the use

24

of his nickname. Men always like her, when she can be bothered to try. Cath seems less friendly now. Polly will need to watch for that. She has no use for women, which is why she has to make sure to befriend them. Women never like her. They feel threatened by her, which is silly. She'd never take another woman's man, doesn't even want that much attention from men. The problem is, when a man wants her, he usually won't stop trying to get her. They wear her down, men. She starts off by taking pity on them, ends up feeling sorry for herself.

"When can you start?" Mr. C asks.

"When do you need me?"

"Let's try you out now, see how it goes."

When Mr. #3 comes in, there's now more space between them than before, the breadth of the bar instead of a couple of stools. He wasn't counting on that, she can tell. But now she has to talk to him, indulge his quiet, not-quite flirtation, because it's going to make the difference in where she sleeps, what she eats. Tips. You have to swallow a lot to make good tips. She's already started reading the *PennySaver*, looking for a cheap place to live. Today, she checked out a big apartment over the empty Ben Franklin store on Main. Walking distance from here, although it's not a great walk, a lot of highway with narrow shoulders, few sidewalks. The apartment's not anything special, but it's huge, and only $300 a month. She likes the idea of those two big empty rooms, only for her. She wouldn't fill it with furniture even if she could.

She leans over the bar. Max and Ernest have already made the inevitable top shelf jokes, snicker, snicker. It was strange, how she got skinny but her breasts stayed the same size. But just because her breasts don't look as if they belong on her body, it doesn't mean they belong to the world, either. Every time she waitresses, she swears it's the last time. But she's good at it, and she loves taking home cash at night's end. There's nothing like cash.

"So you're sticking around?" Mr. #3 asks. Adam, the first man, only this one is into pears, not apples.

"For now."

"You going to keep living at the motel?"

"Probably not."

"We'll miss you."

"I'll come back to visit. If I'm invited."

She waits for him to pick up on the suggestion, the hint of a question mark. She tells herself that she's bored enough that she might as well take him up on the inevitable pass. She's going to end up with someone in town, why not this Adam. It's a hard habit to break, gravitating to a protector, even if she's never quite found the right one. She's like Goldilocks—the first one was too rough, the second too weak. But isn't it the third one that's always just right? Unless, of course, you break it, like Little Bear's chair.

In her mind, she's already sitting on the edge of Adam's bed, drinking bourbon and Coke out of a plastic cup, stretching, arching her back, touching the back of his hand. Men are so easy.

He doesn't ask her back.

Screw him.

Maybe she will do just that, after all.

5

When Polly-the-Pink-Lady hints that she might be interested in being invited back to his place, Adam overreacts by not reacting. He plays dim, not a play he can carry. Maybe he should have let her come over. You don't have to sleep with a good-looking woman just because she comes to your motel room and has a drink after work. It's not a law or anything.

Not that this one respects laws or rules. That's why he's here. And he was warned. *She'll have sex with you if you get close to her. It's what she does.*

He has decided not to ask how the client could be so sure of this.

Then again, this Polly doesn't always do what she's expected to do. Who could have predicted she would decamp in the middle of a beach vacation, just up and leave her family? The plan had been to make contact with the husband during the Fenwick trip, get to know him, do some man-on-man bonding. *Oh, you live in Baltimore? Whereabouts? I'm on the northeast side, too.* The plan was to find out what the husband knew. Go figure, he knew less than nothing. Adam was thrown when she left the beach Sunday morning, went up to the house, and packed her bags.

Except—he must have had an inkling something was up, because he left the beach, too, kept watch on the house, saw her come out and start dragging the duffel down the highway, then jump in that guy's car as he followed at a discreet distance.

Luckily, there are only two ways west from the beach, Route 50 and 404, and almost everyone leaving the Delaware beaches takes 404. When she got out in Belleville, he did, too. Good thing he always has an overnight bag in his truck, packed and ready to go. Sure, he had to drive back to Fenwick the next day and check out of his motel there, pick up the rest of his things, risking that she would move on in the interim. But she was there when he got back, hanging out at the High-Ho.

Now she has a job at the bar and she has all but invited herself into his bed and he made the wrong move. She's pissed at him now.

What can he do? He continues to go to the bar, continues to make it sound as if his truck is like some goddamn Maserati that can't be easily serviced even in big-town Salisbury. She pulls his drafts with as little commentary as possible. The two old guys get more attention and they barely tip. Her cold shoulder isn't obvious; she's too much of a pro to frost a regular. She *neutralizes* him. That's the perfect word. He's invisible, an outline of his former self, drinking beer, leaving a respectable tip at night's end. Overtipping would be a mistake, even if it's not his money. She's ignoring him, he's ignoring her ignoring him. It's exhausting and much less fun than their slow dance toward each other when they were on the same side of the bar. It makes him think of a Japanese horror film he saw as a kid, one that no one else seems to remember. He describes it all the time to people and never gets a flash of recognition. The setup was like *The Blob,* only it was a stream of hot atomic liquid that flowed through the streets of Tokyo and if it touched you, that was it, you were a goner, you were vaporized in a flash.

How much longer can he linger here in Belleville?

Fate intervenes in the form of a cardboard box of San Marzano tomatoes that someone left in a damp spot. The case, weakened by moisture, breaks open. The cans drop in quick succession on the line cook's foot, ill-protected in flip-flops of all things. The poor guy might have survived the broken toe, but not the index finger sliced open by the knife he inadvertently grabbed as he fell. The owner—Mr. C, although Adam has yet to learn what the "C" is for—puts up a sign looking for temporary help. Cath says the boss can cook, in a pinch, but he prefers not to in the summer. Hard to figure what he does with his days given how ghostly pale he is.

So Adam's after-school job in "Uncle" Claude's diner in San Mateo, his time at the CIA—Culinary Institute of America, not the spy agency—is going to save this gig. He also spent a season cooking on a rich guy's yacht, but his instincts tell him not to share that part of his résumé.

Mr. C takes the HELP WANTED sign down after talking to Adam for five minutes. He says he'll do most of the cooking, use Adam for the scut work, but he's lazy and by the third day, he's letting Adam do everything.

Customers begin saying nice things about the food. Adam, who can't phone anything in, pushes Mr. C to upgrade some of his suppliers. To let him use local produce when possible, although it's still early for tomatoes, and spend a little extra on the things that matter, like beef and seafood. Cheap chicken is fine; people who order a chicken sandwich in a place like this have no taste buds. Besides, the locals seldom order chicken. Adam can't figure if this is out of fealty to the Kiwanis, who sell barbecue by the roadside on weekends, or because this is chicken country. You drive past those long, low coops, inhale—it puts you off chicken, all due respect, Mr. Perdue.

Business picks up, which is good for everyone. Mr. C needs both waitresses most nights, one for lunch. The tips are bigger.

And through it all, Adam keeps it mild and professional with the new barmaid, "Polly Costello."

"Polly want a cracker," he says, shaking a bag of oyster crackers at her, deliberately being cornpone. It doesn't get a smile. "Is Polly short for something?"

"No," she says.

They don't speak again, beyond the shorthand of short-order speak—Adam and Eve on a raft, et cetera. Their first real conversation begins with an argument over a steak. Customer orders it medium rare, then complains it's too red.

"That's what medium rare is," he tells her, maybe with a little more heat than the situation requires. "Medium has some pink. If there's no hint of pink, it's on its way to being medium well. Truly rare is closer to blue, maybe a bluish purple."

"The customer is always right," she says.

"You don't believe that."

"I believe that the customer leaves the tip and the tip is my real pay. So the customer is *my* boss."

And you're not, she's telling him. Like a little kid: You're not the boss of me.

"But I'm here day in, day out. Your customer will only be as happy as my food makes him."

"The food was shitty before you got here. It will be shitty after you leave. I'm not worried about the food."

"So you think my food is good?" He can't help feeling a little flattered.

"I didn't say that. It's not as bad as it was. It's okay. I wouldn't know. I don't eat meat."

"I can make you a nice salad."

"I don't eat salad."

"You don't eat meat, you don't eat salad. What do you eat?"

She doesn't bother to answer. "Look, *please* cook it a little more. Is that so hard?"

"That's all I needed to hear. 'Please.' Was *that* so hard?"

The kitchen closes at 9:30, the bar goes to 11:00, but Adam, a neat freak who obsesses over the hood, needs that long to clean and prep for the next day. When Polly closes the register at 10:55, he slides a plate across the bar to her. It's the most perfect grilled cheese and tomato sandwich that ever was. The brown stripes on the buttery white bread are so perfectly symmetrical they could have been put there by a painter. Inside, there is finely chopped bacon, his own secret. Fry the bacon, then chop it. Otherwise, it tears up the sandwich as you bite, fights the cheese, gets stuck in your teeth. He mixes it with some bacon paste, calculating there may be a day when he wants to add this to the menu; the version he prepares for Polly is about as practical as a hand-whittled clothespin. On the side: fries made from fresh potatoes, not the ones in the freezer, blanched in 250-degree oil, then sprinkled with rosemary. A cup of ketchup, but also a cup of homemade aioli, although he'll call it mayo on the board. With good fries, you want mayo.

She eats without commentary. She eats every bite, though.

"There was bacon in there," he says.

"I know," she says. "You testing me?"

"My sister's a vegetarian and she says she misses bacon every day."

"I didn't say I was a vegetarian. I said I didn't eat meat."

"I just thought I knew what you would like."

"You thought that, huh?" She eats a french fry.

The bus boy–dishwasher, Jorge, is working in the back, a cramped space overwhelmed by the beat-up Wolf with six burners, a broken salamander, a deep fryer that Adam loves, and a microwave he detests, but relies on more than he likes to admit. They're not really alone. Adam reminds himself. They're not alone.

"This was nice of you," she says.

"Thanks."

"What do you want?"

"Nothing. That was just lagniappe, as they say in New Orleans. A little extra something-something."

She laughs as if that's the most ridiculous thing she's ever heard, a man wanting nothing from her.

"You've been kind of standoffish with me. Like we got off on the wrong foot or something. And it's nicer if people who work together get along."

"We get along fine."

Every instinct warns him not to reference that one night, when he didn't ask her back to his room. In fact, he has to turn it around, make it a story about how *she* gave him the brush-off. Her pride demands this. In her head, that might already be the story.

"Look, you're a good-looking woman. You can't blame men for getting a little mopey around you."

She's interested now. "Mopey? That's your word for it?"

"I worry you're going to make me your friend. Tell me all about the guy you really like."

"Not really in the market for a boy *friend*," she says. He thinks there's a pause between the two words. "You still at the motel?"

"Yeah."

"With rent as cheap as it is in this town? You could do better. You should see my place. It's huge."

"I'd like that. To see your place. One day."

Bait.

"I need some furniture. Can you get off next Saturday? During the day?"

Hook.

"Maybe." It will be hard, but if he comes up with a good excuse, promises to be there for the dinner rush, it should be okay. They don't really do a good lunch business on Saturday, so Mr. C could be persuaded to cook. Schools are out and the roads are clogged with traffic because most of the weekly rentals change over on Saturday. Locals can barely get out of their driveways on the weekends. The people bound for the beach are too close to those salty sea breezes to stop by the time they reach Belleville, while those who are headed home feel as if they're too early in their journey to abandon their momentum.

And next weekend is the beginning of the long Fourth of July weekend, so the traffic will be worse than usual.

"There's an auction, over to Mardela Springs. I might be able to pick up a few things I need for my new place. But I'd need someone strong. Someone with a truck. You drive a truck, a big one, right?"

"Pretty big," he says.

"Well, let me know. If you can get off on Saturday."

33

She has eaten every bite of the food he put in front of her. The plate barely needs to go in the dishwasher. Who eats like that and has a figure like hers?

He finds himself thinking of the folktales his mother liked to tell him. Greek and Roman mythology wasn't enough for Lillian Bosk. She had studied Slavic languages, written a dissertation on Eastern European folktales. She loved to tell him about the *ala* and *Baba Yaga,* and what happened when young women came to visit them. The stories differed in key parts—the ala wore a horse's head while delousing her "human" head; Baba Yaga, in her heyday, was almost a goddess.

But the stories always ended the same way, with the demon devouring her nosy visitor in one bite.

The Saturday of the auction is hot, but not humid. Adam's truck has air-conditioning, but when he asks if they can drive with the windows open, she says yes. Polly always plays the good sport, the girl—*woman*—who doesn't mind if her hair gets tousled. Being a good sport sounds like such a good thing, but there's no good thing that can't become bad for you. Polly looks at the skies, remembers some tiny shred of poetry from grade school, something about blue skies arching. She never got that. How can a sky arch? It doesn't touch the ground.

"What do you need?" he asks her.

"Everything." She doubles down on that one word, gives him a quick glance, but level, not through the lashes. She hates women who do that, peer through their lashes.

"You got a budget? Easy to get carried away at an auction. There's something about someone else trying to get what you want, even if you don't want it that bad, that can make you crazy."

Tell me about it. She's been clocking Cath clocking Adam.

She's wearing a sundress that she found in the Purple Heart on

Main Street. In a vintage shop back in Baltimore, this same dress might cost $50, $75. Here, it was $12. Her body is made for clothes like this—fitted through the bodice, then a big swirl of a skirt, patterned with bright fruits. She found a pair of earrings—purple glass grapes that dangle from her lobes. A little matchy-matchy, but it works. She wears flat sandals and when she starts roaming the dusty rows of furniture and housewares at the auction, it feels as if something is nibbling at her ankles. What kind of bug can live in such dry dust?

More than once, she feels his gaze on her shoulders. She knows she has a beautiful back, her bones clearly visible, but not in a way that makes her look underfed or scrawny. Her shoulder blades look like wings. Or so she's been told, by more than one man. Two, to be exact. Both husbands.

This one says nothing, though. Today, he seems determined not to compliment her.

Focus on what you need, she tells herself, *not what you want.*

She shouldn't be buying anything, but she did the math: The motel, at $220 a week, was $880 a month. So she's saving $580 by taking the apartment, which means she can get out west by September, wrap things up mid-October. But she can't live in a completely empty apartment for two months. She needs utensils, a kitchen table, a couple of chairs.

She wants an iron bed, a full set of jadeite, a quilt in the log cabin pattern.

Right off the bat, she finds a little deco table—white-and-black metal top, painted white base, no matching chairs, so it will go cheap, and it does, only $65. Now to find two chairs. There are two white painted ones made of cane, but she passes on those. No man will want to sit on those chairs. Why is she thinking about men, anyway? Then she has the brainstorm of buying only one chair, a lonely wooden chair from some old schoolhouse, which gets his attention.

"Not planning to entertain?" Adam asks.

"I never *entertain*."

She has the resolve to pass on the jadeite; she's not much for cooking and, as she just told Adam, she doesn't entertain. But she can't say no to the quilt. It's so much like one that was on her frau-frau's spare bed when she was a child. *Hot chocolate and strudel for breakfast, making a tent with cousin Annie, playing War by flashlight.* Even though Polly is not planning to spend a single winter's night in Belleville, she has to have it.

Then an iron bed comes up. Oh, it's a beauty. White, with gold details. Polly has a tricky back, prone to going out. Sleeping on a mattress without a box spring isn't good for her.

"Looks awfully small," Adam says.

"You don't often find them larger than full," she says. "People didn't used to think they needed so much room in bed."

"I like a king myself," he says.

"Then you'll probably never have an antique bed."

She has set her limit at $150, which is $150 too much. She tries to put up her paddle as if she couldn't care less, but she feels her heart thrumming in her chest as the price rises. Another woman is bidding—a little older than her, definitely richer. Polly sees the flash of jewels on the other woman's hands, at her throat. She hates her, she wants to kill her. They are at $175, $200, $225. She wants this bed so bad.

"Do you have any cash on you?" she asks Adam.

"Don't get carried away."

"Did I ask your advice? Do you have any cash on you? You know I'm good for it."

"You can't spend more on a bed than you do on your rent."

"Don't tell me what I can do."

The choice has slipped away during their argument and the other woman has won the beautiful bed for $275. Polly's so angry she has to stalk away, fuming. She's not sure who she's angrier with—the woman who got her bed or the man who argued with her over what she could afford.

Or herself, for caring so much about a damn bed.

But in her mind's eye, she already owned that bed, covered with the quilt, and, maybe, thrown over the foot, a man's silk bathrobe that she bought at the Purple Heart. It's purple, covered with dragons. Too big for her and too hot for the current weather, but it makes her feel like royalty when she pulls it over her naked body, walks around her empty rooms.

She cools down, returns to the auction. When he raises his eyebrows in a question—*You OK?*—she raises hers as if she has no idea what he's asking. She doesn't bid again, but when they go to collect her purchases at the end of the auction, there's the bed, waiting with her table, chair, and quilt.

"What the—?"

"I asked the lady if she wanted to make a quick profit."

"How much do I owe you?"

"Two hundred twenty-five."

No way she let it go for fifty less than she paid.

He answers her unvoiced skepticism. "She thought she could come back and get it later. But this auction is strictly cash-and-carry. Would have cost her at least fifty dollars to haul it away and that's assuming she could find someone with a truck who wanted to drive all the way to Oxford today. And it's strictly no refunds, so getting two twenty-five from me meant losing only fifty bucks. Pricey mistake for people like us, but she didn't bat an eye."

Polly doesn't believe a word of it, but it's not the first time someone has gone out of the way to pay her tribute. Men have always done things for her. *People.* And she never asks. That is, she never seems to ask. He won't even remember that she hit him up for a loan. He won't want to remember. He's her savior, Mr. Magnanimous. It's a special art, asking people to do things, yet making it seem as if you never asked at all. There are talents she would prefer to this one, because favors often carry a hefty penalty when it's time to return them, but it's the skill she was given, the hand she has to play.

So he bought her a bed. It's funny, when she was mad at him, she was thinking that she just might get him to make a move tonight. Tonight or on the drive back home. All it would take is a hand on his thigh, about halfway up. But now that he's bought her a bed, she's going to have to deny him a little while longer. It would seem too much like commerce, tit for tat, quid pro quo. Bed for bed.

He bought her a bed. On the drive home, she keeps her face turned toward the cornfields and those arching blue skies, not wanting him to see how wide her grin is.

Gregg lets Jani have chocolate cake for breakfast. Why not? In the end, what's the difference between cake and a muffin, or even cereal? Besides, he'll do anything to avoid whining. Pauline was always going on and on about schedules. *Kids need schedules, they thrive when life is orderly.* But Jani's doing fine. Other than the fact that her mother disappeared four weeks ago and hasn't been heard from except for a letter that arrived four days ago, postmarked Philadelphia. If he's sure of anything, he knows Pauline's not in Philadelphia. Someone probably mailed it for her. She had that way about her, of getting people, strangers even, to do her favors.

She certainly got him to do her a lot of favors. Marry her. Become a dad. Buy a brick house near a park. This whole setup was all for her, and now she's left him holding the bag.

The letter's not even addressed to him. It's to Jani. A greeting card with a bear on the front, the imprinted message: "I can't bear being away." Then, in her tight, up-and-down script: "I love you, I miss you." *Lies, lies, lies.*

Well, today's the day. It's been four weeks, and she's clearly not coming back. Maybe she's certifiably insane. Wouldn't that be just his luck? At any rate, he needs to find her and get her back to Baltimore to take care of Jani. He's made an appointment with a private detective. A woman. He wouldn't trust any man around Pauline. No, it's not the men he doesn't trust. It's Pauline. She's just too good at getting what she wants. Why did he ever fall for her? She's not that pretty. Her shape is good, but not crazy-insane great.

The sex *was* good, though.

The private detective's office is up in Towson and he's arranged to come in late at the office, although things are crazy busy. After spiking up last year, interest rates are back down. Not 1993 levels, but under 8 percent for a thirty-year fixed and lower still for the adjustable-rate mortgages that are so popular now. Everyone's trying to sell and buy before school starts up. Summer's barely started, and people are already thinking about fall.

He drops Jani at his mom's. He thought grandmothers were supposed to love their grandchildren to the point where they could never get enough of them, but his mom's getting a little cheesed off about all the babysitting over the past month. He hasn't told her the exact truth about Pauline. He dropped a hint that she had to go somewhere to take care of a family member, but he didn't provide many details. He's not sure why he's lying to his mother. It's not like he and Pauline are going to get back together. He guesses he just doesn't want his mother to say, "I told you so." She hated Pauline from the start. Said she didn't seem like wife material. But Gregg hadn't been looking for wife material. He tried to make the best of it when she got pregnant, but it was foolish to think that you could marry a party girl and she would figure out how to be a party girl by night, a mom and wife by day. Now he knows it doesn't work that way.

The detective's office is in a beige building off Joppa Road, a place with a credit union on the first floor, and a lot of "professional" places above—dentists, podiatrists, urologists. But only one private detective. Not how he imagined it. Then he realizes he was imagining an old movie: venetian blinds behind a glass panel with the agency's name stenciled in gold letters. *This gun for hire.*

Here, there is a plastic nameplate, SECURITY ASSOCIATES. Inside, Sue Snead—wait, did he pick her for the name, without making the association, Sue Snead/Sam Spade?—is small and nondescript, an asset in her work if not her life. *Probably a lesbian,* he thinks, taking in her short hair, button-down shirt, khakis.

"Office buildings are air-conditioned for men," she says.

"What?" Her voice is gorgeous, unexpected. It's like listening to beautiful music pour out of some kid's rinky-dink toy piano.

"That's why I wear pants and long-sleeved shirts, even on a day with temperatures in the nineties. Because the business world, its thermostats are set to temperatures that are comfortable for people who wear suits. The women come in bare legged, in sleeveless tops, then complain that they're freezing."

"Interesting," he says. It's not, but what does it cost him?

"I think the first thing we need to do is a background check on your wife, which means I'll order a search of all legal databases through Chicago Title."

"She's got no legal troubles."

"How do you know?" Her tone is kind, her eyes round and serious. She's not challenging him.

And for the first time he thinks: *How do I know?* You meet a woman in a bar. She's fun. You tell her your best stories. She laughs and tells hers—only Pauline Smith never did, come to think of it. Tell stories. She laughed and asked for more of his. In Baltimore,

42

people always start with *Where did you go to school?* They mean high school, not college. But she always said she wasn't from Baltimore, that she grew up in West Virginia. And the weird thing about West Virginia is that, although you can drive there in two hours, it feels like it's a million miles away. There's a reason they have those bunkers at the Greenbrier Hotel in case D.C. is ever nuked. Gregg plays the license plate game on road trips, a hangover from childhood, and you seldom see a West Virginia tag east of Hagerstown. Less often than Vermont, even. About as often as Utah, he reckons.

"Let's start with what you do know," Sue Snead says, her pen at the ready.

"Well, her name. Her birth date. Her social. And the social has to be right, because we file a joint return."

"Where does she work?"

"She doesn't." Oh, he remembers—you're supposed to say it differently. "She didn't have a job outside the home, I mean. She was a full-time mom. A good one, too. She loves our little girl. Or I thought she did."

They talk for almost an hour and, while part of him is clocking the cost, there's another part of him that enjoys the conversation, all those questions in that honeyed voice. Usually, talking to a woman this long is a prelude to sex. Maybe this is what going to a therapist is like. She seems so *interested* in him, kind and supportive. No detail is too small, she keeps telling him. He finds himself talking about what it was like, at first, the sex with Pauline, how great it was, and then she got pregnant and everything changed. Like, she would be up for sex in odd places—outdoors, the spare bedroom at a party, but she scoped it out first, made sure it was unlikely they would be seen. Did that mean the wildness was a calculation? Or something she had learned to control?

43

He doesn't mention the hitting, though. He admits to Sue Snead that he was thinking about leaving, but the only thing he cares about now is finding Pauline, making sure she's not in trouble, helping his little girl, who's brokenhearted. Divorce is inevitable, but it can be civilized, he says.

Gambling problem? Drugs? Alcohol? He shakes his head no to each question. Sure, she's bought a lottery ticket here or there, done a bump of cocaine on special occasions, enjoys a cocktail. But she's the opposite of an addict, the only person he's ever known who could smoke three or five times a year, then let it go. It's impossible to imagine her in thrall to anything, anyone. She calls the shots while pretending not to. Even in motherhood, she has shown this steely control. She was never the type of mother to get gooey about it, or make those comments about how the tops of babies' heads smell.

"Maybe there's another man," he blurts out. Until he says it, he hasn't really considered this possibility. But what else can there be? Sure, she took two thousand dollars out of their savings account the week before she left, a smart play on her part. But how long can she go on two thousand dollars? Someone has to be supporting her. She's not fit for much work beyond McDonald's.

He writes a check for the retainer and Ms. Snead promises to be in touch within the week. He knows he should go to work, but he calls in with a "family emergency" and goes to Wagner's Tavern, the bar where he met Pauline. A beer at lunch isn't really drinking, not in a place like Wagner's, a cop bar tucked into a corner of Joppa Road.

That was the first thing Pauline ever said to him: "You a cop?"

"Do I look like a cop?" His hair was on the long side, his jeans tight.

"That's not a no. You could be undercover. You've got *that* look."

44

"What kind of look is that?"

"Like a guy who's trying not to look like a cop."

Forty-five minutes later, they were having sex in his car. It was weeks before she believed he wasn't a cop, just a guy from a title company less than a mile up the street.

Today at Wagner's, one beer turns into two turns into three and then he has to drink a big cup of coffee before he gets behind the wheel. Pauline'd kill him if he drove tipsy with Jani in the car. Well, too bad. *You want to set the rules, you can get your goddamn ass home.*

And then I'm going to leave. Maybe she thought she was clever, that if she left first, he would change his mind about leaving. How had she even figured out what he was planning to do? A witch, that one. She's a witch.

Sometimes, he used to wake up in the middle of the night and find her looking at him. The light from the streetlamp threw a stripe across her eyes, and it was as if she were wearing a mask that allowed her to read his every thought.

He turns on the radio and it's that goddamn song that's on the radio all the time this summer, the one about chasing waterfalls. No one *chases* a waterfall. You go for a swim and next thing you know, the current catches you and throws you right over.

8

A new convenience store, a Royal Farms, has opened near the spot where the bypass will eventually join the beach highway. It's a big deal in Belleville and Polly has heard people in the bar talking about it. The old-timers claim they will never patronize the convenience store, the first to open in Belleville, where one family has long had a lock on the grocery trade. They see it as a symbol of everything that is wrong, with Belleville and the world beyond. Open for twenty-four hours, undercutting the local gas station with its prices, a place where teenagers can be idle.

As a local, at least for the time being, Polly should stay away. But there's something about the store's bright, shiny newness that promises anonymity, a rare commodity in this town. In the mornings, she finds herself walking more than a mile there to buy a Diet Mountain Dew or a Good Humor bar, the one with toasted almonds. It's a strange breakfast, to be sure, and she has to be careful about sweets: she wasn't always thin like this and it was hard, getting the weight off after Jani. But there's something about having an ice cream bar for breakfast that makes her feel truly free, maybe for the first time in her life. How thoughtlessly she squandered her freedom, taking up with Gregg and getting pregnant. If anyone knew her whole story, that might be the truly shocking part, the way she ruined her own second chance.

But no one knows her whole story. She plans to keep it that way.

She eats the ice cream bar in the store's little alcove of preformed tables and benches, where almost no one else ever lingers. Only 9 A.M., it's already hot enough that the ice cream will melt quickly if she takes it outside, and she wants to eat it as slowly as possible. She catches a glimpse of a familiar face from the bar, one of the locals who claimed he would never come here. He's drinking a cup of coffee and eating some kind of breakfast sandwich made with a croissant. He registers her gaze, shrugs. Hard to know if the gesture is a sheepish concession to his hypocrisy or a kind of hello, the kind that says, *I see you, I like you, but I want to be alone.* She thinks it's the first, but decides to believe it's the second. What does it matter? The same nonresponse is fine for either one.

A young woman comes in with two fretful children, boys, no more than eighteen months apart, maybe both still in diapers, although the bigger one is walking alongside the double stroller. "Can I have?" he keeps whining. "Can I have?" Polly studies the children intently, waiting to see if she feels anything. No. She feels nothing. She is not an indiscriminate lover of children. Wait, that's not quite right. She feels intense empathy for the mother, who looks miserable. The poor thing has large, fleshy thighs, dotted with a scarlet rash. Her hair is almost half and half—six inches of dull brown roots, six inches of a brassy blond that looks slightly greenish. She can't be more than twenty-two or twenty-three, but she moves with the shuffling tread of a much older woman.

She picks up milk, a carton of eggs, and, with a quick look over her shoulder, a bag of off-brand chips, then pays with a card. Probably a welfare card, loaded with her food stamp benefits. That's the reason for the nervous look. She thinks someone is going to bust her for buying chips. Allowed, under the rules, but taxpayers always think they have the right to look over a welfare recipient's shoulder, dictate her choices.

All the while, the older boy is whining, *Can I have, can I have, can I have?* It's like a high-pitched saw at a construction site.

"I wan' treat, too," the younger boy says.

"I'll share my chips."

The older child: "I don't like those chips. Too spicy."

Polly can almost feel the woman's palm itch with the desire to slap him.

Polly was on welfare once. Very briefly. And very fraudulently, as she claimed a child she didn't have. It was a risk, doing that. But she was stuck. She needed money to start a new life, so she borrowed a few things from another life—a name, a birth certificate, a daughter.

Daughter. She should get another card to Jani, but it's tricky, finding someone to mail it, someone westward bound, with a soft heart and no curiosity about the woman who doesn't want a Belleville postmark on her letters.

Her fake daughter and real name had been enough to get temporary benefits from an emergency fund at the county level. She learned about food pantries, even took the bus to the occasional soup kitchen. Every dollar she could get her hands on, she had to use to put some kind of roof over her head—a room in someone else's row house, strictly cash. She had the good sense to settle in Baltimore County, although at the north end, and shopped around until she found a male social worker. He got her into a motel that was taking homeless families, never asked to see the daughter she claimed to have, not even the one night he came to "check on her" and brought a bottle of white zinfandel.

Then she went to Legal Aid, where she told the truth straight up, and that was good enough to get her the name change she needed. She kept it simple, going from Pauline Ditmars to Pauline Smith, and then Pauline Smith became Pauline Hansen when she married Gregg. But she had been Polly as a kid, so it's no stretch, answering to that again. She had thought about changing her name to Pollyanna, thought about using it again when Adam Bosk first asked her name. A little in-joke because she's pretty much the opposite of Pollyanna at this point.

But a Pollyanna calls attention to herself, whereas a Pauline doesn't. The point of becoming Pauline Smith four years ago was to disappear and start over.

So why was she in that bar, Wagner's, the night she met Gregg? It was within walking distance of the motel, no more than a mile or two, although that strip of Joppa Road wasn't very friendly to pedestrians. Dark, with cracked sidewalks leading past stores with dusty windows, places that sell things like blinds and suitcases and tile. She wasn't officially Pauline Smith yet, but she was on her way, trying the name out in anticipation of the day the paperwork came through. Still, it was dangerous to go to that bar. She could have been spotted by someone who knew her well enough not to be fooled by the red hair, long as it was by then. She couldn't have long hair when she was married to Ditmars. Too much like a leash, too easy to grab.

Gregg was very ordinary trouble at least. Fun, at first. She didn't expect to see him again after that first night—and maybe she wouldn't have if she hadn't gone back to Wagner's two nights later.

Of course, she could never take him to the motel, she saw that right away. And she didn't have a phone. She told him that when he asked and he laughed, thinking she was making a joke. "I don't," she said. "Give me your number and I promise I'll call you." She made good on her promise seventy-two hours later, calling from a pay phone outside the Bel-Loc Diner. When he asked her out for a real date, she told him that she worked at the mall and he could pick her up in the food court. They went to a movie, had pizza. Then came the question she dreaded: "Can I take you home?"

"Take me for a drive," she said. "Out into the country."

Fifteen minutes later, she asked him to pull into the deserted parking lot outside a greenhouse, led him into a copse of trees. He actually believed that this was her thing, that she didn't want to make love in a bed, hardly ever. All summer long, they did it outdoors and when fall came and her new identity was under way and she could get a for-real job—waitressing, at a decent place, a Crab Imperial kind of place with fat tips, although the cab fare ate up too much of her earnings for the job to be practical—she started taking him into bathrooms and, once, the dressing room at Nordstrom. Sometimes they used his bed, at his crummy apartment over on Loch Raven, but the pilled sheets, even when clean, felt itchy.

She put a deposit down on a sweet little place over the city line, near Belvedere Square. It was an old Victorian cut up into apartments, so the appliances were half-assed and the closets tiny, but she didn't mind. It was hers, the first place that had ever been hers. Still, she wouldn't have sex with Gregg there. Force of habit, she guessed, although maybe there was something deeper going on, some part of her mind trying to tell her that her new life was here and it was time to leave Gregg behind, the last station on her journey to becoming Pauline Smith.

Then she peed on a stick and her life was over. Again.

She had misread him, badly. She believed him when he said he wanted their child. She told herself she had to stop thinking that every man was Ditmars, acted like Ditmars, thought like Ditmars. But maybe they were. She remembers when Gregg spanked her the first time. She went numb, limp, terrified that she was going to do something crazy. But then it turned out that was all he wanted, just a few light slaps, nothing more. She still wants to laugh when she remembers his face when she asked if *he* wanted a few whacks. That was something to behold. This gander wanted no sauce, but he had to take it or be exposed for the bully he was.

"*She's* eating ice cream for breakfast!" The older boy is pointing a finger in her face, almost touching the tip of her nose. It takes enormous control not to swat that finger away.

"She's a grown-up."

The boy continues to glare. Polly levels her eyes on him. He holds her stare for an impressive amount of time, but he finally folds.

The woman struggles to get him into the two-seater stroller with his brother, to roll out the door into the already burning hot day. She and Polly have the same number of hours ahead of them. But for Polly, who is on her day off, the hours feel like a long, slow bath in which she can luxuriate, whereas this young woman is confined, caught. Down in South Carolina, a woman is being tried for drowning her own kids, letting a car roll forward into a lake with them still strapped in the back. She claimed she was carjacked, but it turned out she just wanted to start over without the kids. A new man had entered the picture. A horrible thing to do—and yet what would you have her do? Men leave their kids all the time and no one thinks them unnatural for it. Not great guys, but not deviants. Women seldom have that option.

Everyone likes to tell that story about the mom who was able to lift a car off her toddler, how maternal love can give you super-strength. Polly's pretty sure it's bullshit. Besides, what if you're under the car with your kid? What do you do then? You can't save a kid if you can't save yourself.

She grabs a *PennySaver*, heads out into the long July day.

dam is enjoying life more than he should. At least, that's the opinion of his boss—his real boss, not Mr. C—who is skeptical at the lack of results Adam has posted. But what can he do? It was never his intention to wind up here in Belleville. And he's keeping expenses to a minimum. His client actually has the nerve to suggest that Adam's earnings at the High-Ho should be counted against his per diem.

"Yeah, it doesn't work that way," he tells him. He cannot believe this guy wants to nickel and dime him all of a sudden.

"I don't know," the client says with a sigh. "Maybe I'm wrong. Maybe there's no money. Remember, 20 percent of nothing is nothing."

Yeah, that's why I'm charging you expenses plus forty hours a week, Adam thinks. *And I could be charging you for my time 24/7, but I'm a good guy. You're only paying me for the time I'm actively with her.*

They are talking on his room phone. Adam has a mobile, but he tries not to use it and keeps it in his room at all times. A guy who takes a job working as a short-order cook wouldn't have a phone like his. He did opt to use his real name, Adam Bosk, to keep things simple. If she got suspicious, she could go to the DMV over the line in Maryland and do a search—but why would she be suspicious? And how would she get there? Besides, all she would find is his address and his spotless driving record. Tell as few lies as possible, that's his rule.

He knows he's lucky now that he wasn't able to strike up a friendship with Gregg at the beach, per the original plan. Because if he had started hanging out with her husband before she split, there's no way he could have shown up here, too, in Belleville.

Why is *she* here? Does her husband know where she is? Does the husband know anything? Why did she leave him? And her little girl, how does that work? *Feral,* his client says of her. *No capacity for genuine emotion. She's out for herself, always.*

"Whatever you do," his client says, "don't turn your back on her." Then he chuckles in an odd way. "Even face-to-face, you might not be safe with that one."

Adam cannot reconcile these dire warnings with the woman he sees at work. No, she isn't warm, and she seems to have only two speeds with men, interested and uninterested. With him, she has flipped the switch so many times now, he's almost dizzy. Not that he cares. He's strong, he's not going to muddy things. But that day at the auction, when he helped her to carry her new purchases into the apartment, even set up the bed for her, he had expected her to say something suggestive, throw him a signal. She couldn't get him out of there fast enough. And since then she has been so cool. Nice, pleasant, but Max and Ernest get more attention from her than he does.

That night at work, the other waitress, Cath, catches him sneaking peeks at Polly through the pass-through for the food. Business has been picking up, and Mr. C now needs both women working Wednesday through Sunday. Cath, who has seniority, gets most of the tables. Polly has the bar and two tables near it.

"You like her." Cath's tone is almost accusing.

"What do you mean, I like her? I barely know her."

Cath smiles. "I said *you're like her.*"

"How so?"

"Mysterious. Not offering up much of anything. Not sure if you're staying or passing through."

"Oh, I'm pretty sure I'm passing through."

"What could entice you to stay?"

She cocks a hip, gives him a look. She's cute if you like that all-American type. He thinks about it, the pros and cons. If he takes up with Cath, he won't have to worry about making a mistake with Polly. And Polly strikes him as someone who would find a guy much more interesting if she definitely can't get to him. It could be messy, though, if Cath became attached. He has to be clear, say, *This is just for fun, no strings.*

Not that there's a woman in the world who can hear those words if she doesn't want to hear them.

"It's out of my hands," he says. "I got a job I have to get back to, come fall." God, he hopes this job is over by fall, that he's secured his bonus and is off on a trip. "But I like to have fun, if you know anyone who's open to having fun, but not being serious."

That night, Cath makes a big deal of parking her car behind the motel, waiting fifteen minutes before she comes to room 3. "It's a small town," she says. "People will gossip soon enough."

Once inside, she comes on pretty strong, almost too strong. He wouldn't have minded working a little harder. But she's good company, quick with a wisecrack while they watch baseball, then blessedly quiet when they go at it a second time, eager to make him happy. Still, when he studies her shoulders, her back in the moonlight, it's only a back, fleshy and earthbound. No wings.

"This is all I'm good for," he says to her back while he massages her shoulders. "I'm not looking to date or have a girlfriend."

"You took Polly to that auction."

"She doesn't have a car."

"I know. You ever wonder how she got here, without a car?"

He doesn't wonder because he knows. "Bus?"

"Even if she did take the bus, why here?"

"Sign says it's one of the ten best small towns in America."

"Sure, if you're married with kids. Or if you grew up here, I guess." She sips her beer, takes on a way-too-casual tone. "What's your excuse?"

"My truck was starting to overheat. I stopped rather than pushing it, risking the whole engine. Took a week to get the part and by then, I landed this job. I have the summer free, I can be where I want and here seemed as good a place as any."

"What kind of job do you have to go back to?"

"Sales." True enough. "It's seasonal work." Also true. "I'm an independent contractor. I don't get benefits, but I get lots of free time."

All true. Adam makes top dollar, always has more work than he needs.

"What do you sell?"

"Depends on who hires me."

She lets it drop. If a person is determined to be vague enough, almost no one has the forbearance, the curiosity really, to keep asking questions. She doesn't ask about his parents, although Adam would be happy to talk about them. She doesn't ask about why he went to the CIA, much less why he dropped out. (The instructors were assholes.)

No, Cath wants to talk about herself. Most people do. So he asks her questions—not too many or she'll get too attached. Women can't help themselves when men ask them questions. So he listens, asks a little, but not too much. She has a younger sister, and he gets the sense that Cath feels she is a little bit in her shadow. The sister is married, just bought a house, and Cath still doesn't have a degree, although she drops in and out of the nearby community college. She got into some trouble when she was in high school—not a big deal, but it derailed her college plans and, somehow, she never got back on track, but she's trying now, she has dreams. She's not going to be a waitress forever. She might not even stay in Belleville.

When it gets so boring he wants to scream, he gives her a little kiss and they go at it again.

The next day at the High-Ho, she drops by during lunch hour, although she's not on the schedule. At the first opportunity, she reaches over and flicks an invisible something from his T-shirt, makes sure Polly sees. Oh, Polly sees. The rest of her shift, she's switched back to interested, which amuses Adam to no end. He's pretty sure that she's going to ask him to come by and see her apartment. He's also sure that he's going to say yes to that, then no to whatever happens next. He enjoys the anticipation, plays the scene several ways in his mind, but the fantasy becomes impossible to keep in focus once a short, squat woman with a butch haircut comes in and orders a chef's salad. He knows the second he sees her that she's a private investigator and she's looking for the woman who's calling herself Polly Costello.

Because like calls to like, and that's what he's doing here.

10

The chef's salad at the High-Ho is better than Sue expected, but then—Sue's expectations aren't very high. Sue Snead always keeps her expectations low. Yet, somehow, she still ends up disappointed. By chef's salads. By people, professionally and personally. It's like there's a wall in her head and nothing she learns about human nature from her job can get through to the other side. Sue the person is going to end up hiring Sue the investigator one day.

Still, it's a really good salad. Crisp romaine, real bacon.

It has been three weeks since Sue and Anna broke up. She saw it coming for a long time. But it was like a blizzard in the weather forecast and she kept hoping she was wrong, that it wouldn't materialize, or that it would swing to the north or south. Baltimore has always had snowstorms like that. She remembered the last prophesied big one, the grocery stores and liquor stores and video stores denuded, everybody preparing to hole up for days. Philadelphia got thirteen inches, Baltimore woke up to pure sun and dry sidewalks.

You might sidestep one blizzard, but another one will come for you. Anna was never going to be Sue's happily ever after. They had embraced the lesbian cliché, renting a U-Haul six weeks after they met to bring Anna's motley assortment of possessions to Sue's house. Anna brought new meaning to *doesn't have a pot to piss in.* Maybe that's why Sue had never expected her to stay and maybe that's what doomed them, Sue's inability to believe that she could be enough for someone like Anna, a newly hatched baby-dyke, fresh from a bad marriage. Anna wanted to romp for a while, and who could blame her?

No, it was fair for Anna to leave her. Not so fair of her to raid the little safe where Sue kept some cash, or to take the Le Creuset Dutch oven that they had picked out together, but for which Sue had paid. It had been a nice winter, making stews and Bolognese in that bright-red dish. Then Anna had started complaining about her weight. *I'm getting fat, look at me.* She would grab her nonexistent belly with two hands while Sue contemplated her undeniable apple of a midriff, wondered if Anna's distaste for her own body extended to Sue's.

Anna then began carping about Sue's house. A neat, well-kept, but undeniably suburban house, a brick one-story that had the potential to be transformed into a midcentury marvel, but only if one spent twice as much as the house was worth. Baltimore's housing market was flat, flat as Anna's belly. The house hadn't gained a dollar in value since Sue bought it five years ago and it seemed crazy to Sue to take a second mortgage, harvesting what little equity she had managed to build. Anna brought home brochures for the condos going up along the waterfront, the promises of new developments where canning factories and shipyards had once stood. *As if,* Sue wanted to laugh. But Anna wasn't from Baltimore. She didn't know how often these dreams had been floated, how seldom they materialized.

The Pauline Hansen case was a nice distraction from her thoughts about Anna, although she doubted it would end happily. She can find almost anyone, she told the client, but she can't make them *do* anything. It is not, alas, illegal to stop loving someone, as Sue knows all too well. Odd, sure, to walk away from your own daughter in the process. Maybe even creepy. But legal. Sue has been clear with Gregg that she won't try to engage his ex if she finds her. She's not a go-between, she's a pointer. I find, you shoot.

God, she hopes there's not shooting involved. But while the guy has a hothead vibe, he's never been arrested for anything violent and there have been no police calls to the house on Kentucky Avenue.

He probably hasn't told her everything, but that's okay. They never do. She hasn't told him everything, either, the ramifications of the name change that popped out of the Chicago Title investigation. Maybe that's why Pauline Hansen ran, to put more distance between herself and her past. Again, it's legal to change one's name, legal not to share everything with a new partner. This lady wanted a fresh start, and Sue won't deny her that.

If only Gregg Hansen knew that losing his wife could be the healthiest thing that could happen to him.

Sue steals a look at the photo in her wallet, glances back at the woman behind the bar. Yeah, it was her, no doubt about it. She'd done nothing to disguise herself. Probably too vain to lose that amazing red hair. Still, it was a lucky break finding her so swiftly. She's been careful not to create a paper trail. No charges on the joint credit card, no withdrawals from the ATM. Finding her had been a bitch, but that just meant more hours, more money for Sue.

She's going to buy another Dutch oven. Only not red this time. Maybe blue or hunter green.

Sue had started the week in Bethany, showing Pauline Hansen's photo around. If you work hard, you make your own luck and, lo and behold, Sue found a geezer who copped to giving the redhead a ride, saying he offered to take her all the way to D.C., but she surprised him by getting out of the car only an hour into the trip. No, he couldn't remember where. A hundred dollars later, he gave up the name. Belleville. He had dropped her off in Belleville.

Once in Belleville, Sue made the tactical decision not to ask questions because it was way too small. Her queries would have gotten back to her quarry, could startle her into running again. So she walked around town, studying the shops, the restaurants. It's summer. Strangers aren't normal here, but they aren't completely unknown this time of year. There's a neighborhood of pretty Victorian houses and nineteenth-century stone homes. She pretended interest in those, all the while going in and out of various businesses. There's only a few places where a person's going to be able to work off the books and this dump, the High-Ho, was so clearly one of them.

And, bingo, there she is. Better looking than her picture. Or maybe just sexier. Sue can tell that this one would sleep with a person if it advanced her agenda. Not a moral judgment on Sue's part, merely an assessment. Sex is currency to this woman. Sue knows the type. Sue dates the type, although she doesn't mean to.

Sue doesn't try to talk to her. She doesn't want Pauline to remember her, even in hindsight. There's no real reason to do her job this way, except it amuses Sue to be invisible, to use her seeming deficits as assets. In a day or two, maybe a week, the husband will show up here and this Pauline Hansen will search through her mind, try to remember the moment she was caught. She'll never find it. Sue Snead. Sue Stealth, moving through the world without attracting attention. She knows what people think when they see her. Dyke. Dyke, dyke, dyke. They file her away under that heading and forget her. Great, makes her job easier.

"Refill?"

Pauline Hansen looms over her with an iced tea pitcher.

"Sure," Sue says. The woman has an almost literal scent on her, but it's not perfume. She smells like June itself, on its best day, warm and wild and promising. She reminds Sue of the tiny strawberries she used to find on that hill near her house, the ones she could never decide if they were safe to eat.

Sue didn't grow up dreaming of being a private detective, but that was only because she didn't realize girls could be PIs. Sure, she read Nancy Drew and Trixie Belden, but did anyone notice that those girls never got paid? Sue wanted to be Mannix or Barnaby Jones or Paul Drake, the investigator that Perry Mason used. Instead, she started out as a middle-school English teacher. But she was scared to have any kind of social life as long as she was teaching, even a secret one. She decided she had to find another gig. Around this time, her cousin, who had a small insurance agency, asked her to follow a guy claiming a back injury. Just that easy, Sue found her new vocation. She started in another PI's office, apprenticing until she could get her own license. She loves her work. It is the perfect job for people who are curious *enough,* but not randomly, promiscuously curious. An incurious person—this target's husband, for example—could never do it. But a supercurious person would also fail. You have to be willing to leave some doors closed, to focus on the task at hand. Some people are like rabbit holes and you can fall a long, long way down if you go too far.

Sue has asked herself repeatedly whether the husband is ill-intentioned. Sue doesn't want to deliver up a woman to a vengeful man. Had he hurt her? Is that why she ran? Would Pauline, who changed her name legally to Pauline Smith, then hid Pauline Smith inside Pauline Hansen, make that mistake again? Of course, to hear others tell it, she hadn't made that mistake the first time, that had been a lie she used as a cover. Still, Sue thinks she was telling the truth. Word on the street is that her first husband was dirty, maybe even a killer.

Ugh. Gristle on the ham. But, if she's fair—and Sue is always fair—the salad is outstanding in every other way, the proportions graceful, with lots of the things most places skimp on, turkey and bacon and chopped egg. And although a classic chef's salad is served with the ingredients set in decorative rows along the top, someone has taken the time to chop it, the way they do at Marconi's back in Baltimore, so each bite is perfectly dressed, with a little bit of everything, Sue's favorite kind of salad.

The cook keeps coming to the door and sneaking looks at her. Homophobe or xenophobe? Sue can't read him, but something is amiss. Is he jealous? Does he feel protective of Pauline? There's definitely a vibe there.

Sue pays her tab and leaves, feeling her hackles rise. When she drives away, the cook is standing outside, pretending to smoke, studying her car. If he were to run the plate—but why would he run the plate?

Her job is done. Almost too quickly. She thought she'd get a few more billable hours out of this one. If she were sleazy, she'd play both sides, ask Pauline Hansen how much it's worth to her not to be found, if her ex knows she used to be Pauline Ditmars and all that entails. But that would be wrong and, besides, Pauline Hansen clearly has no money. Sue shakes her head at her own foolishness, decides to go to a bar she knows, a discreet one in Little Italy where the locals pretend not to notice the women with good haircuts and well-tailored clothes. She needs to hold someone tonight. A dance or two would be enough, but maybe someone will want to come home with her. That would be nice.

Once in the bar, vodka in hand, she finds herself looking for red-heads, trying to find someone with that same sweet, wild strawberry scent of June.

Gregg walks into the High-Ho three days after the visit from that salad-munching PI. Polly probably doesn't make the connection, but Adam does. And you don't have to be a private detective to know that the man who slams the door open at 4:30 P.M., standing there backlit for a moment, all shadow in the afternoon sun, has a claim on Polly. Even Max and Ernest pick up on it.

Yet Polly couldn't be calmer. "What can I get for you?" she asks, drawing drafts for Max and Ernest.

"You can get your butt in the car and come home to your daughter."

"*Our* daughter. And I wager she's all I'm coming home to. You've got one foot out the door, Gregg. Can't blame me because I got both feet out before you did. Saves you the postage on the child support, the way I see it."

"Dammit, Pauline. I can't take care of a kid and work. She's your job."

"Yeah, well, I quit. Sorry I didn't give you two weeks' notice."

Unnatural, Adam's client had told him. He still doesn't believe it. She seems the opposite to him, almost too natural. The weirdest image pops into his head. Botswana, three years ago. He always travels after a big job, but when he got an unexpected bonus, he went really big, did the safari thing at a high level. Lodges with air-conditioning, great food, all the South African wine you could drink, and South African wine turned out to be darn good. But he was there to see wildlife, didn't miss a chance to go out with the guides. One night at dusk, riding back to the lodge in the setting sun, they saw some odd weasel-like animals darting across the road, mama and a brood. She was pushing and herding most of her children, but she was indifferent to the smallest one, resigned to its slim odds for survival. He could see Polly doing that, giving up on a lost cause.

Or maybe the kid's actually her stepchild? He never thought to ask about that. Yeah, probably a stepchild, like the other one.

Other than Max and Ernest, no one else is in the bar and Gregg probably doesn't register Adam, a headless patch of white T-shirt in the rectangle of the pass-through. If things get rough, Adam will step out, but he has a hunch Polly can take care of herself.

Sure enough, when Gregg grabs her arm, she doesn't shake it off. She levels her eyes on him in a way that demands: *You sure you want to do this here?* Is she counting on Adam to come to her rescue? Or simply assuming her husband won't get rough in front of witnesses? Max and Ernest are watching the couple with the same rapt attention they usually reserve for the television. This scene has much more of a plot than anything on CNN.

He drops her arm.

"I'm sorry, Gregg, but you can't make me come home. If you're not cheating on me already, it's not for lack of trying. You'll be dating someone soon as we have the 'talk.' Right? A weekend at the beach, one last family fling, then we were going to go home and you were going to sit me down and tell me what's what. Probably have some- one picked out. Well, good news. You're in a better position to take care of our kid, at least for the time being. You've got the job. The house is in both our names, but I'll waive my equity in it."

"We don't have any equity."

"The economy's not my fault."

"Isn't it? Isn't everything your fault? You're the one who wanted the kid."

This last seems to get her in a way that his presence, the phys- ical aggression, didn't. She turns away, out of arm's reach now, and busies herself behind the bar.

"Dammit, Pauline."

Max and Ernest don't notice the slight variation in her name. Adam does. But then, he has known her real name all along.

Her voice gets harder, although not louder. "Get out, Gregg. Get out or I can't be held responsible for what happens next."

And he does. Wuss. How did such a pansy ever land a woman like her? But Adam knows that she landed *him.* She just let him think he was in charge all these years. Cast, hook, reel.

The question remains why she wanted him in the first place.

Because the kitchen closes before the bar does, Adam and Polly leave about the same time. He's still in the motel across the road, while she has to walk about six blocks into town. Hard to imagine a safer place than Belleville. In the early days, he asked to walk her home and she always said no. Since he started sleeping with Cath he's pretty sure Polly wants him to ask again. He doesn't.

But Cath's not there tonight. Had to go see her sister up in Dover.

"You sure he's gone?"

"No," she says. "But he doesn't scare me."

"I don't think you should walk home alone."

"He's a coward, don't worry."

"That's why I do worry. No one's more dangerous than a coward."

They walk single file along the macadam that borders the old highway, then turn onto the main street. Called Main Street. Not much imagination in Belleville.

She must be thinking the same thing. "Always Main Street. Never Primary Street, for example."

"Central Avenue sometimes. And in the UK, they call it the High Street."

"You've traveled a lot." Statement, not a question.

"Yeah."

"I've hardly been anywhere."

"Most people's lives don't allow them the time to travel, really travel. If you're going to go places and get to know them, you need to take three, four weeks. Maybe six. I'm lucky to be able to do it that way."

"Because your work is *seasonal*."

Had he told her that? Maybe the day they went to the auction? Why does she make it sound as if she doesn't quite believe him?

"It can be."

"You make enough to travel, being a line cook?"

She knows he's not telling her the full story. But all he says is, "You'd be surprised."

"I bet I would." Sultry, suggestive, four ordinary words taut with meaning. Maybe tonight—

Gregg steps out of the shadows ahead. He has a gun. The stupid fucker.

"Maybe I *can* make you do what I say, Pauline."

"Dude—" That's Adam. He's more scared than he wants to be,

but a guy this stupid, he's likely to fire the gun by accident. It's bizarre the image that comes to him, Polly in his arms, eyes unfocused, her face vacant with shock.

"Stay out of this. It's not your business. Even if you're fucking her, it's not your business."

She sighs, calmer than both men.

"Oh, Gregg. You can't keep a gun on me 24/7. I'll be gone again the first minute I can. And this time, I'll do a better job hiding."

Adam does wonder how the private detective, the woman, found her. Polly's getting paid cash by the bar, doesn't have credit cards or a phone. Utilities on her apartment are probably paid by the landlord.

"Why, Pauline? Why?" Gregg's voice is whiny.

"I'm done, Gregg. Sorry, but I'm done. Let it go, let bygones be bygones. You've got your mom. You'll be okay. Jani will be okay, too. Eventually."

He takes a step forward and Adam instinctively shoves him, knocking him back over a bramble bush. Gregg still doesn't drop the gun, though, not until Adam stomps on his hand. Gregg screams, but not many people live along the old Main Street, so the scream attracts no attention. Polly picks up the gun, but Adam doesn't stop stomping on the guy's hand until he hears the crunch of bone. Probably would have happened sooner if he wasn't wearing the rubber clogs he prefers for kitchen work.

"You didn't need to do that," Polly says, but her eyes are feverish. She loves it.

Adam takes the gun from her and tosses it into the sewer, and they listen to it clattering down, making its way toward the bay, then on to the ocean.

"What about the money, Polly?" Gregg asks, getting to his feet, left hand cradling the damaged right one. If he has a stick shift, he'll have a hard time driving home. But a guy like this doesn't drive a stick shift. Probably doesn't know how.

"What money?"

"I know what you did with the insurance check."

This pricks Adam's interest.

"Nothing illegal."

"Forgery's illegal."

"I didn't forge it. Not my fault you'll sign anything I put in front of you during a football game."

"That check was made out to both of us."

"And it was deposited in our joint account. Then withdrawn—by me. All legal. I left you half the money, even though it was my car and you wrecked it. I'm fair."

Oh, a car, penny-ante stuff. Still, she does know her way around an insurance check, doesn't she?

"I got you another car."

"That broken-down Toyota. There are holes in the floorboard."

"You're not right."

It's unclear to Adam if Gregg is contesting the issue at hand or something larger, making a pronouncement about her general character. At any rate, Gregg gives up, stalks away holding his damaged hand.

Adam sees her to her door. He doesn't offer to walk her to the top of the stairs, though. This stairway is an afterthought, small, the carpet smelling faintly of mildew.

Polly lingers in the little vestibule. "You want to come in? See that bed you helped me get?"

No. Yes. No. *Yes.*

"Sure."

70

He convinces himself that it's weird *not* to go up, that she will suspect him if he doesn't. In cartoons, devils and angels argue it out on a guy's shoulder, but he's long past a fight between right and wrong. There's nothing to be done.

The walk up the stairs is the longest walk he's ever taken. He goes in, stands in the doorway to her bedroom while she lingers behind him in the large room that serves as kitchen and living room. Amazing how cozy she's made the place with just a few possessions. Lucky she likes old things—the stove and fridge look to be at least forty years old.

"Yep, that's a bed," he says, looking into her bedroom. It's staged as if she knew he would be here tonight—a bedside lamp draped with a pink scarf, a silk robe tossed over the rails at the foot of the bed. There's a vase of wildflowers on the bureau. They didn't buy a bureau that day at the auction. Was it already here? Or did she get some other guy to take her to another auction? It makes him crazy jealous, thinking about her at another auction with another man.

When he turns around, she doesn't have a stitch on.

"I asked if you wanted to *see* the bed. You want to get in it, you're going to have to earn it."

She goes over to the little metal table from the auction, hoists herself up on it, never taking her eyes from his. She's excited and he knows why. It's the violence, the sound of her husband's hand under his foot, his whimpers. Well, Adam's not going to let her call the shots. He picks her up and carries her to the bed. She fights him, bites and scratches. It's shaming how much he likes this. They haven't even kissed yet, and she's drawn blood on him.

"We do it my way first," he says. "Maybe later I'll let you call the shots."

She smiles and he realizes she's still in charge, that everything is happening as she wants it to. He tells himself that he wants it this way, too, and then he shuts down the voice in his head, the one worrying about the job and ethics and where he goes from here. He convinces himself that this is the only way to do the job. *Follow her. Get close to her.* Those were his instructions.

He can't get much closer than he is now.

12

Polly's first test for Adam is to make him break up with Cath. Of course he's going to stop seeing her, that's a given. But that's not good enough. Polly needs him to break up with Cath in a way that will be at once humiliating and baffling. Only he has to think it's his idea.

It helps that he brings it up first.

"So," he says. "I was seeing Cath. I guess that will have to stop."

It is ten hours later, and they have been on what can only be called a bender, one of those sex hazes where one stops for a little food, a little sleep, maybe a shower. Taken together, of course. Her shower is the one mean, dark room in the apartment, a rigged-up thing with one of those cheap detachable hoses. It's hard enough for one person to get under the spray from the cracked, handheld showerhead. But they are in that mode where nothing matters as long as they can touch each other.

How long will this last? she thinks.

How long does she want it to last?

How long does she need it to last?

He brings up Cath after they step out of the shower, towel each other playfully. She is ashamed of her towels, although they are new. Thin, cheap, inadequate. All she has ever wanted is a *home,* a place with things that bring comfort. Thick towels, deep chairs, soft rugs. That doesn't necessarily mean having money, but it means having more money than she's ever had. So far.

"You can't stop *seeing* her. She works there every day. What are you going to do, shut your eyes?"

"Very funny," he says, kissing her neck. For a while, everything she says will be funny, wonderful, profound. For a while.

"I don't like fake words. *Seeing.* Yeah, I see her, too. But I don't have sex with her. Don't use a word to make something sound nicer than it is."

"Euphemism."

"I guess you went to college, huh?"

"So did you."

Her impulse is to snap her head around, stare him down, but she fights it. Looks in the mirror, runs her fingers through her damp hair. The shower has a knack for getting nothing wet except the things you want to keep dry. "I never said that."

"I just assumed—I meant—sorry. You're clearly smart as a whip."

"That's a weird phrase. Whips aren't smart. They *smart.*" She raises one eyebrow, hoping this gives the impression that she has firsthand knowledge.

He laughs. "See what I mean? That's pretty good wordplay. Cath couldn't do that. Cath couldn't find her way out of a room with no walls."

She decides to risk a little cattiness, knowing it will read as jealousy and he'll be flattered. "But even she can find her ass with both hands. She's got quite the caboose. If you could move that thing to her hip, she'd look like she had a sidecar."

"Sidecars," he says. "You never see those anymore."

"I don't think I ever saw one in real life, only movies. And maybe in that cartoon, from when we were kids? The one with Penelope Pitstop?"

"Oh, yeah. What was that called? With the bad guy and the dog who tried to cheat. Anyway, you know where you see sidecars? Cuba. Havana."

"How'd you get to Cuba? I thought that was illegal."

"I spent some time in Jamaica and there was a resort that arranged day excursions, did it in a way that you didn't get your passport stamped. Havana was fascinating."

"Yeah, but—what is there to see?"

"There's always something to see. Don't you want to travel?"

She's pretty sure what she's expected to say: *Of course. Who doesn't?* The truth is that this town, Belleville, the Delaware shore— that's about as far as she's gotten from Baltimore in her time. And Frostburg, but she doesn't count that. Not like she got outside much.

"Where'd you go to school?" she asks.

"Oberlin. That's in Ohio."

She wants to say, *I know.* Except she didn't.

"You're not from Baltimore."

"I'm not, as it happens, but going to college in Ohio doesn't mean you're not from Baltimore. What makes you think I'm not a Baltimorean? I've lived there almost three years."

Almost three years. Good to know.

"You ask a Baltimore person where they went to school, they tell you their high school. Dundalk for me. I started community college, then I dropped out. So, yeah, I guess you can say I went to college."

They are dry now, but still naked. She moves to the kitchen, stands in front of her refrigerator. She can't figure out if she is hungry or thirsty. The only appetite she can gauge is her desire for him. Eggs. She should make him eggs. No one ever cooks for the cook.

"Why did you drop out?"

She shrugs, taking out the carton of eggs, cracks four into a bowl. "I was young and stupid. Didn't see what the point was. Maybe I'll go back one day. Anyway, what are you going to do about Cath? Don't be unkind. It's not her fault—"

He has crept up behind her and she turns, kisses him. He gets almost too excited and she backs away, goes to light the stove. It's a fussy old thing, often takes two, three match strikes to light. The Bakelite handles are loose and will be impossible to replace if they strip all the way. But she thinks it's beautiful, rounded in a way that stoves aren't anymore, the white enamel faded to a yellowish ivory. It reminds her of a pickup she saw once and coveted, a 1950s Studebaker. But maybe it was the man who drove the truck that she really wanted. All she saw was his forearm and a bit of his face, but he looked like someone who would take care of a woman. For days, she daydreamed about jumping into the bed of that truck, going home with that man.

"What are you going to do," she repeats. "About Cath."

"I guess I'll call her, ask her to meet me somewhere."

"You think that's the kindest way?"

"Isn't it?" Genuinely confused. Good.

"I know, it seems like it should be, but—my two cents, as a woman? Act as if y'all were never together. Like it was all in her head. Be courteous, but don't get drawn into conversations. If she asks to talk or calls you—keep it short. When she asks to get together, say you can't, no explanations. That's a clean break. I hate to say it about my own sex, but women see any scrap of kindness as a promise. You've got to do whatever it takes to keep her from thinking she has a chance with you." Tiny pause. "Unless she does? Maybe this was just a onetime thing for you?"

He doesn't speak for a while and she's worried she's misjudged him, that last night and today have been nothing more than the passion and excitement fueled by the encounter with Gregg. It won't be the first time she's read a man wrong. Yet she was sure this man wanted her, although there was something he was fighting in his own nature. A wife, probably. His story doesn't add up. The travel, the "seasonal" work, the shiny new truck. Yes, there's probably a woman and a kid or two somewhere. Maybe he has families stashed all over the country and that's why he's so big on traveling.

"Okay," he says. "I want to do what's right."

He has to know what she's saying is too good to be true. Good Lord, if this were the kindest way to break up with a woman, that would be the greatest thing that ever happened to men. Maybe she should write an advice book for men, one that tells them everything they want to hear, as opposed to all those books for women, which tell them to be the opposite of what they are, no matter what that is.

If she wrote an advice book for women, it would basically say: *Tell men what they want to hear.* What they *think* they want to hear. But it wouldn't do anyone any good, because most women aren't her. It's not her looks or her body. Her looks are only slightly above average, her body didn't come into its own until she had all those long empty days to exercise. Besides, she would never invest so heavily in a commodity that won't last forever. It's how she is on the inside that makes her different from other women. She fixes her gaze on the goal and never loses sight of it.

The goal is never a man. Never. Men are the stones she jumps to, one after another, toward the goal. She's getting closer. Thank God she's patient. She never figured this to take so long, but you can't plan for every contingency.

And now she's thrown a monkey wrench into her own works. But he's planning to leave this fall and that suits her just fine. She'll have moved on by then, too.

He eats the eggs from the pan, standing up. She starts kissing him again, but gentle, sweet ones, as if she doesn't know where it's going to go. She doesn't want him to think, *I'm being rewarded*. If he makes the conscious connection, that's no good. Moaning, he picks her up, carries her back to the bedroom, tosses her on the bed. The sheets are damp, almost as if dew has fallen on them. She's going to have to get to the Laundromat at some point today.

The morning is warm, but not unbearable, not yet. She doesn't have AC, not even in the bedroom, only a box fan in the window. Set to high, it's loud enough to drown out the noise he's about to start making.

She asks innocently, "Don't you want coffee? I can—" Then lets him cover her with him. There's always a quick moment of panic when a man is on top of her, but she gets through it.

"One more thing," she tells him, not sure if he's the kind of guy who can hear or understand anything at this point. "At work, we're a secret. Which means we're a secret in this town. This will be the last time you leave my place in daylight."

He grunts. A yes? She's pretty sure he would agree to anything she said right now.

By the end of the week, Cath's eyes are red all the time, just big and sad and wretched looking. Polly takes her into the bathroom for a confidential talk.

"Adam won't even speak to me," she sobs, sitting on the closed toilet. "I think he's seeing someone else, but he says no. He acts like he doesn't owe me anything. It's like we were never together at all."

"Men," Polly says, tearing off a piece of toilet paper and handing it to her. "You're better off without that asshole. He probably thinks he's being kind, but this is anything but."

13

Adam tries to tell himself that Plan B is superior to Plan A in every way. No, he shouldn't be sleeping with her, but she's the one who wants to keep it a secret. He didn't see that coming. Most women like to stake their claim publicly. His client doesn't have to know that he's crossed the line. His client won't care, as long as the job gets done.

Adam's the one who cares. He's an ethical guy. He's never done anything like this. But he can't stop. When he leaves her at 3 A.M., 4 A.M., never later than 5 A.M., he sometimes has trouble remembering why he was supposed to get to know her in the first place.

And although his client doesn't have a clue what's going on, he's not exactly pleased with Adam.

"What's taking so long?" the client demands in their next phone call.

"First of all, this whole thing is an improvisation, right? If I didn't get a job in that place, I couldn't keep tabs on her."

"But you must have learned something, working alongside her."

Working alongside her. Sure, let's call it that.

"She doesn't talk much," Adam says. "And she doesn't have a car. So unless it's stashed somewhere here in Belleville—"

"That's an idea."

"No. She's never been here before in her life."

"I thought you said she didn't talk."

"Doesn't talk *much*. Some things come up."

He has started using the pay phone outside the motel to call his client, just in case the phone in his room isn't secure. Not that he thinks anyone has him bugged, but he has to assume the front desk has records of the numbers he calls, even if it's billed to his calling card. It costs too much to use the mobile and that's what a straight shooter he is, has always been. He doesn't run up costs no matter how deep the client's pockets. He *is* ethical, he reminds himself, under the red hood that shields the pay phone from the elements. It's not a full-on phone booth, but it provides all the privacy he needs. There's nothing weird about being a guy who uses a public phone, right?

Monday. He has the night off. She doesn't. He tries to ignore the feeling that is demanding to be heard, this feeling that he can't wait until her shift ends. He no longer walks her home, of course, and she doesn't let him come over every night. He pretends that's mutual, that they both want a little space. They have devised a system, their own one if by land, two if by sea. If they're working the same shift, she passes a fake check to him—*Adam and Eve on a raft, whiskey down.* That means come over. He told her to use that because no one in this place ever orders poached eggs with rye toast.

No fake check, no visit, no explanation. It pains him to admit how much he yearns to see that rectangle of lined green paper being clipped and rotated toward him. The words are just old-fashioned diner slang, innocuous should anyone else see it. *Adam and Eve on a raft, whiskey down.* Never has the thought of two poached eggs on rye toast excited him more.

On Mondays, when there's no dinner service at the High-Ho, she takes a smoke break as close to six on the dot as possible if she wants to see him. Standing here at the phone booth, the sun still hot, Adam misses a few things his client is yammering because he's waiting to see if she's going to come out. 6 P.M., 6:01, 6:02—it's not always exact because she has to have someone cover for her.

At 6:03, she walks out, and it scares him how glad this makes him.

"I hear you," he says to his client, having heard nothing for the past three minutes.

Five hours later, 11 P.M., he approaches her apartment. Belleville is the kind of town where what few sidewalks they have would be rolled up by eleven or so. He never sees anyone, not even a lone insomniac walking a dog. So he has to assume no one sees him.

They have already agreed that she will leave her entry door, the downstairs one, ajar; her actual door is always unlocked. Only in a town like this would he allow such an arrangement. Besides, he likes that she's in bed when he gets there. With the exception of the quilt, folded over the footboard of the bed, the linens are all white and she makes him think of a flame, with her long pale peachy body, the red hair at top, the piercing blue eyes. He used to prefer women with a little froufrou and airs. Lingerie, heels, garters. She doesn't go for that. She likes to be naked and not just because of the warm nights, when even the breezes and her window fan can't do much but push the hot air around. "I think it's silly," she says, "putting on stuff only to take it off."

He thinks he understands. She wants him to believe that she's naked, transparent. *What you see is what you get.* She is so clearly the opposite. He still can't quite believe she's done what his client says. But she's done it before, no? Left another man, another kid, in the lurch, then stole money from the kid when the guy died, disappeared with the life insurance. Hers, free and clear, but a shitty thing to do. "She's capable of anything," his client has warned him. Adam doesn't think that's quite true. Like most people, she's rationalized her poor decisions, come up with a reason that she feels entitled to cut and run, treated herself to a bonus on her way out the door. It would be okay if she just ripped the guys off. But there are kids in the mix, too. Is she pulling the same scam again? How will that work, given that her husband knows where she is? Could she really have blown through all the money she stole the first time?

But if she blew it all, what did she blow it on? And if she's got her new jackpot stashed somewhere around here, what's keeping her from trying to claim it? What is she waiting for?

Her eyes flutter when he heaves his body into her bed and the mattress shifts beneath them. But she doesn't say a word, simply opens her arms, her mouth, herself to him.

The next day at work, Mr. C tells them the bar has to close for one day for an exterminator's visit. "Routine," he adds quickly. "State law. No big deal." Everybody gets Wednesday off.

"Off" as in: you don't get paid. Adam can afford it, but he notices her face falls a little. Wednesday is Polly's night to work the big room on her own, her best tip night.

But all she says is, "Want to go to Baltimore?"

"D.C. is a better place to spend a day," he counters, curious to see what she'll reply.

"I got business in Baltimore. It won't take long."

Bingo.

She's not a chatty woman, that's part of her charm, but she seems unusually quiet even for her, especially as they cross the Bay Bridge Wednesday morning.

"You scared of the bridge?"

She shakes her head, unconvincingly. "Not really. Although, one time, I did that bridge walk, the one in the spring. A shuttle bus takes you to the eastern side and you walk back to Sandy Point. When you do that, you realize how high up it is. And it moves, the bridge. Sways like a hammock. Now I can feel it, every time."

Her sentences are landing like questions. Not usually her style. Something about crossing the bay seems to have made her tentative, less herself. Returning to the scene of the crime?

"Of course it moves. It's a suspension bridge. If it didn't have some give, it would collapse."

She gives him an impatient look as if that's some masculine spoilsport bullshit. She doesn't talk again until they're on the Beltway, about fifteen minutes out from downtown. With her, it's hard to tell if she's miffed or being her usual silent self.

"Drop me off at the Hyatt," she says.

"I thought we were spending the day together."

"I got this one thing I need to do," she says. "I told you. Then I'll meet you for a late lunch in Fells Point. Where you wanna go? John Steven's? Bertha's?"

"John Steven's is fine," he says. "But where—"

"It's a family thing," she says. "I gotta do it alone. It's no big deal—but I have to be alone."

He thinks, but doesn't say, *You told Gregg you don't have any family*. His client told him the same thing. Parents dead, not in touch with any blood relatives, no friends.

He drops her at the Hyatt, watches in the rearview as she gets into the line for a cab. His truck is too noticeable. He can't follow her in this. But he makes note of the cab's number, watches it head north, and figures he has a chance of catching it, given the slow-as-syrup traffic. He swoops into the driveway, hands his truck over to the valet, hops into another cab and promises a $50 bonus if the driver can find cab number 1214. It's on his client's tab, after all.

Four blocks up Calvert Street, they spot 1214.

"Hang back," he says. "Don't get too close."

"You a spy?" the guy laughs. He's in his sixties, a big-boned African American man, the kind of guy who seems to find all white people mildly ridiculous. He's right, Adam has to admit, although not about Adam, of course.

"Following my wife," he says.

"Oooh, intrigue. I got you. I got you." Jolly, as if it's all a game. Adam feels a stab of anger for the man he just pretended to be. If he were a husband following his wife, it wouldn't be a joking matter.

Her cab cuts right, gets on the JFX going north. Adam hunkers down in the back seat, not that he's too worried about her noticing him. Three miles up, her cab takes the exit to Northern Parkway, heads west. The track? Sinai Hospital? When her cab turns right onto Rogers Avenue, he tells his guy to continue straight. He knows the area well enough to recognize that's basically a residential street. Two cabs on that winding two-lane road? Too suspicious.

"Stay on Northern Parkway, make a U, and take me back to the hotel," he tells his guy.

"Ah, man."

"Don't worry. You'll get your fifty."

"But I wanted to know the end of the story."

Don't we all.

He ransoms his car back from the valet, $20, another receipt to file with the client. He can see things from his client's point of view. What's taking so long? But he honestly doesn't see what he could do better, faster. Was she headed to a personal residence? There's no way she was going to a bank or a business, not in that neck of the woods, and he's sure she didn't know she had a tail to shake.

Tail to shake. He thinks about her rear end. She's so slender above the waist, then that wonderful swell of flesh below, like a summer peach.

He hopes his jones for her passes by the end of peach season.

Adam walks around Fells Point to kill time. He finds a neck-lace in a vintage store that makes him think of her, a coral-colored flower on a chain. Bakelite, 1940s. The shopkeeper asks if he wants it wrapped, but he thinks that's overkill. Then, when he sees her face at John Steven's, he wishes he had gone to a little more trouble. She tries to keep her sunglasses on until the last possible moment despite the overcast day, but when she removes them, it's clear she's been crying—and clear she's tried to cover it up, maybe with some cold water, a little makeup.

The necklace makes her smile and he feels as if he's won the lottery. "This is exactly my kind of thing." She puts it on right away. But being happy for even a moment seems to make her sadder. She doesn't want to eat anything, drinks only one beer. Some day off this is.

The sun is almost down by the time they hit Annapolis. "Pull off here," she says, pointing to the last exit before the bridge, where there are a couple of fast-food places.

"You hungry? We can do better than this."

"I want to drive your truck across the bridge. Maybe in something this big, I won't feel it."

"Do you really feel the bridge move?"

"I think I do. That's all that matters."

They change places in a Roy Rogers parking lot. She doesn't get out, just crawls over and sits in his lap, making him squirm out from under her to get to the passenger side. She is literally white knuckled, but otherwise composed. He doesn't talk, doesn't try to change the radio, despite the song that's playing, the one about chasing waterfalls. Not his thing, this song. Toward the end, as the bridge flattens out and delivers them safely back to land, she exhales as if she's been holding her breath for the entire five-mile span. He's not surprised when she glides off at the first possible exit on the other side.

He *is* surprised when she keeps driving, going deeper and deeper down the country road. The world has gone dark around them. Two minutes ago, there was a fiery sun in the rearview mirror, flattening on the horizon, made more brilliant by today's clouds. Now the sky is blue black. She pulls over next to a cornfield, unfastens her seat belt, and lifts up her skirt. Look at that. She's wearing the kind of gear she normally disdains. The whole megillah, although there are no stockings connected to the garter belt, which is weird.

"You're not the only one who went shopping today," she says, crawling on top of him. She pulls down her top, so he can see the matching bra. It's coral, almost the exact same shade as the rose now nestled between her breasts. They both know what suits her.

He wonders what happened to the underwear she was wearing this morning, did she put it in her purse? Can you say in a lingerie store, *I'll just wear this out*—and then he stops thinking for a while.

When they're done, she has a smoke. She doesn't smoke much and her mouth doesn't taste of it, not like Cath, who tried to mask her chronic tobacco breath with mouthwash. Polly smokes maybe once or twice a week, and only then because that's their code.

Unnatural.

He tells his client to get out of his head. The husband, too. Didn't he use those same words or something similar? *Shut up, everybody.* She's the most natural woman he's ever met. She's all the elements. Fire, water, earth, air.

"I feel safe with you," she says. "With you, I *wanted* to feel the movement of the bridge. I know you won't let me go over the edge."

And he feels awful because his job, in a sense, is to push her over the edge.

14

Irving curses silently when he sees the latest invoice from Adam.
His curses are Yiddish—*behema, putz, schmuck*. No one who works
for him—the plump, gap-toothed black woman who sits at the desk
by the front door, Susie, or the young handyman, Johnny, who does
a little of this, a little of that—would understand these words if he
spoke them aloud, but he still will not speak them outside his head.
He has never liked crude language and he has no respect for those
who use it.

But Adam Bosk! Adam Bosk, who came so highly recommended.
Behema, putz, schmuck. Look at these bills. Mileage to and from
Baltimore, yet also a $75 cab receipt for the same trip, plus parking.
Irving isn't blindsided by these charges. Adam, dutiful man that he
is, explained what happened before he sent the monthly invoice on
Friday. He played it well, Irving has to give him that. And thank
God he didn't follow her up Rogers Avenue, because Irving knows
where she was headed even if Adam doesn't. If Adam had seen her
destination, he might have asked some questions, and while Irving
is quick on his feet, he hasn't figured out how to make a few pesky

facts go away. It's not as if Adam needs to know *everything*. The basic outline of what Irving has told him is correct. This *nafkeh* ripped him off. Now he has a chance to make her pay him back, but he needs leverage first. That's Adam's job, even if he doesn't quite know it. Find what she fears losing.

The trip to Baltimore, her little game with the cab, is also proof that she's keeping Adam in the dark—and not just about her real name. That pleases Irving, because if she's bothering to keep such little secrets, it means he must be right about the big secret. But how much more money can he expend when he's not 100 percent sure of any return? Maybe he should cut his losses, admit that this whole quest is as much about pride as unfinished business.

He doesn't usually let emotion dictate his business moves. But it seemed so simple at first. Gather some intel on her current situation, then blackmail her. He wasn't greedy, but a 10 percent finder's fee seemed about right. Twenty, to make up for what she did ten years ago. Only who could anticipate that she would walk out on her family? That husband better watch his back, Irving thinks, and maybe the kid, too. Ditmars once suggested to him that the issues with the other kid, those were her fault.

Eight weeks ago, the plan had seemed foolproof. Buddy up with the husband, then blackmail her with the threat of exposure. When the family took off for the beach all of a sudden, Irving had agreed with Adam that such a friendship would be easier to jump-start at the shore. Easier for strangers to come into your life on vacation. Then they would return to Baltimore and Adam would insinuate himself into the family's routines, maybe start double-dating with them, whatever people do. The husband, even if he knew about her current scam, was the best way in. She was a sharp cookie and her life as a stay-at-home mom didn't offer her much exposure to new friends, male or female. That's another reason Irving thinks he's right about her. The very lack of friends, the way she keeps to herself. She has secrets. And now that she's left the new husband, she has to be on the verge of leading Irving—finally, finally—to an almost literal pot of gold at the end of the rainbow.

So why hasn't she? Is he throwing good money after bad? What does that phrase even mean? If you've spent bad money, you continue to spend bad money, right? The money doesn't become good once you realize how foolish you've been.

He walks to the front of his office, peers out the window at Route 40. This strip of commercial highway was never nice, but it had been respectable in his childhood. There had been a Korvette's across the street—whatever happened to Korvette's? Also a reliable place for steamed crabs, back in the day. Then that soft ice cream place closer to Ingleside. Gino's, Hot Shoppes Jr. Now everything's just a little sleazier, a little trashier. Through the 1970s, there was a girls' school, looked like a castle to him, near the city-county line. But that closed long ago. Why do things have to change? And why is it always for the worse? Yes, he gets that the world has to keep moving, but movement is not necessarily progress. They put a man on the moon, so what? They still can't cure cancer. If they could cure cancer, he wouldn't be a widower at age sixty-three.

He turns to Susie, typing away.

"You know what never changes, Susie?"

"What, Mr. L?" she asks, still typing. Such a good girl, industrious, capable, never idle. Is it okay to call her *girl*? You can't call a black man *boy*, he knows that. This world makes his head hurt.

"*People*. What they wear changes. How they talk, maybe. But people never change and that has made me a rich man by most people's measure."

Although not, he thinks, as rich as he should be and that's on *her*. She stole his money, he can't help seeing it that way, even if no cop would agree. Would have gotten away with it, too, if it weren't for that chance encounter last fall. Then she surfaced, hiding inside a suburban mom, and he saw that she was playing a very long game. Maybe waiting for him to die? She was going to be disappointed then. He's only sixty-three, which might seem old to her, but his people are long-lived, their memories sharp to the end. Now and then, especially when he's paying Adam Bosk's invoices, he starts to forget why he wants to get her back, why it matters so much, then he reminds himself: *It's the principle.* Even if no one else knows or remembers what she did to him, he does—and he's going to get what was his. That's the thing about being rich. You can afford a few principles.

He just hopes that wherever she parked the money, she's getting a good interest rate.

Interest. Yeah, she always got a lot of interest. Is Adam sleeping with her? Probably. Unprofessional, but that one does things to men. She's a witch. He tries to tell himself he doesn't get the appeal, but he can't lie. Back in the day, even when she was heavier, she had a glow about her. He would try to prolong his visits to the house, arriving when he knew Ditmars wasn't there yet, asking for a glass of water, acting kindly toward that scary, sad kid. He was never sure how much she knew. At the time, she seemed kind of dumb to him. Incurious, to be more accurate. Her entire life was that house and that kid. It was grim, and being married to Ditmars didn't make it any better, although Irving doesn't believe all those things they said about Ditmars, after. Guy didn't have it in him. Sure, he was probably a *putz* in a lot of ways, and a bully, too, but he wouldn't have hit a woman. Besides, she could have left, anytime. It's not like he had her chained to the radiator.

When Adam sent him the photos from the beach, he was stunned by how much better-looking she was now. At first, he wondered if that meant she had started tapping into the money. Transformations like that, when a woman's in her thirties—they don't just happen. But, yeah, she probably did drop weight, given her circumstances. In her case, that was enough. Lost the weight, grew her hair out, let it go back to its natural color. Ditmars had made her dye her hair blond, the stupid oaf. The way she looks now, she could have done better than the second guy she married. Apparently she got knocked up. Again. He wondered why she just didn't decommission the equipment once and for all. But some women worry that they'll stop being women if they do that.

He goes back to his desk, pulls out those photos again, a treat he tries to indulge no more than weekly. Okay, daily, as of late. She's wearing a one-piece, cut very low in the back. She's helping her new kid build a sand castle. The way she's posed—her rear end tilted up in the air—it's like she knows someone's watching her. Not necessarily Adam, who took these photos. Boy, if she had any inkling who Adam is, who he's working for, she'd pull up stakes and leave that sleepy little Delaware town. He's starting to think that may be the point for her, seeing how long she can go without leading Irving to the pot of gold at the end of this endless rainbow.

Then he wonders if she thinks of him, ever.

He remembers their one time. It was her idea, but it wasn't really that great and he realized—later—that it was a part of setting him up. "Could you help me get a policy on Ditmars?" *Sure, of course, but doesn't the FOP*—"It won't be enough. Because of Joy. The thing is, Ditmars doesn't want it, says it's a waste of money, but I'm smart with the household budget, I can carve out the payments monthly and he'll never know. I just need someone, you know, friendly. Who won't sweat the signature. Who will let me slide on whatever medical tests are required. You must know someone like that. It's mainly for my peace of mind. You know how, if you take an umbrella, it never rains, but when you risk it, you get soaking wet? Besides, Ditmars is healthy as an ox."

Of course, even an ox can't survive a knife through his heart. But Irving wasn't deconstructing her words just then. Irving was on top of her, showing her how friendly he could be. *Sure, I'll find someone to write you a policy. A million dollars for some dumb cop's life.* Why not? It wasn't like an arson investigator put himself at that much risk, not one like Ditmars. The only way Ditmars put himself in danger was by sleeping with other cops' wives, hanging out with drug dealers and murderers. Irving doubted she'd be able to make the monthly payments anyway. Then, when Ditmars did die, he assumed she wouldn't be able to collect, given the circumstances.

But she had outsmarted him by making the daughter the beneficiary of that policy. And now she has outrun him, or tried to. She seemed so weak, so vulnerable. She had needed him. Briefly, just for one afternoon, he let himself think that she wanted him. He knows better now.

He sighs, writes a check to Adam Bosk for his July expenses, then pays the August retainer. He'll give him until Labor Day, then pull the plug.

Maybe in the end, all money is bad money.

15

The trip to Baltimore wasn't a good idea. It was never a good idea. It felt terrible to go. It felt terrible not to go. When she goes, she feels defensive, forced to see herself as others see her. But *not* going makes her that person, too. She can't win. And now she's doubly awful, with two trips to make, two burdens to carry in her heart.

Her low mood continues for days. She can hide it at work. She has to. There's no percentage in being a sulky waitress. But she finds she's snappish with Adam. She wishes he would disappear for a few days. She revealed too much of herself on that trip. Not her actual secrets, but the fact that she has secrets, which is bad enough. She should have concocted a cover story, been nonchalant, let him drive her right up to the front door. *My niece. My cousin. My half sister.* There were a dozen lies she could have told, convincingly, any one of which would have been better than taking that taxi, all but announcing: I AM HIDING SOMETHING FROM YOU.

Which wouldn't matter if she didn't care about him. She can't afford to love any man. But she does, or is beginning to. It's a dangerous game, trying to convince someone you love him. Sometimes, the person you end up convincing is yourself. She's supposed to be leaving by Labor Day.

And so is he.

She finds herself looking for him, at work. Happy for a flash of his forearm as he hands plates through the pass-through. Wanting to make eye contact as she rattles off special orders, as if "Whole wheat, no mayo, no lettuce, extra pickles" is a love song. She tells herself sternly that she is not in love with him. How could she be in love? She doesn't know him and he doesn't know her. He will never know her. To be *known*—there's nothing riskier. She stands behind the bar, listens to Max and Ernest say the same things they say every day, about the Orioles and the Phillies and how late the tomatoes are this summer and do you think OJ did it.

Burton—always Burton, never Burt, he got angry if you called him Burt—had known her since childhood. They had come up together in the same neighborhood, the good part of Dundalk, although some ignorant people laugh at the idea that Dundalk has a good part. But there are beautiful old houses in Dundalk and they were both the children of steel workers at a time when steel workers did quite well. Their families had nice two-story brick homes, memberships at the swimming club.

Five years apart in age, Polly Costello and Burton Ditmars hadn't traveled in the same circles growing up. Five years is huge when you are a kid; it might as well be fifty. Then the summer she was fourteen going on fifteen, she bought a two-piece bathing suit. Yellow, no straps, scandalous by the standards of the day. And a bad choice for a girl who was a little overweight and always burned before she tanned. But she wasn't fat, just not model thin, and Burton cared only about the top half of the bikini. He liked a little heft on the bottom, too. Later, when he began to cheat on her, it was always with bottom-heavy women. Prostitutes, usually. When he was caught, he insisted his choice was chivalrous, made in consideration of her feelings. Because no wife could be jealous of a Wise Avenue whore, right? That was sheer release, that was natural, and she was so exhausted all the time. It was the most considerate thing he could do, if you thought about it. Or so he argued. No, not even argued, said blandly as if it were a fact she had to accept. *I don't like onions. We'll go to my mom's for Sunday dinner. I'm going to cheat on you.*

"You know why I'm exhausted, Ditmars," she would say, sitting at their kitchen table, weeping. Early in their marriage, she had started using his surname, the way all his buddies did. Not that they were buddies. Anything but.

The house alone was enough to make her cry. It was okay, but small and cramped, with only one bathroom. She had thought they would enjoy a better standard of living, him being a cop. Crime, unlike the demand for U.S. steel, didn't have huge fluctuations.

And crime didn't crawl into the lungs and skin of men, destroying them. Her father had died before the young couple's first wedding anniversary. Her mother had opted out of the class-action suit, accepted a settlement, moved to a small town on the Gulf Coast in Florida. When she died less than a decade later, people said politely that some marriages were like that, the partner can't go on, but Polly knew she had killed her mother.

"It was your choice," Ditmars said when she dared to feel sorry for herself.

"No, not this. You can't say this is my fault." She was scared to tell the truth, that she thought he was the one who was accountable, for his indifference and his slowness to respond that horrible day. *If they had gotten there sooner, if he had been more forceful.* But one night, she did, she said the things that were never supposed to be said and, sure enough, he hit her. Only once, but with a closed fist straight to her stomach, hard enough to double her over.

"I hope nothing ever grows in there again," he said. "If it does, I'll make sure it's not in there for long."

She would lie in bed at night alone, trying to remember Burton, the shy young nineteen-year-old who had dared to flirt with the fourteen-year-old in the yellow bathing suit. He hadn't known she was fourteen, not at first. He assumed sixteen, would have been fine with fifteen, and, when he learned fourteen, he said, "Wow, there are laws." Then he set out trying to persuade her to break those laws. All summer long, in the backs of cars, on blankets spread in spots he said no one could see. *I'm dying. I'll die if I can't. No, really, I'll truly die. I'd die for you.* Always some variation of death. Until, finally, he decided he could not, would not wait. He raped her. Not that anyone would call it that. Not even her father would call it that. She had brought this on herself. Burton said as much, when he was finished: "I didn't want to do that." Weeping, as if she had forced him to be a lesser version of himself.

Then: "I love you." So it was okay.

They went together for three years. She was too young to go on the Pill without her parents' consent, but she was careful, truly careful. So they were both surprised when she turned up pregnant at age seventeen. He was twenty-two then, in his last year at UB. "There goes law school," he said. He had never mentioned law school before. He joined the county police department, and they got married in her third month. In her sixth month, she lost the baby and he was enraged, accused her of faking the pregnancy. Then, he decided he wanted her to get pregnant right away. He didn't want to admit he had made a mistake, that he could have gotten away without marrying her. He could never be wrong, about anything. In some ways, that was the most dangerous thing about him.

By the time she got pregnant again and had the baby at age twenty-one, he had lost all interest in her, left her alone to care for their child, began running after women. And it wasn't just the whores of Wise Avenue. He slept with neighbors, a coworker's wife.

He was an awful person. That was his true calling. Being awful. It was inevitable that he and Irving would form a partnership. The things they did—she tried to stay as ignorant as possible, but she knew they did terrible things. She tried to figure out how to make it right, how to tell someone, make it stop. But she knew he would kill her. He would smell the betrayal on her, kill her, and then what would happen to Joy?

After that first punch, the one to the gut, he began giving her little slaps if she dared to say anything contradictory. Even something as mild as, *No, honey, it's the eighteenth, not the nineteenth,* brought a reflexive backhand, sharp and stinging.

On the rare times she dared to actually disagree, to stake out an opinion opposite his, he would throw her to the floor and lower himself on top of her, as he had done on that blanket in the cemetery the first time they had sex, only now pounding and kicking and choking her until she passed out, or he lost interest.

She was stuck. Circumstances being what they were, she couldn't leave him. Besides, he had these friends now, dangerous men. He boasted about what these men would do for him. She was so scared of him by then, she didn't even allow herself to think mean thoughts against him when he was in the house. Her fantasies of escape were saved for those quiet moments, 1 A.M. to 2 A.M., when he was still out and she was too exhausted to sleep.

Imagine if we could leave, she would think, then cry at the impossibility of it.

Then came the night in 1983 that the Orioles lost what seemed a crucial game. They would go on to win the World Series that year, but that knowledge would arrive too late to comfort Burton. He picked up the kitchen radio and heaved it through the kitchen window, then told her to clean it up.

"I'm so tired," she said. "I'll get it in the morning." Not saying no because she never said no. Not pointing out that he was the one who had tossed the radio, only appealing to him to recognize what her days, her life, were like.

For a moment, he seemed to soften. He went outside with the dustpan, came back with the fragments of the window. Smiling at her, shy as the boy who had first tried to get her attention at the pool, he emptied the dustpan into the kitchen trash.

Then reached in, pulled out a shard, and held it to her throat.

"I'll kill you if you ever fail to do what I say," he said. "I'll kill you and burn this house down in such a way that they'll never know what killed you."

She thought she was going to die that night. That freed her to say what she had never dared to say: "What about Joy? Without me, you'll need someone to take care of her."

"I'll kill her, too."

She considered spitting in his face. He would kill her, but maybe it would be better to be dead. She was tired. She was trapped. This was her life and it was never going to get any better.

But—Joy. He said he would kill Joy, too. And she believed him.

She begged, she babbled: "I'm sorry. I don't know what got into me. I'll be good."

Impulsive acts are a luxury. She needed a plan. Days went by.

Weeks. Months. She balanced the checkbook, cooked his favorite meals. Seasons went by, years.

Winter 1986 was mild, temperatures reaching the seventies a couple of days. She made him his favorite dinner and let him have his favorite sex, although it was never really a matter of *letting*. He fastened his hands around her throat, claiming all the while that it was for her pleasure. She turned her face to the wall—he preferred not to see her face during sex, the better to imagine others—and wondered at how her body still could respond to him at all. Muscle memory, she guessed.

She waited for him to fall asleep, then got up, took a shower, knowing she would have to shower again. She stood there looking at him a long time—on his back, limbs splayed, snoring. His arms and legs were still the limbs of the boy she had once known, Burton, hard with muscle and tanned year-round. But Ditmars was soft around the middle. He blamed her cooking. He was thirty-one. She was twenty-five, almost twenty-six. They would celebrate their ninth anniversary later in the summer.

Except they wouldn't because she raised both her arms above her head and plunged a kitchen knife into his heart with all the force she could muster. His eyes flew open at the impact, but her aim was true. It had to be. There would be no second chances.

At her trial, the medical examiner testified she almost cleaved his heart in two with one thrust. Her lawyer, court appointed, had tried to use this to prove that her initial story about an intruder must be true. He was a little bit in love with Polly by then. He asked a jury to contemplate if Polly could have mustered the force, even if she was lucky not to hit a bone on the way in. But he knew and she knew that she was more than capable. Just another of those super-human feats of strength that a mother can summon, like lifting a car or leaping from a burning building. Polly was surprised the knife didn't pierce his back, pinning him to the mattress as he had pinned her there time and again.

She did not take the stand in her own defense.

16

Adam can't stop singing.

He sings in the shower, hums while shaving. Little tunes bubble out of his mouth at work, snatches of songs he doesn't remember ever learning, show tunes and pop tunes, all with one word in common: *Love*. Love, Love, Love. As in: *You're not sick, you're just in love*. As in: *I can love you like that*. And once, before he stopped himself: *I'm in love with a wonderful—*

His food sings, too. People begin talking about it. How good the grilled cheese is, the burgers, the fish. He convinces the boss to take advantage of the summer bounty—the good tomatoes, the beautiful varieties of silver corn. People who think silver corn begins and ends with Silver Queen have no idea what they're missing. He makes towering BLTs with his own cured bacon and aioli. Mr. C is skeptical: "Why bother making mayo from scratch?"

A couple stops by one day, deciding they'd rather have a long lunch than fight the beach traffic. Turns out they write a column for the *Baltimore Beacon* called the Dive Club that reviews bars and restaurants off the beaten path. The High-Ho gets a rave. Adam can barely believe it's his food they're describing, even though he knows how good he is. Belleville was always the place no one wanted to stop. But this August it becomes commonplace to see out-of-state tags in the parking lot on weekends, and not just Maryland. Pennsylvania, New Jersey, Virginia, D.C. Now Mr. C is the one who wants to sing all the time. "I can't lose you, Adam," he says.

You won't, he thinks, stealing a look at Polly. *Not yet.*

"You have to hide it better," she says to him that night in bed. "We're a secret."

"Why?" he says. "It's been almost a month. Cath can't expect me to not date at all."

"It's not just Cath. It's *better* if it's a secret. Besides, people don't like it when people at a job date each other. Especially when there aren't a lot of people working there. Max and Ernest are grumpy enough that the bar is so busy now. Come Labor Day, it'll be a small-town bar again. Remember that."

Come Labor Day. He's paid up through then. How long can he stay on this job? When will Irving pull the plug? Should he quit, tell Irving that he has determined she has no funds and he's sorry it took so long to establish this? Maybe she had money once, but it's clearly gone. Why would she stay here otherwise?

"I don't think anyone would mind. I think you just like secrets." Once he ends the job with Irving, he thinks, he'll want to go public with her. He's trying to do the right thing, but things happen. Love happens.

"That's true," she says agreeably. "I do like secrets. A little mystery is good for a woman."

"So, what, you got a husband and kid or something I don't know about?"

He's more startled by his words than she is. Did she tell him that

Gregg was her husband? He's pretty sure Gregg mentioned a kid at least. She sure never mentioned a kid to him. They don't talk about their pasts. Easier that way.

She says, coy as a kitten: "What if I do?" He's spooning her so he can't see her face, but her body is relaxed and loose in his arms, no tension at all except in her neck. There's always tension in that one spot. She will let her entire body melt into his, but extends her neck so far forward he can't bury his face in her nape, as he would like to do. She smells wonderful there.

"Were you married?" he asks. "You and that guy? Are you going to divorce him?" She doesn't encourage questions, but it occurs to him that normal lovers ask such questions. He probably should ask more questions, even if he knows the answers. Heck, maybe he'll even ask questions to which he's supposed to be finding the answers. *Where's the money, Polly?*

"What do you think?" she asks back.

"I don't think a woman like you has been roaming free all this time. Someone tried to slip a harness on you a time or two."

She yawns. "Amazing women often remain single into their thirties. Men—men are the ones who are suspect if they haven't married by forty. So what about you?"

"I've got a couple of years until I hit your deadline."

"But have you ever been married?"

"Once. Really young. The kind of marriage that doesn't count. When we broke up, we didn't even argue over stuff because it was so clear what belonged to whom."

"*Whom.* Listen to you, Mr. Fancy Pants. Mr. College."

"Nothing wrong with proper grammar."

"Yes, that's why you come over here every night. To teach me grammar." She arches her back, that's all, arches her back and

105

twitches her hips, and he's gone. Then, suddenly, it's 5 A.M., and there's a glimmer of light and she's saying "Go, go, go" as if this is a fairy tale where something dire happens at sunrise.

He meant to ask her about the kid, but she distracted him.

Because she has no AC, the outdoor air feels refreshing as he walks home. Not driving to her place is another one of her rules. People go for walks in the middle of the night, she says, but no one drives anywhere after 2 A.M. unless they're up to something. So he walks. There's one stretch where he has to cross a vacant lot, and the dew is heavy enough to drench his shoes through and through. He's in love. He has a job. Is there any way he can do the job and not risk her? He has to quit. That's it, plain and simple. He has to call Irving and tell him she has no money and it's time to wrap this up.

———————

"So nice of you to worry about me wasting my money," Irving says on the phone, in a tone that suggests he doesn't find Adam nice at all. "How can you be so sure I'm wrong about her?"

"Because she clearly has no money."

"No, she's not *spending* any money. That's different. You watch me for—how long has it been since she hit Belleville? Nine weeks? You watch me nine weeks and you'll think I have no money, either. I dress like crap, I drive a ten-year-old Cadillac, I eat ready-made egg salad sandwiches from the deli, with a cream soda. But I'm rich, Adam. Rich enough to pay you for weeks on a job that shouldn't take anywhere near this long."

"We've been over this. No one could have foreseen her picking up stakes and starting a new life somewhere other than Baltimore."

"Fair enough. I didn't hire you for your psychic abilities. Although maybe I should have gone to that fortune-teller, the one at the corner of Northern Parkway and Park Heights. Everything in that neighborhood changes, but she's been there forever, so she must know something. A scam artist, but I bet her customers don't know it. They're happy. Me, I am *not* a happy customer. But then, I don't enjoy being scammed."

Adam takes offense, despite the fact that Irving is right to doubt him. But how could he help falling in love with her? It's not his fault that he thought he could enjoy the sex for what it was, get the info he had been hired to find, and then move on. It wasn't the sex that made him fall for her. It was something in her eyes, when they went for lunch in Baltimore that day. She needed him. Needed *someone*, and why not him? He could take care of her—if she would only let him. He *is* taking care of her, even if she doesn't realize it. Irving promised to keep things clean, no violence. Adam never would have taken this job if he thought someone could be hurt. What if Irving hires someone who's willing to be a little rougher? Adam will be here to protect her.

"You can't prove a negative. It's impossible to prove someone *doesn't* have money stashed away. But I've gotten close enough to her to feel confident on this score."

"How close, sonny boy?"

Irving speaks in the rhythms of a grandfather, which he is. But Irving never sounds more dangerous than when he's trying to sound affectionate, paternal.

"We work together. At the bar. I told you that."

"What else you do together? Am I going to have to hire a PI to follow the PI?"

"Look, I'm trying to be responsible about your money. It may be time for you to terminate this job."

"And if I do, I guess you'll come back to Baltimore?"

What does Irving know? Nothing. Yet Adam is getting nervous. "I usually take a big trip after a long job. New Zealand, maybe. Or I'll join the peepers in New England, come fall. I want to go to Egypt."

"I hear Belleville is beautiful in autumn."

"Irving, you got something to say to me?"

"No, but I got some info for you. Maybe I should have shared it from the start. But in my own way, I thought I was being fair to her, that it would color your interactions if you knew too much. You like movies? I'll send you a movie."

"I don't have a VHS—"

"I'll send one of those, too. You really need to see this movie."

"Irving—"

"*Watch*," he says. "Listen. Then we'll talk. Fast-forward to the thirty-seven-minute mark or you'll cry from boredom."

———

A package arrives at the motel the next day, Adam's day off. "Heavy," says the guy at the front desk, who's always into everyone's business. It's a bitch, figuring out how to connect it to the old-fashioned television and Adam has to drive to the Radio Shack in Salisbury twice to get the right cords. It's almost nine o'clock when he pops the unmarked black cassette into the slot and sees a not-very-professional title card. "In the Name of Love."

"What the—?" He remembers Irving's advice, fast-forwards. Goes too far, but he recognizes her, jumbled as she is, her brilliant red hair covered with a scarf. The name on the screen, though, isn't one he remembers. Pauline Ditmars. *Who's Ditmars?* He realizes then that Irving never told him the name of her first husband. He said it wasn't important.

Irving also said he had run a LexisNexis on Pauline Hansen and given Adam the full results. Adam believed him. Why wouldn't you believe a client who ran an insurance brokerage, had access to all kinds of info, especially a tightfisted one like Irving, who wouldn't want to waste money paying Adam to do things he could do for himself? He said she had cheated the stepdaughter from her first marriage out of a life insurance settlement and that she was probably working another scam now. Irving had it on good authority that she had swindled someone out of millions. *Irving said.*

Polly's voice in the movie is toneless, almost robotic. He can barely believe it's the same woman. She's beaten down, joyless.

"By the end, he was hitting me almost every day. No, I didn't tell the truth to the cops. He was a cop, no one was going to believe me. So I said there was an intruder. Well, they saw through that right away. Then when I tried to tell the truth, I had no credibility. They thought if I would lie about one thing, I'd lie about the other. He was a cop. I guess no one gets to kill a cop, not even his own wife."

A narrator's voice takes over: "Pauline now freely admits that she stabbed her husband while he slept. But she is a classic case of 'battered women's syndrome,' driven to kill Burton Ditmars because she could not imagine any way to end the cycle of abuse, especially after he threatened to kill their disabled daughter."

Disabled daughter? Irving had said *stepdaughter,* Adam is sure of that. But then, Irving also said the father had died of "heart trouble" and that Pauline had rigged the medical exam so it didn't show he had a preexisting condition when she forged the life insurance papers.

Well, being an abusive husband is a preexisting condition of sorts, although it's rare for men to die of it. And a knife through the heart is definitely a kind of heart trouble.

Adam starts the video from the beginning. Woman after woman, telling the same sad story. Boring in the way that only such mundane viciousness can be. *He hit me here, he hit me there.* At the end, there is an epilogue, noting that the governor's decision to commute these sentences resulted in a *Beacon-Light* investigation that determined some of the women had not been properly vetted and probably should not have been released.

Pauline Ditmars, whereabouts unknown, is named as one of the three women that the governor regrets releasing, in part because the large insurance policy she took out on her husband, three months before his death, did not come to light during the vetting process.

17

He's changed.

Polly can't put her finger on it, but something is different about Adam. She had him. He was hooked, addicted. He was almost too far gone on her, gazing at her when he thought no one was looking, humming all the time.

Now he steals glances when he thinks *she* isn't looking.

They still follow their same routine—friendly colleagues at work, secret lovers at night. Adam and Eve, whiskey down. If anything, he seems more passionate during sex. But out of bed, it's as if a transparent screen has fallen between them. She catches him with his arms folded, considering her. He studies her face when she speaks. His food is getting crazier, as if he's trying to impress her.

He is trying to figure out if he can tell when she is lying.

The next day at work, she oozes charm for the customers, turns it off when she's talking to him. She doesn't do the cold burn, shooting daggers at him with tight-lipped denials. *I'm fine, I'm fine.* That's for amateurs.

She smiles. She is polite and kind. Sweet, even. But there's no fillip of teasing in her eyes or her smile. She's his oh-so-professional colleague. When he says, "You okay?" she replies with buttery sincerity, "Why wouldn't I be okay?" She pays special attention to Max and Ernest, who love it, not that they'll ever tip well. She giggles with Cath when she comes in to pick up her paycheck.

"Summer's almost over," Cath says. It is mid-August, blisteringly hot. Hard to believe it will ever be cool again, yet somehow things always cool down.

"It's gone by fast."

"Always does." Cath fans herself with her check. "So what are you going to do?"

"Do?"

"There won't be enough work for both of us, come Labor Day. I told you that. It's a seasonal gig."

"Even with Adam's cooking getting all this new business?"

"That's temporary. Watch. Maybe they'll let him stay if he wants because the boss doesn't like to cook and he usually takes over in the kitchen come Labor Day. But they won't need *you*. I guess you'll be moving on."

Cath says the last part a little hopefully. Maybe she's begun to suspect that Adam moved on before he broke up with her. Maybe she knows something else. How? It's been years since anyone cared who Polly was and that Polly had a different name, Pauline Ditmars. A different body and different hair, too.

It's funny, all her life, she wanted to lose ten pounds. She wasn't fat, but she wanted to be a size or two smaller. Nothing worked. She tried every diet, every form of exercise. Turns out all she needed was living on pins and needles while waiting to see if she was going to get a pardon. She's glad now, in hindsight, that Ditmars made her dye her hair that awful blond color while they were married, that she wore a scarf during the interviews for the movie. Sometimes, she was so smart she was ahead of herself. She came out of prison ten pounds lighter, lost another ten pounds, let her hair grow. She was unrecognizable. Even if you remembered who Pauline Ditmars was, you couldn't recognize her in Pauline Smith.

She had never worried about Gregg putting two and two together. Gregg could barely put two and two together on his best days. One time, they had been out drinking with friends, and they had talked about her case right in front of her. She had made all the right noises. *Oh. Ah. What an awful person. Killed him in cold blood, then made up a story when she caught wind that they were looking for battered women to pardon? And then they couldn't take the pardon back, so all she did was jeopardize the women still in, the ones who really were battered women?*

She had yearned to tell them the truth. Yes, she had lied, at first. In part because she was scared of Irving. She had killed Irving's cash cow, tricking Irving into paying for it in a sense, not that a dollar came out of his pocket. But he knew the signature was forged, yet couldn't rat her out without implicating himself. It was a double betrayal and he took it personally. He was probably still out to get her, but there was no way that Irving knew where she was. The day the Baltimore paper sent a photographer for that article on the restaurant, she had kept in the background, made sure that Cath got all the glory.

No, it must be Cath who has come between Adam and Polly. Has to be. She might not know anything, but that didn't mean she couldn't make trouble. *She* probably told the boss to cut Polly loose at summer's end.

"Labor Day is two weeks away" is all Polly says to Cath. "Maybe I'll find something else in town."

"Don't count on it." She seems to realize that she's been a little too quick, too vicious in her triumph. "I mean—it's a small town, quiet in the winters. Maybe you can find some work up at the chicken plants, but that's a nasty business. Or the prison might be hiring. Good jobs, union jobs, but not my thing."

Not mine either, Polly thinks.

At closing time, Polly tells Adam not to come by, that she's got plans with Cath. He looks hurt, so she says: "I had to say yes or she'd get suspicious, ask me too many questions about why I never do anything with her. I can't put her off forever."

Cath lives in the trailer park. It's a nice one, better than some of the houses around here, with flower beds and sweet little "patios" created by pull-out canopies. People are sitting out, enjoying the relatively cool night, having one last beer. She knocks on Cath's door.

She doesn't look happy to see her.

"Kinda late to be dropping by."

"Well, I just got off."

"There's this thing called a phone?"

"I don't have one." Brandishing her paper bag. "I do have vodka."

"There's a pay phone at work."

"I don't know your number. Are you mad at me? You seemed a little mad at me today, when we talked."

It's hard, sounding sincere about her concern. She's not used to this kind of girlish chitchat. The reason she doesn't like women is because they're exhausting. If this is how they treat men, no wonder they all have relationship problems. *Do you like me? Are you mad at me?* So much emotional folderol. Maybe she was like other women, once, but Ditmars changed her. He made her weak, he broke her down until she had no choice but to become strong. It was get strong or die. Because *not* dying, not giving up, required the greatest strength of all.

"No, I'm not mad," Cath says.

Because women aren't allowed to be mad, right?

"You seem awfully anxious for me to be out of town."

"Not exactly. But we're not really friends, are we? I thought we were going to be. You were so nice when Adam—well, you know."

Polly walks past her and enters the little trailer without being asked, takes a seat on the plaid sofa. Cath's not very neat. That's kind, actually. Cath's a slob. She follows Polly in, lights a cigarette from her stovetop burner. The woman cannot go much more than fifteen minutes without a cigarette. Her trailer reeks of tobacco, and there's a film on everything. Even Cath.

"What do we really know about Adam?" Polly asks her.

"What's there to know?"

"I mean, it's so mysterious, isn't it? He's like—Clint Eastwood in those old westerns, a stranger who just shows up. A great cook, someone who's traveled a lot. How was he supporting himself before he took the job cooking?"

"I don't know." Cath shrugs, but Polly can tell her incuriosity is feigned. She longs to talk about him. She's been denied that basic female right, the relationship postmortem. Polly doesn't usually indulge this kind of talk, either. But then—no man has ever left her. *She* leaves, one way or another.

"I think he has secrets," she continues. "If I were you, I'd poke around."

"What's it to me?"

"Oh, come on. I know you still like him."

Cath wants to deny it, but can't. "Yeah, but, it's like that song from a few years ago, right? I can't make him love me."

Polly has to be careful. She doesn't want to point Cath in her own direction. "Well, I'd start with his license plates. Check to see if they lead to a different name, or an address. And you're a local. I bet the motel people would tell you anything they know."

"Mainly wetbacks over there these days, doing the cleaning."

Ugh. She really is a terrible person. If she had ever said anything like that in front of Adam, he would have dumped her on his own. "What about the front desk? That nosy guy, Marvin, can't help knowing some things. Like—I bet Adam pays his bills in cash."

"So? From what I hear, you do, too."

Oh, it is a gossipy little town. She's been as careful as possible to keep the relationship with Adam a secret and, so far, so good. But it will get out if it keeps on. She's going to have to break things off with him, leave town as she planned. The thought saddens her more than she thought possible.

Fuck it, she's in love. She can't afford love. No matter how much money she ends up with, it won't be enough to have love, too.

"You're right," she says. "I'm just making trouble. Let it go. You've handled this whole thing with a lot of dignity. Do you have a mixer for the vodka?"

Cath rummages inside her little refrigerator. "Only Coke, and that's gross."

"I can drink it on ice if you can."

They sit outside with sweating tumblers of vodka, swap stories. Polly's are all made up. Maybe Cath's are, too, although they're certainly boring enough to be true. *Younger sister was the pretty one, made the good marriage. I made some mistakes when I was a teen and my family never lets me forget it.* Blah, blah, blah.

Maybe everybody lies, all the time.

18

On her next day off, Cath goes up to Dover to see her younger sister. She loves June, but she wouldn't wish a sister like her on her worst enemy. June is a little prettier, a lot more accomplished, everyone's favorite. She has a career as a court stenographer, while Cath's still trying to figure things out. June has a nice house, too, and it's the house that Cath envies the most. Not the husband, who is the reason that June could afford a house. Cath thinks she can do better than the husband and is secretly pleased that her sister has settled.

But she loves their house, which was brand spanking new when they moved in a year ago. The kitchen is huge, with a family room alcove and one of those big islands with a marble top. Everything is white. It's like something out of a magazine. June even has white roses in a milk-glass vase. Cath sits on a white wooden stool, watching June cut up vegetables for a salad while they both sip white wine.

"Be careful," June's husband, Jim, warns. "You could blow a

.01 with even one glass of wine in you. And there's only so much that I—"

"I know my capacity," Cath says, but not too pertly. He did her a favor, after all. That's why she's here, to find out what her brother-in-law, a state trooper, can tell her about Polly and Adam.

She knows they're together. She's not dumb. She's confused why Polly is pretending to be her friend, though. And when Polly showed up at her place with no explanation, then tried to plant the idea that Cath should be checking out Adam, Cath realized it was *Polly* she needed to research.

"So how do you know this person?"

Some instinct tells her to lie. "She's looking at a lot in the trailer park." *God, I hate that place,* she thinks, glancing covetously around her sister's gleaming kitchen. So Martha Stewart. "She seemed—off to me."

"Your instincts are good," Jim says. "She killed her husband."

Oh, this is even better than she dreamed. Cath takes a big swig of wine.

"Then what is she doing running around loose?"

"Sentence commuted four years ago. Governor wanted to show women some mercy in his final term, I think. Picked thirteen inmates he was told were victims of abuse. But the nonprofit he worked with didn't vet them well. There were some straight-up killers in that group. She was one of them."

"Huh. When was this?"

"Been almost ten years since she killed him. She stabbed her husband in the heart while he slept. *While he slept.*" Jim brings his arms up, miming the thrust of a knife into his own heart. "Do you know how cold-blooded you have to be to do that? Then she tried to claim he was killed by a burglar while she was sleeping in her kid's room."

"Are you sure?" She wants to believe it, but it doesn't jibe with the woman she knows. A man-eater, sure. A man *killer*? No way. "I mean, if he did beat her and she had a kid, maybe she couldn't imagine any other way." Cath has read everything she can about the OJ case. Of course, if any man ever raised a hand to her, she'd be out the door—or *he'd* be out the door—the next minute. But some women aren't strong the way she is.

"There's more," Jim says.

By the time Cath heads south on Route 13, she figures she has had almost three glasses of wine, but that's because June kept topping her off. Sabotaging her again. June is more invested in being the good sister than even she realizes. Aware that she's a little affected, Cath drives supercarefully. Almost too carefully at times—her speed drops and brights flash in her rearview mirror, warning her that she's driving erratically. But she doesn't think it's the alcohol, not really. She's trying to take in everything that Jim told her. A lot of it is gossip, he says, not written down anywhere, but he knows a cop who knows a cop who knew Polly's ex and this cop swears by his info. Polly-Pauline spun it as if she were selfless, putting her kid above everything. So why isn't she with that kid now? Why is the state paying the kid's bills if she inherited all this money?

Cath knows some people would think she's a hypocrite, dragging up a person's past. But she was only seventeen when she got in trouble, a kid. And it was an accident, awful as it was. If that railing hadn't given way, no one would have been hurt seriously. Her parents found a good-enough lawyer, she did anger management, and the records were sealed because she was a juvenile. That's totally different.

When she gets to Belleville, it's almost eleven. Over at the High-Ho, everybody will be heading home soon. Polly to her apartment above the old Ben Franklin, Adam to his motel room. Cath's torn about where to go. She wants to tell Adam first, see the look on his face, but it won't matter, she thinks. Even if he gives up Polly, he won't choose Cath. Especially if she's the one who tells him.

No, she'll go to Polly's apartment.

"What's up?" Polly says, opening her door to her, but not wide enough to let her in.

"Just thought I'd pay you a visit. Sauce for the goose, right?"

"So am I the gander in this situation, or are you?"

"Oh, I think we both know who the gander is." She pushes her way in.

"At least I didn't come empty-handed when I dropped in on you," Polly says, but her voice is mild, as if she's teasing an old friend. *As if.* Polly opens her fridge, pulls a bottle of vodka out of the freezer. The fridge is ancient, looks like something from the 1950s, with its rounded top and single door, the freezer a metal compartment with ice trays and a buildup of frost. The oven is old, too, one of those white enamel jobs. Metal table with one wood chair, not much else. Cath glimpses an iron bed in the next room, a quilt neatly folded at the foot. Polly won't be here long enough to need that quilt, Cath will see to that. Everything is so old-fashioned, not to Cath's taste at all. Adam probably thinks Polly's quirky, special. She's special all right. Cath studies the magnetic strip above the stove where three knives hang.

"So I did what you suggested. Kinda."

"Yeah?" The glasses are that thick Mexican blue glass. More quirk.

Polly has certainly made herself at home here. But because there's only one chair, she has to lean against the counter while Cath sits.

"I didn't go to the DMV, though. I didn't have to. My brother-in-law is a Delaware state trooper."

"Oh?" Surprised, but trying not to show it.

"Nothing much came back on Adam. His driver's license goes to a place in North Baltimore. Big apartment building."

"That was a bum suggestion on my part," Polly says cheerfully. "I was silly to waste your time."

Cath, looking at her, knowing what she knows about her—she just doesn't get it. How did she wrap Adam around her little finger? Her figure's pretty good, but her face has that narrow, foxy look common to redheads. People are always going on about how women pick the bad boys, but men have similar weaknesses. Is Polly better in bed than Cath is? What really makes a woman good in bed? Cath has a pretty high opinion of herself as a lover. She's enthusiastic, up for almost anything, although she's keeping a few things back for when she's engaged, proper.

"Oh, no, it was a good suggestion. Because he told me some stuff about *you*."

"Yeah?"

Waiting, not even that curious. What kind of person doesn't get nervous in this situation?

A person who knows exactly what she's done.

"This is a small town. When word gets out—"

"Isn't it already?"

"What do you mean?"

"I'm guessing you went straight to Adam, told him everything you know."

"No, I did not." Happy to play the high-road card here, no need to explain her thinking behind it. "I came to you first. I think it would be better for everyone concerned if you left town."

"Really?" She's not getting rattled. She doesn't seem to respect the fact that Cath's in charge here.

"Really. Leave town and—" This is the harder part. "Leave town and maybe pay me a little money."

"Pay you? For what?"

"Not to tell people what I know. About you and your ex. And how you pretended it was all for your kid, but you didn't hesitate to cash in when you could."

"Now I really don't know what you're talking about. Are you drunk? You seem a little drunk, Cath. You should leave your car on Main Street, walk home."

"You have money. There was an insurance policy."

"Right." Polly rolls her eyes, looks around the room where they're sitting. "I'm clearly loaded."

Cath is a little buzzed and caught off guard by how differently the conversation is playing out, now that she's having it. She had imagined Polly weeping, begging her to keep quiet, offering up money. *Gossip,* her brother-in-law said. *A lot of this stuff isn't written down anywhere.* There's a newspaper article naming Polly as one of the women whose sentence shouldn't have been commuted, but the stuff about the money—it was never proven that Polly planned to steal it, Jim says. And would anyone with money live here? Not just in this apartment, but in Belleville. If Cath had a lot of money, she'd blow this town so fast. How much money does Polly have? Cath's decided she'll settle for $10,000, enough for a down payment on one of the new town houses they're building on the little swampy section south of town that they've started calling a lake. Belle's Landing. The cattails are pretty in the sunset. She imagines herself on the deck, having a drink with a nice man, watching the sun go down over the marsh.

"I mean it," Cath says. "I'll give you"—she pauses, then realizes that in pausing she has erred badly—"two days. Then I'm going to tell everyone at the bar about you."

"Everyone? Isn't Adam the only person who matters to you?"

"This isn't about Adam."

"That's good. Because you'll never have him. You could tell him I'm a man, like in that movie everybody was talking about last year. It still won't make him want you. Nothing could."

That hurts. Cath twitches, remembers what it was like, lunging at that girl when she was seventeen, the crack of the railing, then another crack, more of a snap. The girl ended up a quadriplegic, but it was the railing's fault, not Cath's. *Attractive nuisance* was the legal term. The guy who owned the old driving range was the one who had to pay the family, not Cath's mother and father. Besides, the girl had baited her, prodded Cath into losing her temper.

"Two days," she says, rising to her feet. She wishes her hip didn't sway and bump the table, sloshing the vodka from her untouched glass. Her tipsiness undercuts her power.

She drives home at fifteen miles per hour, trying to figure out when the two days begin. She guesses she has to give Polly forty-eight hours, which takes them to midnight Thursday, so it will be Friday before she gets around to telling anyone.

She realizes she really wants to tell everybody. Wants it more than the money, maybe. She wants to embarrass Polly, to vanquish her. She hates Polly in a way she has almost forgotten she could hate. Who is she to come to town, steal a desirable man, act so holier than thou?

Cath decides she's going to take whatever money Polly scratches together and still tell everyone. Hasta la vista, baby.

olly locks the door behind Cath. Adam is planning to visit later, but too bad for him. Let him steal up the stairs, try the door, be surprised when he discovers it is locked. Will he knock? Call out her name in the street below? She has told him over and over again that they must not draw attention to themselves. Even in this block, a ghost town after five, someone might hear.

If he does knock, will she let him in? She's not sure. She needs to think.

It's clear that Cath doesn't know much. She can fish all she wants, but the only thing she has, solid, is that Polly served time for killing her husband and some people think she lied about the abuse. Interesting that the old money gossip follows her. At least, she's pretty sure it's the old gossip, about the old money. When those reporters looked into the commutations, they wrote, semiaccurately, that Ditmars took out life insurance a few months before she killed him. But that policy was in Joy's name and Joy became a ward of the state after Polly was sentenced.

Could someone be gossiping about the other stuff? There's

only one possible source to these rumors, and he's bound by law not to tell anyone. Which doesn't mean he hasn't. Lie down with dogs, as they say. He didn't have the best reputation. But then— that's exactly why she chose him. Polly can't afford men with good reputations.

She can leave, of course. Even absent Cath's threats, there are good reasons to leave. Adam is acting oddly. She never planned to stay past Labor Day. She has things to do. Why not leave? Leaving solves everything. And she won't have to pay Cath a dime. That's how stupid Cath is. She doesn't realize that, with blackmail, it's one or the other. You can't tell someone to leave and expect to be paid off. Why would Polly, once gone, care what anyone in Belleville thinks of her?

Adam. It grieves her to leave him behind, vulnerable to Cath's lies, if not to Cath herself. He will think the worst of Polly. That she's a killer, a liar, a rip-off artist. And maybe she deserves his low opinion, but only if he knows the whole story, not whatever jumbled mess that Cath relates. If she leaves now, Cath wins.

Cath can't win.

Footsteps on the stairs. She watches the knob turn. Even the knob, squeaking in alarm, seems surprised when the door fails to open. Now it rattles, turning back and forth, as Adam whispers her name.

"Polly? Polly? It's me."

Of course it's you. Who else would be at my door this late? She says nothing, just stares at the knob, mesmerized.

"Polly?" Louder now.

She stands still, barely breathing. He knows she's here. Where else would she be? *How much do you want me?* she thinks. It's not vanity on her part. It's vital information.

She hears him retreating down the stairs. Okay, that's it, she has to leave town, he's not going to stand by her. She is already mentally packing. She'll rent a U-Haul, load up her things. She could be in Reno next week.

Then his footsteps roar back, it's like a big wave rolling in after a series of small ones have lulled you into thinking the surf is calm. To her shock and delight, the door flies open with what sounds like one swift kick, the frame splintering.

He rushes in and she is terrified, but only for a moment. This man will never hurt her. She jumps up, her arms circling his neck, confident of being caught.

———————

"What was that?" he asks later.

"What?"

"That stupid game with the door. Did you not tell me to come by tonight?"

"We have trouble," she says. "And very little time to decide what to do. Cath's figured out that we're together. She's willing to do anything—*anything*—to force me to leave town. A woman scorned and all that. You won't believe the lies she's willing to spread."

He doesn't ask about the lies. Interesting.

"I'll go with you," he says without hesitation. More interesting, still. How much does he know? And how? Yet he's loyal to her, still wants her.

"Let's sleep on it," she says. "I don't trust decisions made in the middle of the night." She is telling the truth. Although she killed Ditmars in the middle of the night, she planned it by day. For weeks and weeks she planned. She was planning his murder even before she realized it. The universe all but told her to do it.

It began with a nurse's aide, who came to help twice a week. Respite care, they called it. At first, Polly would use those hours to grocery shop. Then she found the film series at the museum, free on Thursday afternoons, and she escaped the long Baltimore summer in that cool, hushed place. Afterward, she'd go to the sculpture garden, studying the families in the museum restaurant, wondering what it would take to be like them. She couldn't believe that they were the same species on the same planet, that's how far away their lives seemed to her.

The summer of 1985, the film series was all black-and-white films from the 1940s. *Double Indemnity. Mildred Pierce. The Postman Always Rings Twice.* Polly didn't understand at first how they were linked, why the series was called Raising Cain, but then someone explained they were all based on books by a Maryland man who had lived in Baltimore and Annapolis, grown up on the Eastern Shore.

When fall came and the film series ended, she began going to the library and looked for the books that had inspired the movies. Be bold, Walter Huff told Phyllis Nirdlinger—no wonder they had changed the name for the movie. Not even Barbara Stanwyck could play someone named Nirdlinger and make her sexy. Polly began to study the encyclopedias, the ones that didn't circulate. There was a diagram of the human body layered on three color transparencies that showed exactly where everything was. The heart is not really on the left side of the body, although we place our hands there to say the pledge. It's much closer to the center. And it tips slightly, almost as if it were drunk.

Once you know where the heart is, then you need to know where the rib cage is. Because even the best knife could break on a bone. Night after night, Polly slipped her arms around Ditmars, tickling his chest softly. Counting his ribs, willing her fingers to memorize the topography of his body. She needed the best knife she could find, so she squirreled away money, bought a beauty of a Japanese butcher knife, one she never used for carving.

She would get one chance. Only one. She went to sleep night after night next to her husband, praying for the literal strength to kill him.

"Sleep?" Adam asks.

"Eventually," she says, putting her hand in his. They lie on their backs, side by side, like brother and sister. When she tells him everything, he will understand.

Right? Right?

Polly is up with the sun. Adam finds her at the kitchen table, not a stitch on, drinking hot coffee. No matter how warm the day, she always wants to start it with a cup of hot coffee.

"So we go, right?" he says. "There's nothing to bind us here."

"Casper will have a heart attack if you leave. He'll do anything for you."

"Summer's almost over. Doesn't matter how good the food is. No one's going to come to Belleville just for the food."

"They might. If the place were nice enough. A little paint, cosmetic changes. It could be something really special."

"I don't see that happening."

"Maybe not right away. But it's more your place now than his. He'd probably do whatever it takes to keep you. I don't see why we should have to go."

"But if you don't want Cath to tell people about you—"

"Maybe *she* should go."

"She's pretty rooted, best I can tell."

"They say the big trees topple over fastest. Because they don't bend."

"What are you saying?"

"The only power she has over me is what she knows. I'm going to tell you what she's got on me, Adam. What she thinks she's got on me."

"You don't have to do that."

"No, I do. I need you to decide if you want to be with me once everything is out in the open."

He takes the mug of coffee out of her hand, says: "Baby, I do know."

"What, exactly?"

"I know who you used to be. What you did."

"How?"

A pause. "She already told me."

"And?"

Years go by. Dinosaurs roam the earth, find extinction, mankind begins, Jesus dies on the cross. Columbus sails to America, the world wars are fought. All those things happen while she waits for him to reply.

"I don't care."

He loves her. He actually loves her.

"Then I'll tell her tonight that she can say whatever she thinks she knows. I'm not leaving. And today, I'll tell Casper. I don't want him to hear it from her."

"You said she wanted money from you."

"Can't get blood from a stone."

He falls to his knees in front of her, almost as if he were about to propose, which delights and terrifies her in equal measure. But all Adam wants to do is bury his head in her midsection like a child. They remain this way for a very long time, Polly cradling Adam's head, grateful the world has finally sent her the man she needs, the man she deserves.

20

Adam clocks Cath making a beeline for him the first chance she gets at work. It's Thursday, the last day of August, they're busy at lunch and dinner. Mr. C can get by with Cath alone on the lunch shift, but he'll need both his waitresses for dinner.

"Your girlfriend's not who you think she is," she says.

He says, "What girlfriend?" and keeps on working. He's layering mozzarella between local tomatoes, then drizzling pesto vinaigrette. It doesn't really require a lot of focus, but he keeps his eyes on those tomatoes as if he's making rosettes for a wedding cake.

Cath, perhaps mindful of the fact that it's hard to collect black-mail once you've let the secrets out into the air, doesn't say anything more, just cocks her hip, then saunters away, swinging her ass hard. He's dying to learn how much she knows. The facts in the video are the ones in the public domain and her state trooper brother-in-law might have been able to grab some records, especially if Cath filched Polly's social security number. But the money that Irving knows about—*nobody* knows about that, according to Irving. He only found out by accident. Millions, he said, and won on a lie.

According to Irving. Who didn't bother to tell Adam about Polly's past until he decided he wanted to make Adam feel like a jerk. It's funny—knowing what he knows now isn't enough to make him stop loving her. But if he had known all along, it might have been enough to stop him from falling in the first place.

Barn door open, horse gone.

Adam has never had these out-of-control feelings about a woman before, not even the woman he loved enough, for a time, to marry. Lainey. She never even crosses his mind. Polly never leaves it. He keeps thinking this has to end, that it's like a flu or fever that will run its course. He had moments where he believed he could walk away from her, collect his last check from Irving, and enjoy the fall on another continent.

And then he kicked her door in. She tried to act tough, but he wasn't fooled. She was terrified when he came through that door. Memories of her ex, he's guessing. But she also seemed excited. It's a complicated thing, the human brain. No one wants to be abused. But what if, after the fights, some chemical is released? What if the fight is a kind of drug that leads to a high? What do you do then?

They should leave together. And then what? Irving could destroy his reputation pretty fast if Adam takes up with Polly. No one's going to want to hire the PI who fell in love with his target.

Polly told him last night that she doesn't want to settle more than one hundred miles from Baltimore, maybe two hundred, although she refused to say why. He thinks about the trip back to the city, the day he followed her. The answer is on Rogers Avenue, or nearby. Could the money be there? Has she entrusted the cash to a third party she believes won't rip her off? She has no family left in Maryland—*according to Irving*—and she isn't a woman who makes friends easily. The film mentioned a disabled daughter, so maybe that's the stepdaughter she ripped off? If she ripped her off.

Philadelphia, Richmond, Pittsburgh, New York—her two-hundred-mile radius leaves them with a nice array of options. He can't see himself in New York; money doesn't go far there. He doesn't want to live in the South. (He knows Maryland is technically the South, but the D.C.-Baltimore area has been an okay base. Richmond is *South*-South.) Pittsburgh, though—it's a city, but it's easy to get to nature from there. Maybe not the ocean, but he could still hunt in western Maryland. And you can be in Canada in less than four hours.

Canada? Where did that come from? He pauses, knife in hand, tries to nail down his own chain of thought. Escape, running away. They're going to run away from here. Once you start to run, you never stop. Maybe she's right. They should hold their ground. Face down Cath, make her ashamed to think she could use Polly's past against her. Make her the bad guy.

But they would still have to contend with Irving. Adam has to persuade Irving there is no money, that it was all a bullshit story. To do that, he would have to talk to her about what he's been told, get her side of things.

He would have to tell her that it was no accident, him finding her here.

Would she forgive him? Would she ever trust him again if she knew he'd been hired to befriend her, follow her, find this money that may or may not exist?

They need to go. He'll persuade her tomorrow that's the only safe way.

f there is one thing Polly knows how to do, it's waiting. It's her talent, her art. *Waitress* indeed. She's a pro.

Her life began with waiting. But isn't that what all teenage girls do? You put on a yellow bathing suit and you wait for your life to begin. There was Burton Ditmars, tanned and muscled and so grown up. She was fourteen. She cannot blame herself for thinking he was offering her a life.

The next phase was waiting for Ditmars to come home. Then she began waiting even more eagerly for him to go out. The night Joy was born, she waited for the doctor to come, screaming at nurses that it was time, it was time, it was time. She waited through doctors' appointments. Waited for Ditmars to hit her because then she would be in that briefly benevolent "after" phase, all sweetness and gifts and backrubs. Strangely, when she discovered that nonprofit that organized time-outs for women such as herself, she initially found herself watching the clock during her "liberty," longing for it to end. She didn't know what to do with four hours to herself. Shop? She had no money of her own. And it made her jumpy, trying to relax in her own house with another person in it. Plus, Joy knew she was there. Polly had to leave in order to enjoy her "respite," and that was no respite at all.

The longest wait of all had been in the weeks before she killed Ditmars. She was not trying to concoct the perfect murder, per Walter Huff's advice to Phyllis in *Double Indemnity*. She was resigned to not getting away with it, although she did her best. Lord knows, there was no shortage of people who had reason to want Ditmars dead, given the things he had done. Her fear was that she would only maim Ditmars, deal him a crippling injury, and then she would be trapped with him forever, caring for him.

Prison had been easy for a waiting pro such as herself. Unpleasant, cruel, but easy, the affronts predictable and impersonal. Unlike life with Ditmars, it could be managed once she learned the rules and personalities. She assumed she would never get out, so all she was waiting for was one day to end and another to begin.

Then she was released, met Gregg, fucked him, fucked up— fucked up by fucking him—and that was that. She might as well have gone back to prison. Luck, so overdue, finally arrived in the form of a nasal Baltimore voice, shouting at her from the television during an *All My Children* commercial break. She knew that voice, that guy, that *shyster*. Irving used to complain about him all the time, but anyone who did business with Irving had to be a little bent. Look at Ditmars. She called the number that promised to change her life. And for once a man's promise was kept. Then a new wait. She is still waiting. But it's a waiting she has chosen, so she has power. It's her decision to wait a little longer. What will she tell Adam six, eight months from now? She'll figure something out. It's easy to make people believe in good luck, because who doesn't want to believe in good luck?

At work that night, Polly lets Cath's deadline approach, showing no concern. She has no concerns. She tells Mr. C what's what, and, sure enough, he doesn't care.

"He hit you, this man?"

Polly nods. "Hit" doesn't begin to cover what Ditmars did to her, but it's good enough.

"You did your time, you deserve to be out, it's nobody's business," he says. "If my business falls off and I can keep only one waitress—it will be you. You're the better one. And you make my cook happy."

So Mr. C knows about them, too. She and Adam must have been terrible at hiding their relationship. Mr. C is the most oblivious man she's ever met. Not a bad thing in a man. Her preference, actually.

It's a busy night, the last Thursday in August, and Polly makes sure she is on top of her game, putting a little extra into her encounters with Max and Ernest, laughing at their stale jokes and observations. She can tell it throws Cath off her stride, seeing Polly happy and calm.

Toward 10 P.M., Cath corners Polly by the ice machine: "What about that thing we talked about?"

Polly waits a beat, as if puzzled, as if it's so inconsequential as to have slipped her mind. "Oh, *that*."

"Do you have my money?"

"No."

"Tonight is the deadline."

Polly shrugs. "What can I do? You didn't give me very much notice."

"I'm going to tell everyone."

"Fine."

"Not just Adam. *Everybody*."

"Okay."

"You'll have to leave. This is a small town. People won't want to come here once they know. Casper won't be able to keep you on."

She shrugs. "I'll let him be the one to tell me that, if that's okay with you."

Her coolness infuriates Cath. She's the nervous one now, worried that her bombshell is all fizzle, no pop. She has to make good on her threat, or she'll look like a fool. She is a fool. She has blackmailed Polly into doing the best thing. No more secrets, from anyone.

Well, almost no secrets. Just the one, and it's a happy one. Happy secrets are okay.

That night, Polly doesn't slip Adam the usual Adam and Eve note signaling that she hopes for a visit from him. He's puzzled, she can tell, but she needs to be alone and sit in the quiet of this new life. She walks home, finds herself humming. She likes it here, in Belleville. She's happy to stay. Maybe not forever-forever, but for a good long while.

She's having a glass of wine at her metal-top table when she hears a slight tap. She smiles. Adam jury-rigged the door this morn-ing, but it doesn't really lock. She's had her alone time and now she's glad he presumed he could drop by.

"Come in," she calls out. "It's not like I could lock it now if I tried."

Only it's Cath.

"If you're going to stay, you better give me some money," she says without preamble, her words a slurry rush. There's booze on her breath.

"I am staying," Polly says. "And Casper says if he has to let one of us go, it's going to be you."

"I don't believe that."

"Ask him."

"Then you damn well better give me some money."

"I don't have any money."

"That's not what I heard."

"I can't be responsible for what you've heard. I don't have any money." A pause. "Although I guess I'll have a lot more when I'm the only one waiting tables at the High-Ho."

"What about your husband?"

"My husband's dead. As you know. I killed him, and I don't care who knows anymore. My sentence was commuted. I was defending my own life, in a sense."

"Not him. The one who came looking for you. I bet he'd pay something for what I know."

Polly laughs at this. She's not sure what's funnier, the idea of Gregg having money or Gregg giving it up. Does Cath think there's going to be a custody battle over Jani? "Go ask him. Heck, take him, he's available. Make sure you use a condom, though. His sperm is pretty determined."

"I bet you got knocked up on purpose."

Polly sees herself in the bathroom in her apartment four years ago, staring with dismay at a beaming pregnancy stick, so pinkly confident that it was sharing good news. She had killed a man, gone to prison, endured public shame, reinvented herself. But she couldn't bear the idea of an abortion. At the time, she told herself it was because of being raised Catholic. With her parents dead— there were those who said Polly's conviction put the final nail in her mother's coffin—she should have been free of the church. She was already down for one mortal sin, why not another?

Because, in the back of her head, she couldn't help being curious: What would it be like this time? How hard could it be, compared to what she had already done and endured? She felt guilty even thinking such thoughts, disloyal to Joy. But the truth was, she wanted the experience of being mother to a normal kid. Even if the father was Gregg.

And Jani was a good kid, although Polly loved Joy a little bit more. Mothers aren't supposed to say that, feel that, but Polly can't help acknowledging the difference. Jani's a sweetheart, a natural-born winner. She'd be fine. Joy needed her.

When she answers Cath, it's with a heat generated by these memories, the losses she has known. The father who dried up like a cornhusk, the mother who followed him too quickly, her heart doubly broken. The two daughters, neither one with Polly now because she has done what is best for them.

"No, I don't play it that way. But maybe you should. It's probably the only way you'll ever get a man to stay, getting knocked up. Good luck with that. Adam says you're a rotten lay."

The dew is heavy, Polly's feet are drenched by the time she knocks at the door to room 3. The rain that has been threatening all night starts to fall in sheets and there are thunderclaps, full and close, almost loud enough to drown out the sirens in the distance. It's the last day of August—actually the first day of September—and the first true cold front of the season lies behind this storm. Almost every Labor Day weekend, it seems, the first true cold front arrives.

"Rabbit, rabbit," she says to the night air. But maybe it only counts after you go to sleep and wake up?

Adam opens his door, sleepy, confused. He's really handsome.

She considered his looks too bland the first time she saw him, but now she thinks he's the best-looking man she's ever known.

"What the—? What time is it?"

"I missed you."

"But—"

"I told Casper today. He doesn't care. Everyone knows about us now. Everyone who matters. Turns out he knew all along. Guess we're not the supersleuths we thought we are."

"I think you mean stealthy," he says. "Not sleuths." He looks uneasy.

"Sleuth, stealth. Let me in, college boy. I'm soaked."

She is on top of him when the second wave of sirens start.

"Whatever's burning, they must have had to send for another crew," he says, his hands pressing hard into her shoulder blades. "From Millsboro or wherever. I wonder how anything can burn in this rain."

"Who cares," she says, moving faster. "We're safe."

She stays all night, into the morning. He's the one who suggests they go out to breakfast at the diner on Main. She contemplates last night's dress, still damp from the downpour.

"I can't go out in that."

"We'll swing by your place."

She and Adam stroll hand in hand toward the center of town, public at last, rooted at last, a couple. No more shadows, no more hiding. The morning feels as if the world is new, bright and crisp and ready for back to school. But an acrid smoke lingers in the breeze, making her nostrils flare with memories of Ditmars. He used to come home smelling like this. A combination of smoke and chemicals, sometimes even a whiff of death, although he always swore the sweetish scorched smell was from insulation, not people. And there was no question that Ditmars knew what people smelled like when they burned.

Yet, for all her knowledge, Polly is not prepared to turn the corner and see rubble where her apartment once stood. Everything—everything—is gone. Smoke is rising from the debris, the volunteer firefighters still bustle about, their long night still not over.

It's shameful, but she starts to weep for her small array of possessions, the first things she's been allowed to choose for herself. Her bed, her quilt, her table, her blue glasses. The silk bathrobe. The sundresses from the Purple Heart. Tiny things, material things, objects that can be replaced. But they could have been the building blocks of this new life.

Then she sees the gurney, covered by a sheet. It looks flat, but Polly's not fooled. She was an arson investigator's wife. She knows what an explosion can do to a body, how it collapses the internal organs. There's something—someone—under that sheet.

Everyone stares at Polly as if she's a ghost. In a sense, she is. Back from the dead, just that quick. Of course everyone would have assumed it was her, the tenant, in the wreckage. Who else could it be? But as she looks around, she realizes that most of the spectators are horrified in a bland, rubbernecking way. Belleville is a small town, yet few here know her. She spots her landlord, talking to one of the firefighters. He, at least, looks upset in a specific, visible way, but then—he's just lost a significant property. Maybe if Max and Ernest strolled by, they would care that Polly is alive. As it is, only Adam knows this is her former home and he didn't have to worry for a moment that she had been harmed because he's holding her hand, sure of her. He knows it's not her on the gurney.

She wonders when he'll realize it has to be Cath.

PART TWO
FIRE

22

Adam stands at the grill, making the usual lunchtime items. He has his own method of frying burgers: He takes a ball of meat—larger than a golf ball but smaller than a tennis ball—then smashes it with great force, using two spatulas one on top of the other. After flipping, he places a thin slice of American cheese on each patty. There is simply no better cheese for burgers, no matter one's culinary aspirations. He uses two patties per burger, otherwise the customer will feel he's being shortchanged. Almost everyone values quantity over quality. The patties cook very fast when they are this thin, and he ruins two in a row, mesmerized by the way the flames lunge greedily for the drops of fat.

Cath probably did not die by fire. Almost no one ever does. If smoke inhalation didn't get her, then it was probably the explosion itself. A horrible way to die, but quite fast. He hopes it was fast. An official ruling is expected soon.

Polly told investigators that morning she had no idea why Cath was in her apartment. The door was unlocked, a custom of small-town living she had come to appreciate. Besides, it couldn't be locked since Adam kicked it in early Wednesday, although Polly didn't mention that part to the investigators. She did tell them that she and Cath had a habit of stopping by each other's places after work.

"You said that?" Adam asked. "That it was a habit?"

"I had been by her place last week, she came to see me two nights ago and apparently returned. That's enough for a habit, right?"

"You make it sound like you were friends."

"Just being factual. Lots of people saw me sitting with her at the trailer park last week, having a drink after work. Sure, she probably came by to make trouble for me, but I can't know that. I did tell them that she was trying to blackmail me. And I told them that she couldn't, because I had already let you and Mr. C know what she had on me."

The stove was old, faulty, finicky. You had to turn the handles just so. Adam knew that. Cath couldn't go more than thirty minutes without a smoke. Everybody knew that. She had probably used the burner to light a cigarette, then failed to turn it all the way off. Lit another and—

"It could have been my fault," Polly said. "I could have been the one who didn't turn it all the way off. And you know how I keep that scarf on my bedside lamp—what if it slipped, fell against the bulb? I had closed the windows because I knew rain was coming. And if there was already gas and a little fire started—I kept meaning to tell the landlord about that stove, but the rent was cheap and I didn't cook much, not in this summer heat."

Her story makes sense, Adam thinks, tossing the overdone burgers. Some chefs would try to serve them, wait to see if the customers complained, but he would never do that.

He pounds another globe of beef into submission. *Story.* Why did he think of it as a story?

There was so much confusion at the scene. The first responders were the local volunteers, unused to dealing with a blaze of this magnitude, hampered by the heavy rains, which helped keep the flames from spreading to the other buildings on Main, but made a sodden mess of the wreckage. They thought they were doing the right thing, moving Cath's body when they found it in the early morning hours, but they compromised the investigation into her death.

They also began to question Polly on the spot, as she stood there holding Adam's hand. "Where were you?" "Who is this?" She told them she had gone to Adam's place about midnight, that she had no idea who was in her apartment, but she recognized Cath's car, parked right there on Main. Later, they found Cath's key ring, a heavy knob of turquoise, in the wreckage.

When Adam was asked during a more formal interview what time Polly came by his room, he agreed it was about midnight. But the fact is, he doesn't know. He was asleep. He knows what she said to them. He assumes it's true.

He's pretty sure it's true.

It has been five days since the fire. Cath's sister came to town Sunday, husband in tow, screaming and crying and hurling accusations. They told the Delaware State Police investigators that Cath had all sorts of dirt on Polly, that the whole thing had to be a setup. But Polly had already owned her past, said she had told Mr. C and Adam what was what, and that Cath was angry because she had no real leverage. Polly begged police not to let word get out, but it was a small town and the gossip skipped and whirled from mouth to mouth, too delicious not to be shared.

Yet when the gossip settled, all anyone really knew was that Polly had a sad, brutal past. Yes, she had killed her husband. Yes, there was skepticism about her exoneration, but what was done was done. No one could see how Polly, in bed with Adam, could be responsible for an explosion almost a mile away. Maybe Cath had gone there to confront Polly, then decided to lie in wait for her.

"Maybe," Polly told the state investigators. "I should tell you—she had other reasons to be mad at me. She had a thing for Adam. We tried to keep our relationship quiet, out of respect for her feelings, but that was the real source of her anger, the reason she wanted to run me out of town. Adam chose me over her."

There is no daily newspaper in Belleville. Cath's death received a scant mention in the Wilmington paper and was the third story in the second break on the so-called Delmarva stations, out of Salisbury. "Belleville woman dead in explosion." That's that. Nothing's going to happen. Adam doesn't have to say or do anything more.

"I guess you could call it karma," Polly said at one point. "She tried to hurt me, and she ended up hurt."

Karma. That's a name for it. Coincidence, too. Accident.

A check comes in, he flips it around: *Adam and Eve, whiskey down.*

"Very funny," he says. They don't have to plan their rendezvous anymore.

"It's the real thing," Polly calls over her shoulder. "Do we have any rye bread?"

Polly has to cover all the shifts now. Business is still brisk this first week of September. When she's not working, she sits on his bed in room 3, looking at the classifieds. She's circling things. Houses. For sale, not rent, and in the best part of town, where the streets are named for flowers and trees.

"You really want to put down roots? Here?"

"I thought that's what we agreed to."

Did they? He feels his restlessness kicking in. The fall is when he usually travels. It wasn't that long ago that he thought he might go to New Zealand this autumn, catch its spring. Or somewhere on the other side of the equator. Flip the seasons, flip your life.

Flip this burger, Adam. Don't burn another one.

Now he can't imagine going anywhere without her. Still, he has an itchy foot and she's sitting on the bed, circling real estate ads.

"How are you going to afford to buy a house?" he asked her last night. "You don't get the insurance on the building." It's supposed to be a joke, but it becomes a question, a plea for assurance. *Please tell me that you don't have insurance. On the apartment. On your belongings. On Cath.* If what Irving said was true—but maybe nothing Irving said was true.

"I'm going to come into some money soon," she says.

"From what?"

"It's just a feeling I have. Don't you ever have those? Like, a sixth sense about something that's going to happen. It's in my palm."

Her landlord is paying for her to stay at the motel, but Adam never visits her room. She comes to him now. How he misses that apartment. Maybe more than she does, he thinks. Did she know all along that it wasn't going to be her home? All summer, she had said she had to be moving on. But she loved those things, he knows it.

She also loves her freedom. She would not have risked that cavalierly.

———

About midnight she taps on his door. Their lovemaking has become more savage as of late, which surprises him. When a secret romance goes public, things usually get tamer. Even as she circles ads for homes, plots domestic life, she retains this innate wildness in bed. What is their future? He would be crazy to marry her, have children with her.

He will be crazy without her.

Finished, he stares at the ceiling, wills himself not to speak, waits for her to fall asleep.

Then, very nonchalantly: "Was it midnight when you came by?"

"Tonight?"

"Then."

"Oh. I think so. Thereabouts. You know I don't have a watch anymore. And it was humid before the rain started, so I was walking pretty slowly."

Thunderclap, the rain coming down in sheets. He feels as if he heard the thunder first, then saw the lightning, but that's not how it works. Could it have been the explosion that he heard? All he has to do is call the weather service, find out what time the storm started and he'll know what time she was on his doorstep.

What does it matter? As she says, she no longer has a watch. In that conflagration, it melted as surely as that watch in Salvador Dalí's famous painting.

23

Polly loves Thursdays, the day that the area weekly paper is published. She gets up at six and walks to the Royal Farms to buy a copy, then curls up on one of the benches near the window that gets strong morning light. She could take the paper back to her room, but she thinks of the Royal Farms as her "office," a place to tend to business until she has her own place. Once a week, she buys cards, sends them to Jani and Joy, obviously no longer afraid for Gregg to know where she is.

————

She reads the real estate ads as if they were love poems.

> *Cozy cottage with fruit trees*
> *3 beds, 2 baths, your dream house awaits*
> *Two beds, one bath, needs TLC*

She's not naive. She can translate the optimistic real estate speak: *Cramped shack with bug-infested trees; a waking nightmare yearns to scare you; house reviled for good reason.* But she prefers a fixer-upper. She wants her next house to be hers, truly hers, tailored to her particular needs and specifications. Her dream house awaits.

When Gregg bought the house on Kentucky Avenue, she tried to believe it could be her dream house. It had small touches of what felt like grandeur to her—a built-in breakfront, a heavy swinging door between dining room and kitchen, a glass transom over the front door, the house number etched in gold. But it was just an ordinary 1940s house. The neighborhood, even in its glory days, had never been better than middle class. People had expected more, once upon a time. You didn't have to be rich to have a breakfront.

Now, everywhere you look, it's about size. Polly doesn't want a big house, no more than three bedrooms, preferably a rancher. In the decor magazines, she has begun to study photos of places that were considered modern forty years ago. She is fond of uncluttered rooms, as few objects as possible. Smooth wood floors. Bedrooms with nothing but beds, nightstands, a single dresser. She will never buy another iron bed or metal-top table. She wouldn't mind doing the whole house in IKEA furniture, although she would have to rent a big U-Haul to get it all over here from Baltimore.

She's not in a hurry to realize this dream. Good thing, because she's no longer sure how quickly the divorce will come through now that she's decided not to go to Reno. But how much longer could it take, with things so cut and dried between Gregg and her? She'll give him everything he wants. Which, she assumes, is everything. So, six months? Maybe a year? A year's a long time, but she's endured longer stretches of waiting, in and out of prison. Still, it's worrisome. She had planned to be free of Gregg no later than November.

Maybe she and Adam should both leave Belleville and head to Nevada. No one's forcing them to stay here. Cath Whitmire's death has been ruled an accident. They found enough of her skull to rule the cause of death blunt force trauma, consistent with a gas explosion. The case is closed.

Only it's not. Cath's sister and brother-in-law keep agitating. They know people, what with him working for the state police and her a court stenographer. They have complained that the investigation was botched, that Polly should have been treated as a suspect, not a lucky witness who escaped death by paying an impromptu booty call. They pointed out that the volunteer fire department made myriad mistakes at the scene. That was Jim's quote in the *Wilmington News-Journal*—"myriad mistakes at the scene." If Polly leaves town now, with or without Adam, everyone will think she's guilty. That shouldn't bother her, but it does.

Polly wonders if Cath's people have come to regret making a stink. Because while the *News-Journal* has dutifully reported Polly's "life story"—*apartment's tenant was a Baltimore woman who had killed her husband after years of alleged abuse, then been granted a controversial pardon*—it also dug up Cath's past, which is almost as interesting. As a seventeen-year-old high school senior, she had jumped another girl who was taunting her. The two had been on the elevated ramp at an old driving range, a place where high school students went to smoke dope and drink beer. The railing gave way and the other girl had fallen, breaking her neck. Cath went to a juvenile facility; the other girl was in a wheelchair for life. So, yes, there was a record of rage and anger, consistent with lying in wait for a woman she was trying to blackmail. If Polly had known before about Cath's temper—no, she thinks it's better she didn't know.

But the brother-in-law can't let go. When Polly arrives for work on this particular Thursday, he's sitting in the High-Ho parking lot in his state trooper car. His tanned, brawny forearm on the window ledge makes Polly think of a thick snake basking in the middle of the road, one you'd almost go out of your way to slice with your tires. She wonders if it's allowed, using his official car on this not-quite-official business.

"I want to talk to you," he says, without preamble.

She doesn't have to cooperate with him, of course. She could get a restraining order, complain to his bosses. She has been cleared. It's—*unseemly,* the way he uses his job to badger her.

But Polly knows a thing or two about cops. She knows how they close ranks, even behind the worst of the worst. Her husband was a dirty cop and his colleagues had to have suspected as much. There was a pattern, if anyone cared to find it. Beyond his own criminal activities, he was just a lousy guy. He hit her, threatened horrible things. His coworkers had to have known that was true as well. But he was one of theirs and she had killed him, and that wasn't allowed. Killing was a perk that cops kept for themselves. Themselves and maybe little old ladies, shooting blindly toward an intruder in the middle of the night.

"What do you want to talk about?" She stops, but doesn't get in the car, which is clearly his intent. She doesn't want to be in a confined space with him. Then again, she's not going to let him follow her inside, where Adam is already at work, prepping for lunch.

"What really happened that night."

"Only she knows for sure. I wasn't there."

"Why wasn't your door locked?"

"I never locked the door. No one locks their doors here. It's Belleville."

"We could bring a lawsuit against you, you know."

That gets her attention. "For what?"

"Liability. You knew that stove wasn't safe."

"That's on the landlord."

"He says you didn't report it."

"Yeah, well, I'm not sure that trespassers have any right to be assured that the appliances they use are in perfect condition." She goes inside the High-Ho, not in the least bit of a hurry or a fluster.

Still, he has needled her, and she mulls what he has said as she moves on autopilot through the steps of readying for the lunch service. Could Cath's family really sue her? Can she be held accountable? She has heard about cases where people claim civil damages even when criminal liability is unproven. She should ask a lawyer, but no one knows better than she does that you can't even say how-are-you to a lawyer without starting the clock.

There's a famous old saying, *He who steals my purse steals trash, he who steals my good name, etc., etc.* People can do whatever they want to her name, but Polly likes her purse, thank you very much.

"What did he want?" Adam asks. So he, too, saw the car, saw Cath's brother-in-law.

"He's just being a jerk probably to appease that crazy wife of his. Tried to scare me by saying they could sue because I knew that old stove was dangerous. Can someone really sue me? For that?"

"People can sue for anything," Adam says.

She had expected a more comforting reply from him. She stews about Jim's threat the rest of the day, is snappish with Max and Ernest when they come in, not that they notice or care. No matter how she treats them, each man leaves a lone dollar at the end, usually a soft limp one that looks as if it's been dug out of a back pocket. Never more, never less, as if her actions don't matter. Polly is so tired of men deciding how much money she deserves—Ditmars, who kept her on a strict allowance. Gregg, ditto. Even her landlord, who seemed like such a sweetheart, stated flatly how long he was willing to stake her to a motel room while she tried to find a new place. Maybe she should sue *him*. No, better to let that go if she's going to stay in Belleville. The town has been remarkably forgiving of the newcomer whose faulty stove killed one of their own. This is the time to live and let live. For the landlord, if not for poor Cath.

If she and Adam stay together, will *he* police her money? Will she be asked to show her receipts, to account for every cent? *Show me a man's wallet and I'll show you his soul,* she thinks as she pockets Max and Ernest's sad little dollars. Was that a famous saying? It should be.

24

Irving Lowenstein has no voice mail. If someone wants to leave a message for him, Susie takes it down, writes it on one of those pink WHILE YOU WERE OUT slips. This morning there are three, all from the same number, which he recognizes immediately. A tenant. That means money going out instead of in.

Irving owns only a few properties now, mainly on the northwest side. He once had more than forty, thirty-six apartments and ten houses, some commercial in the mix. But it was too much work, and all he ever got for his trouble was labels. *Slumlord,* as if he were the one who made the places slums. They started out nice, his units. Now he's down to one commercial property and three residential ones. He'd like to get rid of those, but he has a soft spot for the tenants, elderly women, good people, if prone to neediness.

Today, it's Mrs. Macalester on Oakley Road, says the hot-water heater is acting up. It's a pretty new heater, so he's not sure what could be wrong. Turns out the pilot blew out, something he can fix, although anything with gas makes him a little nervous. He's in and out in less than fifteen minutes and the day is so nice, the first real fallish day of September, even if the calendar says there are ten more days to autumn. He decides to eat an early lunch in a diner on Garrison Boulevard.

But when he comes out at noon, it's hot again, the day's promises broken. Noon on the dot, he notices on the dashboard clock.

High noon. Yes, it's coming on high noon in more ways than one.

They think he's stupid, those two. Why not? Fool me once, shame on you, fool me twice—but she hasn't fooled him twice. He has been onto her for a very long time. Maybe she's like one of those diseases you get as a kid. Once you've had it, you're immune. He had a little case of the Pauline Ditmars blues, but once she cheated him, he was over it. There are a lot of women in the world, only so many dollars. Irving likes having money, although he permits himself few indulgences. The nice things, such as the house, were for his wife, and Birdy's gone. Irving likes having his money in the bank, in brokerage accounts, in retirement funds. His account balances are proof that everyone was wrong about him—his parents, who wouldn't support him past the age of sixteen, forcing him to drop out of high school. The teachers who gave him Cs and Ds, when he knew he was the sharpest in the class. The insurance agents with whom he works, who put so much stock into appearances, with their expensive cars and suits and haircuts.

"I don't waste money on luxuries," Irving tells new clients when they visit his office. "You see a fancy office, you're looking at waste. I don't have a big nut, so I have no incentive into getting you to bite off more than you can chew. And I'm a broker—I find the best policy for you. I work for *you*."

Ninety percent of the time, every word was true. Ninety, ninety-five percent of his customers paid their premiums, and the policies were there when they needed them. People in insurance sell something that everyone resents paying for—until they need it, and then it's never as good as they think it should be. Doesn't make for popularity. Yet he's the one who's there for them, time and time again. Irving has helped families bury people, send children to college, survive natural disasters. He has consoled survivors and widows.

Helped to create a few widows, too. But that wasn't his fault, not really.

It started in the early 1980s, when he still had properties in the county. He had a tenant in Dundalk, just over the city line. She was okay, but her kids were trouble. Moved in, basically turned the house into a shooting gallery. Place was trashed. But—she paid the rent. Somehow, every month, the rent was paid. He couldn't evict them without cause and he couldn't prove they were selling drugs out of the house. Maybe he should have let it go—they were paying on time—but once they vacated, it was going to cost him a year's rent to get the place back into shape. They let metal men scavenge the appliances, then claimed they had been burglarized. Their hot-water heater was stolen, or so they said. He needed them gone.

He started to spy on them, thinking he would see something that would allow him to kick them out. But tenants have too many rights in Maryland and he never caught them in an open act of thievery. One night, he was wandering down the alley, smoking a cigar, trying not to look too conspicuous—it was a mixed neighborhood, still more white than black, yet Irving felt he stood out here— and it occurred to him that people couldn't live in a house with a little fire damage. He tossed his cigar in the overflowing trash container behind the house. Such pigs they were. And it was a slow-starting fire, the smoke was only beginning to rise in the sky as he pulled away in his Buick. They would have had plenty of time to get out if their senses hadn't been dulled by drugs. Or if the smoke alarms had worked.

Three people died.

That's when Ditmars came into Irving's life.

Later, too late, Irving would come to understand that the guy was always dirty. Ditmars was born dirty, couldn't play it straight even when straight was the better play. He needed to be getting away with something, anything. Salesmen say, *always be closing*. Ditmars just wanted always to be putting something over on someone, anyone.

But the first time Irving met Ditmars, all he knew was that an arson investigator had him in his sights.

"Shame about that fire at your Dundalk property," Ditmars said, dropping heavily into the chair opposite Irving's desk.

"Yeah," Irving said. "A very sad situation."

"No, I mean it's a shame it doesn't happen more often. Druggies. Scum. The kind of people you never used to see in the county, but I guess that's changing."

Irving thought himself a cynical man, but Arson Investigator Burton Ditmars was a new kind of hard.

"Do they know what started the fire?"

"Trash can fire. The front of the house is brick, but the addition on the back was wood. Guess I don't have to tell you the nature of the structure. Something as small as a burning cigarette butt could have done it."

He almost yearned to correct this arrogant man, offer up *cigar*. Instead: "They had smoke alarms. My places are always up to code. But it's not on the landlord to check the batteries."

Ditmars put his feet up on Irving's desk, knees bent so Irving could see the tops of the shoes, which had a formidable shine. Irving could almost see his reflection in the toes.

"I got somebody you should meet," Ditmars said. "Somebody I think you should be in business with."

"I'm not sure—"

"That your blue Buick out front?"

His Buick. There's no reason for Ditmars to ask about his car— unless someone saw him driving away.

Irving watched as his twin reflections nodded hesitantly, trapped in the bulbous ends of those shoes.

A week later, Ditmars returned, this time with a quiet African American man in khakis and a Banlon shirt. Rail-thin and sinewy, with close-cropped hair that was beginning to gray. He looked like a walking piece of jerky.

"Charles Coupay," he said.

"Like the car?"

"Like what you get on your medical insurance, only with a 'u.'" He smiled. "I'm talking your language, huh? I find that's important, to speak to a man in terms he understands."

Irving nodded. He had no idea what Coupé—Coupay—was talking about.

"That fire in your rental in Dundalk. I lost an employee."

"I'm sorry."

"I'm not. He wasn't much good. But now he's gone, taking with him all the time and energy I put into him, and I can't be compensated for that. Ditmars, though, he told me *you* get a check. Because you owned the building. You owned this shitty row house with bum smoke alarms—"

"I put the alarms in. I can't help it if they don't replace the batteries. You know what those people do? They hear the beeping and they disconnect them."

Coupay grinned and repeated: "Those people."

"Tenants like that, I mean."

"How much was the place insured for?"

"Fifty thousand," Irving said. "But I lose the income, don't forget. Nothing left but walls. I have to rebuild if I want to get the monthly income back. Frankly, I'm not sure it's worth it."

"Fifty thousand for a row house that you rented for three twenty-five a month, without utilities. And you bought it, for what—eighteen thousand, twenty thousand?"

Coupay's numbers were eerily on point.

"Man, I'd buy all the row houses I could if I could get money back when they burned down."

Interesting conversation to be having in front of an arson investigator, Irving thought, but said nothing.

"That young man who worked for me, he had children, living with their grandmom, thank goodness. Two kids. Daddy's gone, Mama's gone. Who's going to provide for them?"

"Maybe you could start a fund or ask the church—"

"But they won't get fifty thousand dollars, will they? I was thinking maybe the men who work for me should have life insurance. As a—what's the word—a *perquisite*. I'd like to start offering life insurance policies to my workers. They're young men, in their twenties. Couldn't cost much. Do you understand what I want?"

Irving understood. Ditmars knew he had set the fire, Ditmars had sold him out to Coupay. Could Ditmars prove anything? Probably not. But even an investigation would be disastrous for Irving, an insurance broker suspected of setting a fire in a building he owned.

He could lose his license and what would he be then? A full-time slumlord.

"It can't always be a fire," he said.

"It won't be," Coupay assured him. "Mine is a dangerous business. Employee turnover is very high."

Irving found himself warming to the idea. These young men, trapped in a life from which they couldn't escape—why shouldn't someone benefit?

"You could change it up in other ways. You know what a viatical is?"

"It's where the pope lives." That was Ditmars. Coupay wasn't the kind of man to lean into ignorance, to give answers when he wasn't sure if he was right.

"Why don't you explain the finer points?"

Charles Coupay, who, on paper, was a landlord not unlike Irving Lowenstein, became one of his best customers. He encouraged the young men who worked for him to get life insurance, with Coupay paying the initial premiums. Then, when they had trouble making the monthly payments, Coupay agreed to buy them back at fifty cents on the dollar. Half the time, he didn't even have to arrange for the young men to die; the streets did it for him. And if the young men had the misfortune to suffer crippling injuries, he quietly canceled the policy. When he cashed in, he paid Irving 10 percent of whatever he made, in cash, which Irving collected at Ditmars's house, usually on Friday nights when his wife thought he was at shul.

Ditmars got 40 percent. Irving made a point of not asking him what he was paid for, but Ditmars liked to talk. He would sit at his kitchen table, his big voice booming about the fires he set, the lives he took. Irving told himself it couldn't be true, that he was just a braggart. But it was a relief when Pauline killed him—a relief until Irving realized that she had played him, getting that big insurance policy on a man she planned to kill, but making her kid the beneficiary so the payout couldn't be denied. That sparked the insurance commission investigation he had always feared and he sweated three months, wondering if anyone would spot the pattern, all the claims collected by one Baltimore drug dealer.

Then Coupay got sick, colon cancer, and was dead within four months. Ironic, because he was a disciplined man, ate healthily, never smoked, certainly never dabbled in the wares that his people sold. Ironic, too, because he never took out a life insurance policy for himself. Irving almost missed him. But, mainly, he was glad to be out from under the sword of Damocles. The two people who knew his darkest secret were gone and he was home free. The only person who knew they were in business together was Pauline, and she wasn't going to talk.

In fact, Pauline, who was so quiet that a man could forget she was there, took a trick or two out of his book and wrote some new chapters. Somewhere, she has a jackpot waiting. And if she has money, he deserves some of it. She can give a little bit to him or all of it to the state. Either way, she loses, and isn't that a way for him to win?

———————

It takes twenty-five minutes to get to his office and that's despite knowing all the shortcuts. The strip center is his last commercial property. Twelve stores, a parking lot, a wedge of Route 40 that gets a little seedier every year. His office is modest, as are his clothes, his car. But he paid cash to send his children to college and he'll help to send his grandchildren to college, too. A widower for almost a year now, he's a catch, make no doubt about it. The single women at his synagogue, when he deigns to go, make eyes at him. But there was only one woman for him and she's gone.

And, yes, one afternoon, for about fifteen minutes, he thought a young shiksa fancied him. He thought he was going to be her savior.

He'll settle for being her ruination.

25

W hat are you thinking about?" Polly asks Adam.

They are in bed, looking at the ceiling. She is probably hurt because he doesn't feel like spooning tonight. But Polly would never say anything as needy as that. Polly doesn't push when a man retreats. She pulls back even further. She, too, is lying on her back, hands folded across her chest. Until she spoke, he assumed she was asleep. Her breath, since he rolled off her, has been steady and soft. She won't ask the question again if he doesn't answer. Polly seldom repeats herself. It's odd enough for her to ask what he's thinking.

Adam is thinking about rice. More specifically, he is thinking about risotto. It's a tricky dish in a place as thinly staffed as the High-Ho, but there's a variation that's particularly nice in the fall, with mushrooms and squash, lots of cheese and butter. But risotto requires too much attention in a kitchen where he has only one helper, Jorge, who also has to run the dishwasher, bus the tables. No, he doesn't want to add risotto to the menu at the High-Ho. But he would like to make it for Polly one night. Only when? The restaurant is closed Mondays, but the bar is open and Polly has to work every day but Tuesday. Mr. C has brought in a new girl to help on Fridays and Saturdays, which continue to be semibusy, but he's trying to get by without another full-time waitress until next summer. He doesn't believe the business will stay strong through the off-season. Adam doesn't, either.

Yet Polly has persuaded Mr. C to make subtle changes to the dining room. Nothing fancy. She's too smart to put lipstick on a pig. If anything, she's putting more pig on the pig, leaning into the *jointness* of the joint, playing up its retro features. The jukebox, long broken, has been refurbished, but Polly kept the tunes that were in there, so it's a nice little time warp, 1965–1985.

She also got Mr. C to replace the tables and chairs, but with what appears to be an eclectic jumble of wooden and Formica and one, just one, metal-top table, practically the twin of the one she lost in the fire. Things are cleaner, brighter, but not *too* bright. It's hard to put a finger on it, but the High-Ho is now a place where people might like to linger. She has worked with the liquor supplier to find a few small, affordable wines to offer by the glass, three reds and three whites, all Italian, very drinkable, good with food. "How did you know about vermentino?" he asked her.

"You don't have to go to Italy to have tasted Italian wine," she says, a little affronted.

"I know, but—" He stops himself from saying what he's thinking. *But you're just a Dundalk girl. The farthest you've ever been from home is the beach. The beach, or that women's prison in Frostburg.* But she never told him where she served time. She never tells him anything about her past, not since the last day in August, the day before the fire, when she presumably told him everything.

Adam has been trying to assemble her life story on his own. He can't ask her because he's scared of screwing up, revealing that he knows things she's never told him. He doesn't want to ask Irving if there are other secrets he withheld when he hired Adam because then Irving might figure out the extent of Adam's betrayal. But an old journalist friend has managed to pull together a pretty complete dossier on Polly Costello Ditmars Smith Hansen, whose current legal name is Pauline Smith Hansen. Married at seventeen, a mom at twenty-one. The state has custody of that girl—inevitable, given that her mother was in prison and the father was dead. Adam knows firsthand that she had another kid and abandoned her. She never speaks of her children, never. Sometimes, he catches her with a sad, faraway look on her face, but who knows what that's about.

She's mentioned that they could stop using condoms, but he keeps using them. She's insulted, suspicious. "I can go on the Pill, it's 99 percent." He says only, "I don't think birth control pills are good for women. I won't tell you what to do with your body, but you should rethink all those hormones." God, he sounds like his own mother, but the world finally caught up with her, didn't it? A free spirit who may or may not have had a fling with Neal Cassady, Lillian Bosk would now blend in comfortably with most suburban moms. Adam grew up eating good food, admiring his mother's painting, listening to his father play tenor sax. *Work to live, don't live to work,* that was his parents' motto.

And yet their son has somehow ended up putting in fourteen-hour days in a roadside Delaware restaurant, whose main distinction is that it's too good for most of the people who eat there, but not good enough to get people to drive up from Salisbury or down from Wilmington. What's he going to do, get a Michelin star in Belleville, Delaware? There was a reason he left cooking behind after that season on the yacht. PI work also has its fourteen-hour days, but it pays much better. Then there are the long fallow seasons when he travels. He should be in New Zealand or Argentina right now, watching the world edge into spring instead of fall.

He should be alone. Except he can no longer imagine being any place without Polly and this seems to be where she wants to be.

He argues in his head: *There's no money, Irving. There can't possibly be any money. No one with money would be here, in Belleville, in this garage apartment she found a week ago.*

She seems to love it.

But would someone kill to keep this life? Did she kill Cath?

Shut up, shut up, shut up, shut up, shut up, shut up, he says to his own thoughts, then reaches for her hand.

"Did you say something?" he asks. He's not even sure if she's still awake.

When she replies, her voice is clear and measured, not the least bit sleepy. But also without the edge that most women use when asked to repeat themselves. She is capable of a stillness he has never found in another woman. Stillness. He thinks about hunting. Deer season will be starting soon. Do they have deer in Delaware? Is there a place for him to go and sit in a tree with his bow and arrow? Is there *time*? Tonight at work, doodling on a pad, he found himself sketching a stick figure being pulled underwater by an anchor. The anchor is the High-Ho. The anchor is this town, this life. But not Polly, unless—

"I asked what you were thinking about."

"Rice," he says.

olly asks Adam to borrow his truck. Doesn't say why, doesn't offer to tell him where she's going. Let him show some curiosity, she has answers ready if he wants them. But he doesn't ask. He's terrified to ask her anything, she realizes. He can barely ask her, *How are you?* or, when they're eating breakfast, *Could you pass the butter?*

He thinks she straight-up murdered Cath. Fine. Yet he alibied her, agreed she had been at his door by midnight—which she was, give or take. She didn't ask him to. Didn't need him to. That's his problem. She has her own problems. Which is why she needs his truck.

She's working six days a week, but her pocketbook would be hurting if she and Adam weren't splitting expenses on the garage apartment. Adam never seems to worry about money, though. That must be nice. Polly wonders if people who don't worry about money can ever understand what it's like, fretting over every dollar that leaves your hands. Even if they used to know those circumstances, they forget so quickly. It's like being hungry. You can't really remember it when you have enough food, you can't will yourself to feel it. You're hungry or you're not. You're poor or you're not. Today, for example, Polly has to think about how much gas his truck has, if she can afford to fill it, or at least buy a few gallons of gas after the trip.

Adam being Adam, he gives her the truck with a full tank, kisses her, and remembers to ask, "You going to be okay, going across the bridge?"

"I'm going up to Dover."

He doesn't ask why. She has a lie ready if he does. She's going to say she's taking her driver's exam, that she still has a birth certificate that identifies her as Polly Costello, so she should be able to do it pretty simply. A lie on so many levels, one he'll see through—where'd she get her birth certificate if she lost everything in the fire?—and, again, one she has an answer for. *Oh, you can write to the State of Maryland and request a copy.* Of course, she can't become Polly Costello again until she divorces Gregg. Even then, it's not automatic. She's going to have to go through the Social Security Administration to get her own name back. But Adam doesn't know all that.

Adam, true to form, isn't asking her any questions.

He does say, "You're getting an awfully early start."

It's only six, barely light at this time of year.

"The early bird gets the worm. Place opens at eight, but I want to stop for breakfast."

———

She's in Baltimore by 8:15 waiting near the corner of Harford Road, hoping that Gregg won't notice the big pickup at the curb. Gregg doesn't notice much. He's the kind of guy who can't tell when a woman has an orgasm. And not because the woman's faking it, all *When Harry Met Sally* style. Gregg assumes it's happening and, if it's not, then it's not his problem. He thought their sex life was great. It was. For him.

She can see the edge of her house on Kentucky Avenue from where she's parked, but she can barely remember the woman who used to live there. That woman had been pretending to be so many things she wasn't, had disavowed her past. She is finally herself, Polly Costello. The old nickname, the surname she was born with— they were like some beautiful architectural feature in an old house, hidden by years of "improvements."

She has timed it right. Gregg, who has to be at work at 9:30, pulls out at 8:55. She's pretty sure where he's going, so she hangs back as he drives north, then west. Yep, he's still parking Jani with his mother all day. Savannah Hansen must love that. She's the kind of grandmother who prides herself on how young she looks, used to say things like, *There was this man at the Bel-Loc Diner who thought Pauline and I were sisters, isn't that hilarious?* The guy was legit legally blind and just making polite small talk. Yet if Polly said that, she would be petty. She was expected to ignore Savannah's silly pride, her bizarre competitiveness.

She doesn't risk getting too close to Savannah's house, so all she can see of Jani is her profile. *Brave girl.* Polly's not sure why that word, *brave,* pops into her head, but there's something so upright about this daughter, a little soldier marching on. She always knew Jani would be okay. Gregg lifts her from her car seat and she walks up the sidewalk, her grandmother waiting in the open door. Savannah Hansen is wearing a sundress, way too short, tight and bright.

From there, Polly goes to see Joy. It's unclear how much Joy understands, what she knows, but Polly never doubts that her daughter recognizes her. The staff lets them have thirty minutes alone. Joy's fourteen, and she won't be allowed to stay past her eighteenth birthday, at which point the state will have to find another placement for her. *Soon, sweetheart, soon.* But what is soon to Joy? How does Joy experience time? People thought time in prison moved slowly, and it did. Yet those days were no slower than Polly's days with Ditmars, and much easier to pass. No fear, no lows. No highs, either, but that was okay. What is time like for Joy? Polly spells out "M-a-m-a" on Joy's board, and Joy spells it back. But what does it *mean* to her? The woman who's never there, who could never be there?

Polly's final errand, the real business of the day, is to an office in midtown Baltimore. It's a self-consciously hip place, especially for Baltimore, a converted firehouse. Of course this guy kept the pole, which is at the center of the reception area. He probably makes jokes about it.

Sure enough, when Barry Forshaw ushers her into his office, he says, "How do you like the new digs? I kept the pole for dancing late at night. Want to give it a try?"

She can't even be bothered to show him how offensive that is. "Look, I know you don't do marital law, but Gregg is really dragging his feet now that we're separated. Is there any way I can make *him* file?"

"You want a divorce? I thought you were concerned that he'd leave you if he knew about your past."

Shit, she forgot that she told Forshaw that she wanted to keep the settlement a secret for now because Gregg didn't know she had been married before. Or how it ended.

"It's not going to work out. I left him back in June." She lowers her eyes to her lap. "There are—well, I can't talk about it."

"If you left him, you have to wait for two years."

Two years? She can't believe it.

"Isn't there any way to make it go faster?"

"He can file after one year from the separation, citing abandonment. He has cause. You don't."

Oh, she has cause.

"What would make him file?"

"Christ, Pauline, I don't know. I never met the guy."

"Can you move the money to—what do you call it? Like, a Swiss bank account or something overseas?"

"Offshore. I guess that could be done, but I'd have to charge you for it."

"How much more of my money do you want?"

"I'm a lawyer. I charge for my time."

"You already have 40 percent of my settlement. Isn't that enough?"

"I explained that. If you had let me take it to trial, we were looking at a chance for a much bigger payout. You were the one who wanted a sealed settlement, and that's why the hospital was so eager to give you what you wanted. I could have made two, three million on my usual 30 percent. Instead, that's what we got total. And you can have your money whenever you want."

"If Gregg knows about it, he'll try to take it."

"He can try, but he won't succeed. Look, I don't do marital law, but any half-decent divorce attorney can shield that money from him."

"I'm done paying lawyers," she says. "I just want to get out of my marriage as quick as possible, no complications. I was going to go to Reno, but—that's not going to work out."

"Fine. Do it your way. There's an argument to be made, Pauline, that you're being penny-wise, but pound-foolish. Hire a divorce lawyer."

An argument to be made. He has to think that. He's a lawyer. His livelihood depends on arguments having worth. She looks around his office. It's filled with antiques, stupid things that clearly mean nothing to him, trophies purchased to celebrate cashing in on the misery of others. Babies with cerebral palsy because of botched deliveries, steel workers with destroyed lungs, lives and bodies ruined by drunken drivers.

"Let me just ask you as a man—if your wife walked out on you, left you with your kid, what would make you want to divorce her?"

"If I met a new woman, maybe. I don't know. Your husband probably thinks the divorce is going to cost *him,* so he's in no hurry to get started. Remember, he believes you're dead broke. Maybe if you tell him *you* want to marry again, then he'll think he'll have you over the barrel and he'll tip his hand, reveal what he wants."

She smiles. "That advice is worth more than almost anything you've done for me."

"No charge," he says, waving a hand. Mr. Magnanimous. "We've both benefited nicely from our relationship. It was a lucky day for me when Irving Lowenstein referred you."

Another lie she has forgotten. Irving used to bitch about this guy all the time to Ditmars, which is part of the reason she chose him. Anyone on Irving's bad side couldn't be all bad. She had used Irving's name, let Forshaw assume she was fond of nice old Mr. Lowenstein.

"I probably should have sent him a gift, come to think of it," Forshaw continues. "When I ran into him last fall, he wouldn't even let me buy him a Diet Coke."

"You—ran into Irving? But you didn't mention me, right?"

"Didn't have to. All I did was say medical malpractice and he figured out it was you. Besides, it was a referral. He knew he had recommended me to you, right?"

Polly's nostrils fill with a scorching smell, but it's a memory, the pleasant smell of damp laundry as she presses Gregg's shirts and watches television. "I'm Barry Forshaw and I'm for the law—and for YOU." Irving. Irving Lowenstein. Why had she used his name when she called this stupid ambulance chaser? Because she wanted to sound connected, she wanted to be more than what she was, a dumb housewife, watching soap operas and listening to some guy's Bawlmer accent bleating from her television set. *Barry Forshaw is for the law—and for you.* "How did you find me?" Barry Forshaw had asked her. All she had to say was *television*. But she thought that would mark her as naive, and to be naive was to be cheated, ruined, hurt. She said: "I heard from Irving Lowenstein that you were a fighter. We go way back, Irving and I."

And now, because Baltimore is so goddamn small, Irving has learned she hired Forshaw. Gregg may not know she has money hidden away, but Irving does.

She manages to smile, shake Forshaw's hand, walk out to Adam's truck, but she's shaking too hard to drive.

She hadn't been completely stupid on that first visit, she thinks. It had been a test, dropping Irving's name. She needed someone just a *little* crooked, someone who would agree to pursue a settlement and keep it a secret. Someone who would then bank her money until she was free of Gregg. Anyone who had done business with Irving had to be a little bent. So she had said "Irving Lowenstein" and, abracadabra, Barry had nodded, said he knew Irving, although mostly as an adversary. She remembers thinking that was good, that they were adversaries. He wasn't part of their schemes, then.

The schemes—she straightens up behind the wheel of Adam's truck, takes a deep breath. She's not shaking anymore. There may be a way to solve the Irving problem. Irving's not stupid. If Barry thanked him for referring Polly to him, he'll have figured out she has money. And he'll come after it. "I have 100 percent of the risk, but only 40 percent of the money," Ditmars used to lament. "Irving takes 10 percent for doing nothing. But don't ever try to gyp him out of his 10 percent."

Last fall, Forshaw says. He ran into Irving last fall. The mystery is why Irving hasn't made a move on her yet.

Only maybe he has.

She bangs open the glove compartment, decides she has time to run one more errand before heading east.

think I saw Pauline," Savannah Hansen tells Gregg when he comes to pick up Jani. Late. He's thirty minutes late, and there might be beer on his breath.

"You're always saying that."

"Not always. Sometimes. Maybe three times during the summer." She frowns at a grubby chocolate handprint on the skirt of her yellow plaid sundress, which is brand new. The pattern reminded her of that cute outfit that the lead girl in that new movie wore. Savannah is in very good shape for her age, for any age really. She doesn't exercise, but she watches what she eats, always has, ever since Gregg's father walked out on them when Gregg was not even a year old. She still had some of the pregnancy fat when Curtis left her. Which was her fault. Savannah has always been very honest with herself. She let herself go, got sloppy and whiny, and Curtis wasn't having it. Some women in her situation would have been bitter, but Savannah found strength in seeing what she had done wrong. Being bossy was okay; men secretly liked bossy in her experience. But not naggy and self-pitying. And you can be bossy only as long as, at the end of the day, your man knows he's the king of the castle, the cock of the walk. She raised Gregg to expect nothing less. Go figure that mousy Pauline would be his undoing.

Jani is asleep and Gregg hoists her to his shoulder with a kind of absentminded tenderness. She's a beautiful girl, but then—Jani favors her father. No conceit there, Gregg is a pretty boy, the one thing that Savannah and Curtis did right, with those dark curls and pale blue eyes. Once Curtis left, Savannah never lacked for male companionship but when the men figured out that Gregg was always going to be number one, they didn't want to play second fiddle.

She didn't care. She didn't need 'em. Curtis was good about money, if not much else. She got to raise her boy the way she wanted, which was to be all-man. The way Savannah saw it, if you treated a man right, he could afford to be benevolent, generous. It's only when you pick at a man's power that he turns mean.

She was so disappointed when he brought Pauline home. And not fooled for a minute. She knew the girl—woman, in her thirties already, although she was trying to play it younger—was knocked up the moment she saw her. It was the only possible explanation for the swift marriage down at the courthouse, never mind all that talk about the honeymoon. Eight months later, Jani proved Savannah right.

She would have rather been wrong. Not that she doesn't love Jani, dote on Jani. But she wasn't ready to be a grandmother yet. She was too young, barely fifty when Jani was born. Once, the cashier at the Bel-Loc Diner even asked if she and Pauline were sisters. Oh, Pauline was insulted, but it was right after Jani was born, so she was looking a little puffy and exhausted.

"Girl," Savannah had told her, meaning to do nothing but good. "Don't do what I did. Don't let yourself go. Your man is job number one."

"Really? Then why did you let your man go?" Oh, she had a mouth on her when Gregg wasn't around. She was full of sass, that Pauline.

"I didn't let him go. But when he left, I admitted it was my fault."

Savannah has to give Pauline credit: she starved that baby weight off her. Fact is, she went too far. She wasn't meant to be skinny, Pauline. In a bathing suit, she had those telltale silvery tracks, the sign of a big weight loss at some point.

Ah well, Savannah Hansen's One-Baby Day-Care Center is closed for today. She's going to make herself a kahlúa with a splash of skim milk, then have some Lean Cuisine manicotti while she watches *Entertainment Tonight*.

The woman she saw today, parked across the street in a truck— Savannah was pretty sure it was Pauline. But, as Gregg says, it's not the first time lately that she thought she saw her and why would Pauline be driving a big truck like that. Maybe when you fear something, you see it hiding around every corner. And Savannah has always had an uneasy feeling around Pauline. That look she gave her, when the man at the Bel-Loc said they could be sisters. *She is not a woman who will tolerate rivals,* Savannah thinks, adding some ice cubes to her drink. Which is a problem because Pauline is always going to have rivals. It's not her looks, it's her lack of confidence, pure and simple. She already has a rival in Jani.

Oh, and now come to find out that she had a *past*. Gregg told Savannah that he found out this summer that Pauline was that woman who killed her husband and lied about it. Something like that. Savannah went all over cold, hearing that. Imagine, her sweet

180

son lying in bed next to that woman. Thank God they're getting divorced. They better be getting divorced.

Savannah puts her feet up on her hassock. Her just-so house is beginning to look a little worse for wear. It's no place for a sticky toddler. Much as it pains her, Savannah has to put Gregg on notice that this is a *temporary* arrangement. She loves her grandchild, but she didn't sign up for another round of this every day shit. She has served her time.

28

A song plays in Adam's head as he looks at the gas gauge on his truck. *Where did you go, my Handsome Polly-O?* Half full. That's consistent with a trip to Dover. Only the odometer isn't. The truck has turned over to thirteen thousand miles, which means she traveled more than two hundred miles yesterday. Did she really think he wouldn't check the mileage?

Yes, you sick fuck. Because she thinks you believe every word she says. Which means she either trusts you or she's playing you for a fool.

In which case: *Yes, you dumb fuck.*

Either scenario, he's hosed. If she loves and trusts him, he can never reveal to her the real reason they met. And if she's playing him, he'll end up another chump, abandoned at best.

This much is clear: Polly returned from wherever she was in a mood that is new, at least to him. It's as if she's changed her hair color, but by no more than a shade. Always self-contained, she now carries the air of someone with a secret, a pleasant one. She smiles without seeming to be aware of it, hums in careless moments. They get up, go to work, come home, make love.

Everything is the same as it was.

Or is it?

It takes him a few days to pick up on the changes. She doesn't read the real estate ads anymore. Strange, he used to hate seeing the paper lying on the table, the house ads circled in bright blue marker. But now that she's stopped, he feels unnerved. Why has she stopped planning for the future, their future? She no longer talks about B and Bs, or what the High-Ho could be in the hands of an ambitious young couple. She doesn't push him to add new dishes to the menu. She doesn't brainstorm about specials or theme nights.

In bed, she is more passionate than ever.

Where did you go, my Handsome Polly-O? What do you know, my Handsome Polly-O?

Polly-O. His mother had sung that old folk song to him in her off-key yet pleasant warble of a voice. She had an autoharp. Of course she did. And, once again, the world has caught up to his mother, with people going crazy for this album by a pretty young bluegrass artist. When Adam was young, he hated his parents' music, but then—teenagers are supposed to hate their parents' music. Does it still work that way? If he had a kid, how could the kid dare to say no to the Clash and the Pogues and Elvis Costello? A kid would have to tie himself in knots, making a case against the musicians Adam loved in his teens and twenties, still loves.

But the next generation would do it, if only out of sheer perversity. God, the shit on the radio now, those awful "boy" bands built on a formula as old as the Monkees—a cute one, a brainy one, a quirky one, an ugly one.

He is cleaning up after a slow Wednesday, although business had picked up a bit when early diners reported around town that he was serving "chicken casserole." The dish was, more accurately, a chicken lasagna, made with heavy cream and about four pounds of cheese. It tickles him, he has to admit, when he gets a burst of locals late in the shift because word has traveled about how good tonight's special is. But it reminds him, too, what life in a small town is like. There are three or four families who "matter," at least in Belleville. There's one in particular whose name is on everything, the Langleys. They were here tonight, swanned in like the king and queen of homecoming, their loyal court in attendance. But their approval matters, and he slaved over their plates as if the *New York Times* restaurant critic were out there.

No, the small-town life is not the life for him, which sounds like another song his mother might have sung. How he misses his parents, those sad, sweet hippies who ate macrobiotic, smoked dope, and died before they were sixty—a heart attack for him, a stroke for her—because some people do everything right and still don't catch a break.

And maybe that's Polly, he thinks, looking at her, closing down the register at the bar. Maybe she just had shitty luck all these years. He watches her count the cash. She's so loving with the money. It's as if every bill is a child on its way to school, each one needing a last loving touch—a cap adjusted on this one, a smear of toothpaste wiped from the corner of that one's lips. She is especially solicitous of her tips, tucking them into her billfold snugly.

Why aren't you tucking your own child into bed at night, Handsome Polly-O? Where did you go, my Handsome Polly-O?

And maybe because his thoughts keep going to music tonight, or maybe because she's swaying a little, as if lost in a private dance, he goes over to the jukebox and drops a quarter in. He doesn't want to agonize over a pick, so he punches in a random combo, AA:11. He knows the song from its first notes. "I'd Like to Get to Know You." 1968. A deeply uncool song. But he was eleven in 1968. He would have killed to slow-dance with a girl to this song, to any song.

He turns and opens his arms to her and she doesn't have to be asked. *Oh, how I love you, Quiet Polly-O, with all your secrets and silences.* They move through the restaurant as if it were a ballroom. Jorge comes out of the kitchen to watch, then disappears as if he's caught them fucking. Their dance is that private, that intimate. *I'd Like to Get to Know You.* He would, he would. He wants to know her and he wants her to know him. He was hired to get to know her. Those were his literal marching orders. *Get to know her,* Irving had said. *Insinuate your way into her life. Look for inconsistencies. Is she living large in any way? I need to figure out if she's tapped into the money, or if it's out there somewhere, waiting for her. We have to get to her before she wastes that poor child's money. She's done this before. She and her husband used me to run a very sophisticated insurance scheme.*

He realizes now that Irving planned to blackmail Polly. He thought she would pay to keep her safe new life, that she would be terrified of her husband knowing about her past. When she bolted, he lost his leverage. But it's also evident now that Adam was working for a bad guy. *Had* worked. He ended the relationship the Tuesday after Labor Day, told Irving that he clearly wasn't going to be able to deliver the information Irving wanted—the proof that she even had money, much less where she was keeping it. Adam hadn't started out to work for a bad guy. He thought he was on the right side. He had been told that a woman had stolen money from her stepdaughter. When Adam had confronted Irving with his lies, he seemed to shrug, said he always thought the girl was a stepdaughter because Polly had been so unloving with her, so distant. And, after all, she had in fact murdered her husband. Was it so wrong to think she was capable of screwing over her own daughter?

She did kill a man. That's not up for debate.

What if this woman in his arms killed Cath, set that fire? Did she know that the volunteer fire department would be easy to fool, or did she simply take the risk? But why would she kill Cath when Cath had no power over her? How had she lured her there? By the time Cath died, Adam and Mr. C knew about Polly's past. What more could there be?

I'd Like to Get to Know You. Sing it, Spanky. Sing it. Polly's eyes are closed, her head on his shoulder. They dip and swoon through the restaurant. And when the song ends and the jukebox is silent, they stand there a long time, swaying to the songs in their heads.

29

Polly has taken to slipping out of bed before the sun rises and walking to the Royal Farms for coffee, a little downtime with the *Wilmington News-Journal*. She needs solitude, and that's no longer available to her at home. After the explosion, she was too dazed to consider what it would be like to live with Adam. They were a couple, she was confident of his love for her, it made sense for him to stop paying for the motel when she got the larger place.

But now she's almost never alone, and she realizes how much she craves solitude, a luxury she didn't know until this summer. Even when Adam is sleeping, his presence fills the garage apartment. That used to be comforting, like sleeping next to a lion. She felt safe. Now she notices that he snores a little, sometimes even passes gas. He is, after all, a man. Kinder to her than the other men she has known, but still a man, always a man.

The new place is, by almost anyone's standards, nicer than the one above the Ben Franklin. Modern appliances, one and a half baths. And most people would probably like the wooded backyard, the privacy it provides. But Polly misses the light that filled her second-floor apartment, the high ceilings and almost empty rooms. Even if most of the things in the new place belong to the landlord—the same landlord she had before, giving her a break; he feels terrible about the explosion, Cath's death—they weigh her down. In the Royal Farms, there is nothing to clean, nothing to cook, not even a cup to rinse after she has finished her coffee. She leaves the newspaper behind for whoever sits down next. The *News-Journal* doesn't really mean anything to her, she might as well be reading a paper in a foreign language. The towns, the counties, the elected officials—she doesn't recognize a one. The only thing she knows about Delaware is Belleville and the only time Belleville was in the *News-Journal* was when Polly's apartment blew up and Cath died.

They mentioned her, of course. But no one cared. It was an accident, after all—*that beautiful old stove,* she thinks with a pang. There was even a little backfire of gossip that maybe it was Cath who started the fire but didn't realize how much gas had built up from the leaking stove. It makes as much sense as anything, Polly supposes, but she keeps a polite silence when Max and Ernest try to bait that hook. Best not to speak ill of the dead.

But maybe those rumors are sturdy enough to travel on their own, because here's Cath's brother-in-law, Trooper Jim, waiting in his official car when Polly leaves the Royal Farms just before sunrise.

"May I speak to you?" he asks.

"I need to get home." Adam doesn't like waking up alone. It's really quite endearing.

"It won't take a minute." He leans over, pushes open the passenger-side door. She climbs in, but she doesn't close the door. She doesn't like being in confined spaces with people she can't trust, male or female. Her body is angled so she can move quickly if he tries to grab her.

"You can close the door."

"I know."

He takes her measure, sees she won't be bullied, lets it go.

"So I've been talking to an arson expert. Guy who testifies in trials. He says there's a scenario where it would make sense if someone made that explosion look like an accident in order to cover up a murder."

She says nothing. Ditmars told her a long time ago never to talk to anyone, about anything.

"If there was a fire and the gas was on—yes, it could go like that, kaboom. And if Cath lit a cigarette, maybe, assuming the gas had been leaking for a while. But the scene is consistent with what would happen if a small fire started in another room. Say, from a candle."

Or a scarf, slipping and falling on the bare bulb of a bedside lamp.

Never tell anyone anything, Ditmars whispers in her ear. She never thought she'd be happy to hear his voice in her head. His voice is forever trapped in her head, but it's usually taunting, not helping.

"But if the stove had been leaking for a while, you would have smelled it, right? You said you left to take a walk, then went to your boyfriend's motel room."

"I often take walks at night." Nothing specific, nothing that can be contradicted.

"But, you know, cigarette fiend that Cath is, she's pretty polite. She never would have smoked in someone else's home."

"She lit up a cigarette in my kitchen the first time she came by, even though I asked her not to. And she used the burner."

"Yes, the first time she came by. So how many times was it that she dropped in to see you? Remember, I'm the one she asked to check you out, so don't try to sell me on the friend thing."

Her fault. She has said too much. That doesn't mean she has to keep talking. Ditmars taught her that, too. *You can shut up anytime. The sooner, the better.* If she didn't scream or cry, the things he did to her, they didn't last as long.

"Anyway, it could be arson," Trooper Jim continues. "The investigation isn't necessarily closed. Just so you know. A murder case never goes away. Who knows what kind of technology they'll have in five, ten years? Cath's death has completely fucked up my in-laws. Finding who's to blame may be the only thing that will help them."

"Closure," she says.

Polly thinks about an investigation that had haunted Ditmars, if only briefly. An accident on Christmas Day, in what would be the last full year of their life together. A family that had yearned for an old-fashioned Christmas had been foolish enough to use candles on the tree. But it was a gas leak that made the fire fatal, a fireball shooting up into the sky over Woodlawn. Walking through the wreckage where an entire family had died, Ditmars had a vision. He wanted, briefly, to be a better person. He swore he was going to change, made a resolution to stop drinking.

Three days into the new year, he beat her with a belt, then wrapped it around her neck during sex. Six weeks after that, there was a fire strangely similar to the Christmas Day one, only in the city.

"So you know about my first husband?"

"Some."

"Do you know *everything*?"

"He's dead. Why are we talking about him?"

Polly studies the sun as it rises—there's a stripe of orange red, a low simmer on the horizon, then a perfect round lozenge suddenly popping up. She has never known sunrises and sunsets like they have in Belleville. The flat, open landscape gives the light so much room to spread.

"My husband was a dirty cop. He was an arson investigator. He knew how to make things look like accidents. He never—his words—shat where he ate. He worked for the county. But there were fires in the city, deadly ones, from time to time. And I'm pretty sure he set them."

"He's dead," Trooper Jim repeats. Polly wonders for a moment, *Is he?* How can she be sure? It turns out it is possible to have seen a man's body, a knife sticking through his heart, and still wonder if one will ever be free of him. She can't believe she won. And, yes, she considers killing Ditmars a victory. She lost almost every battle in the years they were together, but she won the war. She won that war and she'll win this one.

"He had a partner. Irving Lowenstein. He arranged for policies, they split the proceeds. He probably suspects I know things—insurance fraud, even murder. He has reasons to want me dead."

"Are you trying to say someone was trying to kill you and killed Cath by accident?"

"I'm saying it's a possibility."

"I'll need more than your say-so. Dates, names."

"I can get them."

30

June pours tomato soup into bowls, puts out goldfish crackers that she bought at the Food Lion on her way to her parents' house.

"Please eat," she urges her mother. When Dorothy "Dodo" Whitmire retired from her job at the state school board, her plan was to start golfing with her husband, pursue her interest in birding, which had been limited to what she could see from their deck. Now she is hunched and ashen as if she has lived years in the dark, immobile. June's father, Dan, never much of a talker, is almost completely mute these days, and he has lost so much weight that his face looks like melted rubber.

Since Cath's death June has tried to visit her parents at least one or two evenings a week. They are only in their late fifties, but the loss of their oldest daughter has aged them, cruelty on top of cruelty. It doesn't help that they had both taken early retirement, which has ended up giving them unlimited time to grieve.

Everyone, even June, always assumed she was their favorite. She was certainly the "good" one, the one who gave them little cause to worry over the years. But she is beginning to suspect that they would be able to make peace more easily with her untimely death for that very reason. Cath was a work in progress, so many of life's most basic milestones left undone. Stuck in a nowhere job she was about to lose. Incapable of getting her act together to enroll in the local community college, no matter how much she talked about it. Cath and her castles in the air. The day before she had died, she had called June with questions about high-end finishes in kitchens, which ones were worth the money, which could be skipped. She said she was thinking about buying a town house in a new development near the marsh, and there were upgrade options. June asked her how she could possibly afford it, and Cath said—coyly, June thinks now—that she was a better saver than anyone gave her credit for, that tip money had been coming in like a bumper crop this summer.

Yet her boss confirmed to Jim that he was going to let Cath go, or at least cut her hours way back, although he also insisted he had not yet told her that. He had been maddeningly unapologetic about his disloyalty to her, indifferent to the protocols of death, in which people agree to act as if the deceased were a better person than she was. "I can't afford two waitresses off-season," he said. "I pitch in, or my wife does."

Could Cath's death have been a suicide attempt? June wonders, leaning against the stove, waiting to see if her parents will eat anything. She cannot imagine her wayward, intense sister taking her own life. But she can envision Cath staging a scene, for effect, getting down on her hands and knees and sticking her head in the oven, then getting bored at her own dramatics. She had done things like that when they were children. Once, on April Fool's Day, she had spread ketchup on herself and sprawled at the bottom of the stairs for June, only seven at the time, to find her. She hadn't been fooled for long, but the image still lives in her head. When she has nightmares about Cath—and she has two, three a week—that's what she sees, a ten-year-old covered in blood.

She feels guilty that she can still go about daily life in a way her parents cannot. She loved her sister, of course. But Cath was exhausting, absorbing so much attention and time. June, settled and happy, felt more and more like Cath's second mother. Cath had begun to borrow money here and there—small amounts, but June kept this secret from Jim. She has a lot of practice, keeping Cath's secrets.

The family never spoke about the "accident"—a word that lives in quotations in June's head because she knows the law. If you attack someone, leap at the person with teeth bared and hands ready to strike, you have intent, even if you're not trying to put them in a wheelchair for life. Yet if the family had dared to discuss this taboo topic, June would never have told them the connection she made long ago: Cath jumped on that girl a week after June won three awards at her middle-school graduation ceremony. June has long believed that Cath yearned to leap at *her,* punch her and hit her, for being the effortlessly good girl. But it wasn't effortless. It was the only role left to her as hellion Cath burned her path through adolescence. When June was a teenager, it felt as if every conversation with her parents started with an almost absentminded congratulations on June's latest achievement, then quickly moved to the problem of Cath, what should they do about Cath? Oh, June believes this woman killed Cath. But the quiet, analytical part of June's mind, honed by hours of listening to court testimony, can't help wondering if Cath provoked her.

"Eat," she urges her parents, who move their soup spoons through their bowls but fail to raise them to their mouths. The goldfish crackers she sprinkled along the surface have bloated and sunk. This was how June and Cath had eaten tomato soup when they were little, putting so many goldfish in their bowls that you could barely see what they called the red sea. The trick was to eat them quickly, while they still had a little crunch and snap. She had thought it might comfort her parents, this unacknowledged callback to a simpler time. Because by the time Cath was eleven or twelve, it was clear she was not going to have an easy life. She wasn't self-destructive, but she was destructive. Things broke around Cath. Things and people. Accidents, her parents always said. Cath had accidents.

But not everything was an accident. There had been a set of china, their paternal grandmother's, in the attic. When June and Jim got engaged and set up a wedding registry, June told her mother that she was happy to take the family china. Her mother, looking embarrassed, confessed that Cath had broken most of it when she was a teenager, just gone up to the attic and flung plates and cups and serving dishes against the wall.

"You have to eat, Mom," June says again. Her mother takes a tiny sip of soup, a larger sip from the Michelob Light at her place. She always seems to have a beer going when June comes by. But it's just the one, as far as June can tell, nursed slowly through the afternoon and evening. She's checked the recycling bins. Her mom is averaging one a day, no more than two.

Desperate to do anything, say anything that will rouse her parents from this dull, zombielike state, June offers, knowing it's premature, "Jim has a lead. Into the, um, explosion. Someone—might be held accountable."

To say that her parents brightened would be inaccurate, but their eyes focus on her, hopeful and curious. They want their daughter's death to have meaning. There is no meaning in an accident. But if

Jim is right, Cath's death was still a kind of an accident, the consequence of being in the wrong place at the wrong time. She won't explain that to them just yet.

"That woman?" her mother asks.

"She's—connected." There will be time enough, assuming Jim is right, to tell them the full story. "But if his information is correct, it would have been someone else who actually did it."

Since that woman—June, like her mother, prefers not to use her name—confided in Jim, he has been almost distressingly excited, talking about how much it will mean for his career if he can link Cath's death to similar arson cases in Baltimore. It's unseemly, that's the word, how Jim is more focused on his future than on justice for Cath. June blames that woman. She does something to men. She took Cath's boyfriend from her. She bewitched Mr. C into giving her preferential treatment over Cath, which makes no sense. Good Lord, Mr. C has known June and Cath since they were kids and he had the soft serve ice cream place on Main Street. And now that woman has Jim convinced that she can help him solve the mystery of Cath's death. It's not sexual, not exactly. She's a pot simmering, full of promises—

Pot. June realizes she has left the electric burner on under the soup and she goes over, turns it off. She pours the uneaten portion into Tupperware, puts it in the fridge, notices all the Tupperware from her last couple of visits. The crisper drawer is full of rotting vegetables and the milk has gone bad. Dutiful daughter that she is, she begins throwing out what can't be saved, rinsing the Tupperware, preparing the dishwasher to run. She boils water for a Nescafé for her drive home, then rummages in the cupboard for sugar. All she can find is the old china sugar bowl from the set that Cath destroyed, filled with sugar cubes. Can sugar go bad? She figures as long as there are no ants crawling in the bowl, it's okay.

As she's bolting her coffee over the kitchen sink, she sees what appears to be a flash of orange and black in the backyard sycamore. An oriole is a rare sight in these parts, especially this time of year, and it's probably just a red-winged blackbird, its coloring distorted by the dusk.

Still, there's no harm in saying, "Mom, I think I just saw a Baltimore oriole."

Her mother doesn't even bother to come to the window.

"Well, it's gone now," June says with staunch cheer. "But I swear I saw one." She will give her mother binoculars for Christmas, she decides, or introduce her to a new hobby. Or they could find something to collect together, maybe those cute little Beanie Babies.

June leaves her parents in the den, watching *Murder, She Wrote*. She worries a little about them watching crime shows, but it was always their favorite program. Maybe it's a good sign that they still want to visit Cabot Cove and follow J. B. Fletcher on her various trips. Murder in J. B. Fletcher's world is almost gentle, bloodless. And there's no follow-up, no future visits from J. B. Fletcher in which the bereaved are staring into space, indifferent to food, conversation, or even a possible Baltimore oriole sighting.

31

Adam is pulling roasted bones from the oven when it first occurs to him to wonder if Polly could be cheating on him. How has he gotten here, from chopping carrots and celery, to questioning her fidelity? He takes a second, traces his chain of thought back to its source: he is making stock and that's one letter off from *taking* stock. Taking stock is taking inventory. At least, he assumes that's where that usage started. But most people now use it as a term for checking in on their own lives. *Where am I? What do I have? What do I lack?*

Adam is in a job with no future or money, in love with a woman he can't trust. At a critical moment, he lied to protect her. But maybe she didn't need his protection. The fire was ruled an accident, as was Cath's death. Polly has done nothing in recent weeks to suggest she's not worthy of his trust.

Although there was the day she borrowed his truck and put two hundred miles on it when it should have been more like a hundred. She later said that she went to Dover to get a Delaware driver's license. Turns out whoever told her that she could use her birth certificate was wrong, because she needed proof of residence, too.

Six nights ago, she borrowed his truck again. A Tuesday, they both had the evening off, and she suddenly announced she was going to go shopping at the outlet malls on Route 50, almost an hour away. She came home empty-handed.

"Nothing looked right," she said. "I hate this year's styles."

Then, this morning, she went to Winterthur, some old estate near Wilmington. She showed him the flyer over the weekend, saying, "The bus leaves from the mall at Dover at nine sharp, comes back at six."

"Doesn't a trip like that make more sense in the summer, when the gardens are in full bloom?"

"I want to see the paintings," she said. "I like art."

News to him.

But this morning he drove her to the parking lot at the mall, near the entrance to the Bon Ton, and watched her get on the bus. He thought about staying until the bus headed out, but how paranoid can a guy be? She was sitting in a window seat near the front, wearing a yellow dress with a jacket, a thrift store find. She's right, old clothes, pieces from the 1950s, suit her better than new ones. She looked excited but was trying to rein it in, act cool. Excited to go to some old house.

Now, back in the kitchen at the High-Ho, he reminds himself that the smallest things are new to her. You could argue she's been a prisoner since she was seventeen, half her life. Married to an abusive fuck. Jail. Rebounding into another unhappy marriage, probably because she was broke. No wonder she seems content in Belleville. Getting up, going to a job she doesn't mind. Pulling drafts for Max and Ernest. Serving his food, which she never ceases to praise.

He remembers the grilled cheese he made for her, back when he was wooing her. Was he wooing her then or just trying to do his job? He can no longer remember how the job faded away, when he first started loving her. Maybe he should add that sandwich to the menu. Not with tomatoes, they're out of season, but bacon and cheese never go out of style. He needs better bread—whole grain, high quality. Better bread means a better baker. Not on-site, but as a supplier. The one place in town—it can produce the quantities he needs, but it's mediocre. Fine for desserts and cakes, but its breads and rolls are clearly an afterthought. What this restaurant really needs is biscuits, good ones, served piping hot. Everybody loves biscuits, and, although no baker, Adam can make those with ease.

Except—he doesn't want to be here, on a highway in Delaware, thinking about biscuits. He feels his world shrinking, rescaling itself to fit this town, this life. Just because she's happy here doesn't mean she couldn't be happier still in a larger, grander life. He wants to take her to Botswana, show her a leopard lolling in a tree. Feed her real mole in Puebla, or fish tacos at a place he knows in Santa Barbara.

They're making love with less frequency. She's started to stay up late, reading, not coming to bed, waiting him out. And he's too proud to ask. If she doesn't want to be with him, okay then. But she was so cute this morning, in her yellow dress, sitting on the bus, another lady going to Winterthur. He glances at the clock. He has to drive back up to Dover to pick her up at six.

_____

When he pulls into the parking lot, he's fifteen minutes ahead of the bus's scheduled arrival. To his amazement, she's there, sitting on a bench outside the mall.

"I told you five," she says, a little peeved, a tone she almost never takes with him. "I've been sitting here for an hour."

"No," he says, "I'm sure it was six. Winterthur is at least an hour away."

"No harm, no foul. I was just worried about you. That feeling, when someone isn't where you expect them to be—anyway, it's a pretty night. And I loved Winterthur. I met the nicest lady on the bus, who lives up here. She asked me if I wanted to be in her book club. I told her I didn't have a car. But maybe I should get one, used. We'll see."

Just like that, the fight over his lateness is forgotten. Polly doesn't go in for sulks. He made a mistake—although he's absolutely sure she said to pick her up at six—and she let it go, right away. She doesn't pout, or try the silent treatment. Of course, it would be hard to notice if Polly gave you the silent treatment. She's not one to chatter. In the early days, he found that restful, but now it unnerves him. There was an Elvis Costello song a few years back, about his grandmother who had Alzheimer's. *What goes on in that something, something head of yours*—Adam can remember the meter, but not the words—*what goes on, something, something in the dark?* Butter literally might not melt in Polly's mouth. She's that cool, that quick thinking.

That cool, that quick thinking.

Tonight, she's unusually lively. Funny, he never noticed her longing for female company or museum trips, but the Winterthur visit seems to have jazzed her up. She doesn't want to be with a book tonight, that's for sure. And she laughs while they're making love—not in a mean way, simply flushed and happy. After, she starts to talk again about opening a bed-and-breakfast, maybe in one of the old Victorian houses near downtown. He flashes on her in the window of the bus, how she looked like a kid on the first day of school, tight with nerves, trying to conceal them. It is touching how little she wants.

But does he love her enough to stay here, restless as he's feeling? How can anyone want to stay in Belleville, where the best scenic view is the sun setting over the cornfields? It's small enough to be boring, big enough to be charmless. *No, my Handsome Polly-O, I do not want to run a B and B here.*

That night, as she sleeps, he goes through her purse. He finds nothing. *How do you go to a place like Winterthur and not have a brochure, a ticket, a receipt for a cup of coffee?* Her purse has an old-fashioned wallet—another thrift store find—a lipstick, a hairbrush, two pens, and a tiny notebook. He opens this, sees a list of numbers. Dates? Accounts? Dates, he thinks, from the 1980s. She has jotted down a series of dates that, best he can tell, correspond to the final months of her marriage.

Where did you go, my Handsome Polly-O?

32

Pauline Ditmars walks through Irving Lowenstein's front door the Tuesday after Yom Kippur, bold as brass. She's wearing a dress the color of marigolds and a lightweight, nubby wool coat, her hair piled on top of her head, like she thinks she's Audrey Hepburn. She even has gloves.

"So," he says, "the mountain came to Mohammed."

"I think we both know you're the mountain here. And I'm no Mohammed. I'm not even sure I know who Mohammed was."

Noting Susie's interest in the visitor, Irving takes Pauline into the back. By any objective standard, she is more attractive than she was when Ditmars was alive. Thinner, less defeated looking. But he preferred her as she used to be, and it's not just because of what he knows now about her proclivities. Still, he has to admit that yellow, the color used for warnings and caution, suits her.

"Why are you here?" No reason not to be blunt. He has nothing to hide. Adam Bosk, on the other hand, has probably concealed his connection to Irving. That's why he was so happy to be fired as of

Labor Day. He tried to make it like he was quitting, but all he did was save Irving the trouble of saying those words.

"I'm here to make amends. I'm in a twelve-step program now and that's one of the steps."

Irving assumes most Gentile women drink, but he doesn't remember that being Pauline's problem. Lord knows her husband was the worst—drink, cocaine, pills, whatever. Whereas Irving drinks only a little sliwowitz, maybe three times a year.

"You going to give me some money? Because you owe me. Even your husband, horrible as he was, knew to kick back something when he used someone."

He sees a flash of anger, something the old Pauline never allowed herself to show. Interesting reaction, for a woman trying to make amends.

"I didn't take that money from you. I took it from an insurance company. And it was to care for my daughter. But if I asked Ditmars to sit for a medical exam—you know he wouldn't have done it. Not because he suspected anything, but because anything I asked for, he said no. It was only a matter of time before he killed me and then what would have happened to Joy? He would have put her in some horrible, cheap institution."

"She ended up in an institution, anyway."

"In a good one. Paid for with that money. That's how I justified it. As I said, I didn't see how I was hurting another person."

"I was investigated by the state insurance board, which wasn't exactly good for my business. And your husband got *hurt,* didn't he? I mean, I think it must hurt to have someone drive a knife through your heart. It's not exactly a mercy killing."

There it is again, a flash of anger, at odds with her penitence.

"You know better than anyone what he was capable of. How many people do you figure he killed while he was on your payroll?"

Irving holds up his hands as if to stop a car coming toward him in a crosswalk. "Hey, hey. I don't know any such thing. I don't know where you get your ideas. For one, he wasn't on my payroll. He worked for someone else."

Glancing down, he notices a stain on his shirt, coffee from his breakfast. Birdy never would have allowed him to go out of the house like this. It bothers Irving that he's been walking around with a stain, even if the only people he's seen all morning are Susie and Pauline. She looks good, Pauline. Healthy, rested. All buffed up with love. Adam Bosk is a schmuck, but it's hard to blame him.

"He told me everything, Irving. To scare me, to keep me in line. You arranged the policies. As a broker, you could spread them among several companies, disguising the pattern. And it wasn't always property, right? Sometimes the guy—what was his name, Ford? He took out life insurance policies. On his own people. Then bought them back at a fraction of face value. He got the idea from you, right?"

"Maybe Ditmars did beat you. I think you got brain damage."

"No, I'm smarter than ever. Wised up. Now I see I should have made a deal with you, offered to give you a percentage instead of rewarding you with that sad little screw in my kitchen."

It's strange, how much that hurts. He's known for a long time that she used him, but he still thought it might have been pleasant for her. Ditmars was no prize. Irving, in his youth—well, not his youth, but he was ten years younger then, well preserved, meticulous in his hygiene—he had prided himself on being a very thoughtful lover. Birdy never had any complaints. She was an animal, this one. The kind that devours her male partner immediately after rutting.

"Again, you have a strange way of making amends."

She lowers her gaze, seemingly contrite. "I'm sorry. It's harder than it might sound, saying you were wrong, taking responsibility. Putting—other things aside, I should have offered you a cut. That's how it worked. I knew that." A pause. "I almost feel as if I need to make amends for Ditmars. He cut you out, sometimes."

"How so?" he asks, adding quickly, "Not that there was anything to be cut out of. But—he talked behind my back?"

"It was one of the last fires he set. He said that you and the other guy—what was his name?"

"I don't know what you're talking about."

"He bragged how they cut you out. They cut you out a lot, went to other insurance brokers. That guy, the drug dealer, he saw that he could buy properties cheap, take out policies, then let Ditmars burn them down. Did you know that? Anyway, the last fire, the one that Ditmars modeled after a real fire he had investigated—open the gas jets, light a candle—was just meant to damage the house as I understand it. He didn't know about the girl sleeping upstairs, with her baby. He was haunted by that. He tried to tell himself that they died from smoke inhalation, but the autopsy couldn't rule out that they had been killed by all that flying debris. That was on Eutaw, I think?"

"Paca," Irving says. Hard to forget Paca. He *wished* they had cut him out of that one. Pauline killed Ditmars two months later. If only she had done it sooner, Paca never would have happened.

"Right, Paca. Winter 1986. A fifteen-year-old girl and her baby blown sky-high. They weren't supposed to be there. It was supposed to be a quick-and-dirty job, a complete loss on the house so—what was his name?"

Irving doesn't provide it.

"Whatever happened to him, that guy?"

"Still don't know what you're talking about—and neither do you, Pauline. So be careful. That's my friendly advice. Don't go around talking about these things. Because some people might wonder how deep you were in it."

"So," Pauline says, rising to her feet. "I'm sorry I deceived you. We okay now?"

"I'm not sure. You hurt my business there for a while. That agent never worked with me again."

"But you're doing okay?" She glances around at his less-than-impressive surroundings and he feels an instinct, quite foreign to him, to justify himself.

"I'm fine," he says. "A rich man by anyone's measure. What about you?"

"Poor as a church mouse, whatever that means. Working as a waitress. It's hard, starting over."

"That why you got a drinking problem?"

"Who says I have a drinking problem?"

"You said you were in a twelve-step program."

"But I didn't say it was for *drinking*. And, you know, we're supposed to be anonymous. In fact, I can't figure that part out. How can I be anonymous and make amends to those I've wronged?"

"Where you living these days?" As if he didn't know.

She smiles, doesn't answer. She was always shrewd, this one.

He walks up front with her, stops to confer with Susie while he watches Pauline head out into the parking lot. Plenty of spaces in front, but she turns to the right and is quickly out of sight. Did Adam drive her here? What was her real agenda? The one thing Irving is sure of is that it's not a twelve-step program, because they don't have those for lying nafkehs.

33

Halloween falls on a Tuesday this year, which means a long buildup to the holiday, starting with a bonfire on Friday night. Bonfires are a big deal in Belleville. Polly finds this charming, but Adam says it's just proof what a hick town it is. The site is still smoldering when they drive by late that night, after work. They get out and inspect the remains, enjoying the heat in the cool October air.

Polly, holding her hands toward the embers, tells him: "There was a movie I saw once—I think it was set in Paris. A man kills a woman. It's not exactly an accident, but it's also not exactly his fault. He's going mad. Anyway, it's the night of a big bonfire, in which people bring anything they want and throw it on the pile. He wraps up the body in a carpet and throws it on the fire, then runs away. But he still gets caught. Something to do with an earring. I think."

Adam doesn't seem particularly interested, but she finds she can't stop herself.

"It was on *Picture for a Sunday Afternoon*. Oh, I forgot—you didn't grow up in Baltimore. That was a local thing. *Picture for a Sunday Afternoon*. Which sounds kind of churchy and nice, but it was amazing the movies they showed sometimes. Horror movies. *The Leech Woman* was a big favorite of mine. She stayed youthful forever by killing men and drinking their blood, but then she killed a woman and the spell reversed itself. They also showed women-in-prison movies." She laughs. "Go figure, those weren't exactly factual."

Polly waits to see if Adam will offer a corresponding story about his childhood. But he doesn't. It's rare for either of them to talk about the past. It's not something they agreed on, merely a pattern that emerged. Once all the secrets—well, *most* of the secrets—were out in the open, there was no reason to talk about the past. What does she know about Adam? He went to college in Ohio, then attended some famous cooking school in New York, although he didn't graduate. Went from there to working on a yacht, first as a deckhand, ended up as the chef. He grew up in the Bay Area. His parents are dead. He liked them a lot, especially his mother.

What does he know about her? Not as much as he thinks he does. Suddenly, it is important to her to let him know that she had a nice childhood, too, warm and safe as his. Her parents were good people, much too nice to prepare their daughter for a world of people like Ditmars and Irving and that guy they worked with.

"On Sunday afternoons, my mom ironed in front of the television in her bedroom. It smelled so good. You know that smell—scorchy and warm. She had a bottle that she filled with water, for the things that needed to be ironed on the steam setting. She put some kind of scent in it. I don't think it was made to be a sprinkle bottle for ironing—there was a tiny picture of a woman on it, but it was starting to flake off. If I could have one thing of my mom's, it would be that bottle. I don't know what happened to it when she moved to Florida."

Better not to mention that Polly was in prison at the time, that her mother died in Florida of a broken heart.

All Adam says is, "I don't think I've ever seen you iron."

"If I had her sprinkle bottle, I think I would. I wish I had her sprinkle bottle and this one bracelet she had, with these flat glass beads with pieces of peacock feathers set inside. My mother loved Halloween. She liked scary movies, too. She would let me watch anything. But then—it's not like anything really scary came on TV back then. I remember *House of Wax*. And *She*—remember *She*?"

"Who?"

"The movie *She*. There's a beautiful woman who's hundreds of years old. She invites a man to bathe in this fire that makes you immortal. But it turns out that if you go into the fire twice, the spell reverses and you age to your real age. She turns into a skeleton, dies, reaching for him. So he's immortal now, but he's betrayed everyone and she's gone. He's going to live forever, but alone."

Adam puts an arm around her, hugs her closer. "I think Halloween is making you morbid. Let's go home."

On Tuesday night, actual Halloween, Polly dresses all in black, in a 1950s cocktail dress unearthed at the church rummage sale a few weeks ago. She has bags and bags of candy—miniature Hershey bars, Reese's cups, small boxes of Dots, because there's always some weird kid who doesn't like chocolate. But the trick-or-treaters don't seem to realize that someone lives in the garage apartment, and they skip her door.

She hopes that's the reason the kids skip her door.

"Adam," she says, the wooden bowl of candy in her lap, "do you think people gossip about us? About me?"

"What do you mean?"

"About my life, what I did before I moved here." A beat. "How Cath died."

"If they do, there's nothing you can do about it, so it's best not to think about it."

"Do you ever think about it?"

"What?"

In her black dress, black gloves, and retro heels, she looks like Joan Crawford or Bette Davis. She feels like them, too. Tough, yet brittle. That's the thing about being really hard. When you do break, you shatter.

"Not even ten years ago, I fed my husband one of his favorite dinners. Turkey and scalloped potatoes, lots of beer. A pie. He didn't like the pie because I didn't have any ice cream, only whipped cream. Fresh whipped cream, whipped by hand. I knew the turkey would make him sleepy, but I couldn't trust it to do the entire job. So I crushed up some sleeping pills, added them to the cheese sauce on the potatoes, to make sure he would be drowsy. Then, when he was asleep, lying on his back, I stood next to the bed—"

"I know all this," Adam says. He's not meeting her eyes. "You told me. Maybe not in such detail—"

"I stabbed him through his heart, Adam. Through his heart. I studied for weeks, making sure I knew where to aim. I had one chance. One chance to save myself and my kid. He was going to kill me. When he did, I knew there was no one who would care for Joy."

"What's got into you tonight?"

"I was looking forward to the kids coming to the door. We didn't get many trick-or-treaters on Kentucky, back in the day." She waits to see if he will ask her about this. He doesn't. "Do you think people think I killed Cath?"

"It was ruled an accident."

His eyes are fixed on the television. He bought it three weeks ago. She hates it. First she loses her beautiful apartment and now this *thing* has invaded. Adam and Eve didn't need to be forced out of Eden, Polly thinks. All God had to do was send down a twenty-seven-inch color television and a cable box. Adam's using the remote to toggle back and forth between a hockey game and a CNN report that a passerby has been subpoenaed to testify about finding Vincent Foster's body.

She drops two words from her question. "Do you think I killed Cath?"

Someone shoots a goal and he gives a short guffaw of approval. Hockey. He watches hockey. She was never one of those people who have lists, questionnaires, to hand out at the beginning of a relationship. She never had the luxury of looking for a relationship, someone who would please her. If she had, she might have remembered to ask: *How many hours a week do you watch sports? Do you care so much that you mope around when your favorite team loses?* Ditmars did that, of course. Gregg didn't really feel passionate about any team, which seemed not very masculine to Polly. Adam, at least, cares, but doesn't take it personally when his team is defeated.

She stands up, begins to shimmy out of her clothes, not trying to divert him. Quite the opposite. This isn't a striptease, it's a disappearing act. Good-bye, Joan Crawford, hello, Polly. She drifts toward their bedroom, pale and cold as a ghost.

Within five minutes, the set clicks off and he is in bed with her. They both play it savage tonight. She pulls his hair, bites him hard. And when he's done and she's still on top of him, she braces herself with her arms on either side of his ears so he couldn't look away if he wanted to.

"Do you think I killed Cath?"

He doesn't answer right away, which she likes. A lie would come quickly. He should have to think about this. He has avoided thinking about it, all these weeks. That morning, when they came onto the accident scene, when he agreed she had reached his place by midnight, he might have been confused, nothing more. It could have been an honest mistake. But if he did lie, it was for love of her. And that kind of love can turn.

"I've wondered," he admits.

"Because of my past."

"Because she was in your apartment and there was a freak accident. It's quite the coincidence."

"Coincidences happen all the time."

"That's true." His tone is agreeable, but that doesn't mean he's agreeing.

She lets it go. Soon enough, he'll see how wrong he was.

34

Bob Riley is eating a turkey sub, extra hots, and thinking about his next week's picks when he notices a new customer, a stranger, walking into Video Americain. Not that Bob knows every VA customer, but most of the customers know *him,* greet him by name—or, rather, the name he uses on his shelf talkers, Baba O'Riley.

Bob's—Baba's—staff picks have earned him a following, mainly with guys. The idea of cults growing up around a staffer's recommendations has gone so mainstream that *Seinfeld* even did an episode about it, but Bob likes to think his picks have an oblique wit that rewards the people who really get him. He's not obscure or arty, but his choices are clever, no obvious or literal connections, similar to the best mix tapes. This week, for example, he's featuring *Songwriter* and *Payday.* Everybody—well, the kind of everybody who rents from Video Americain—knows *Payday* and most of them know Alan Rudolph, although he never lived up to the promise of his early stuff. And even people who love *Choose Me* and *Trouble in Mind* seem to have missed *Songwriter.* Part of it, Bob thinks, is the entrenched snobbery about country music, which shows how ignorant people in the Northeast can be. They think country music is what's on the radio right now—Alan Jackson and Tracy Lawrence and Reba McEntire. They've never listened to Johnny Cash, much less bluegrass. Alison Krauss is fine, but what about Marty Stuart? People mock him for the hair and the sequins, but he's only the best mandolin player ever; he was even in Cash's band for a while.

Johnny Cash. Bob wishes Cash would act more. Have the old *Columbo* episodes even been released on VHS? He could add the season with "Swan Song," featuring Cash as one of the best *Columbo* villains ever. Because you can tell Columbo kind of feels for the guy, gets that he got a raw deal. If he had killed just the harridan of a wife in the plane crash instead of taking out the wife *and* the girl, the Cash character would have been almost heroic. Bob goes over to the television section, which is not his specialty, but no luck. There are not a lot of old television shows on VHS. People don't want to rent things they once saw for free.

The new customer is browsing the mystery section, clearly trying to figure out the store's classification system, which is deliberately offbeat. Bob scored a job here two years ago, which gives a guy some bragging rights in Newark. The owner won't hire just anyone. There's a hundred-question test. And film knowledge isn't enough. You have to have people skills, too. A lot of would-be hires ace the test and fail the customer relations part of the interview. They can tell you every film that Bernard Herrmann scored, but they can't make eye contact with a human being.

"I'm looking for a movie," the guy finally admits to Bob. He's probably the kind of man who doesn't like to ask for directions unless he's desperate.

Bob gestures at the walls with his sandwich. "I think we got you covered."

The man smiles. He's got a Sergio Leone man-with-no-name vibe; you can almost hear the Morricone music coming up. Is he the good or the bad? He's definitely not ugly. Bob's always a little confused, as most men are, about what women find attractive, but he figures this guy checks all the boxes. Tall with broad shoulders, strong jaw, pale blue eyes, olive skin, sort of James Caan crossed with Paul Newman. Bob is medium height and lanky with sandy hair, not a hunchback, but not swoonworthy on first sight.

"I'm looking for a movie that my"—long pause, as if he's lost his train of thought—"that my girlfriend described to me. Only she doesn't know the title or the stars."

Bob doesn't sigh, not even inwardly. On a slow afternoon, this kind of challenge is what he loves. "Does she remember when she saw it in the theater? A year would help narrow it down plenty."

"She saw it on television, when she was growing up in Baltimore, so I'm guessing it's older. Fifties, no later than sixties."

"Black and white?"

"I didn't ask, but my hunch is that her family had a black-and-white set, so she wouldn't know." The guy has the self-awareness to be chagrined. "She did remember one scene in vivid detail."

"Have at me," Bob says. "Graduated UT-Austin six years ago with a film degree. Still unclear how I ended up in the land of the Blue Hen."

"The Blue Hen?"

"That's the mascot for University of Delaware. I've gone from Hook 'em Horns"—he does the fingers—"to who gives a cluck?"

The guy's smile is polite but he's clearly not much on small talk. "Anyway, all she remembers is that it's in Paris and there's a bonfire. A man has killed a woman, but maybe it's by accident? Or she deserves it? And it happens that there's a big bonfire that night, so he rolls her body up in a carpet and goes out, throws the body in the bonfire."

"Does he get away with it?"

"What?"

"In the movie? Does his plan work?"

"I don't remember. I just thought—well, I thought it would make an impression, if I found this movie she was talking about." This smile feels more genuine. "At least it would prove that I'm listening to her, right?"

Bob nods, as if he has as much experience with women as this older man. He hasn't had a girlfriend for eighteen months. He's dated here and there, but his job is a catch-22 when it comes to a social life: Women want to date Baba O'Riley at Video Americain, but if he wants weekends off, he can't be Baba O'Riley at Video Americain. He's going to be Bob Riley again.

This guy could probably get women if he worked the midnight shift at the sanitation department.

"Did you say Paris?"

"Yeah."

"Could the guy be a musician?"

He shrugs.

"Paris. A bonfire." Something is flicking Bob's imagination, he can almost hear the movie's soundtrack in his ear. *Bernard Herrmann.* He's hearing Bernard Herrmann, but not this film, yet he's also seeing an actress who is integral to a pretty famous film with a Herrmann score. "Are you sure it's Paris?"

"I'm not sure of *anything.*"

Bob pages through some of the video guides they keep behind the counter. His mind is racing along, hearing music again, but this time he has finally identified it—the score of *My Darling Clemen-*

tine. Everything clicks into place, cylinders sliding into a tumbler. *My Darling Clementine. Chihuahua.* Linda Darnell. Linda Darnell, with her pout and her put-upon act.

"*Hangover Square,*" he says, snapping his fingers, as pleased with himself as if he were a doctor solving a medical mystery. "Not Paris. London. It's whatever that day is in England when they celebrate that guy not blowing things up."

"Guy Fawkes Day," the customer says. "So do you have it?"

"I'm not even sure it's out on video. The director didn't have much of a career, I don't think. But if you really want it, I can look into it."

"I live downstate, in Belleville, almost an hour's drive. If I opened an account—could I overnight the movies back to you? There's nothing near us like this, of course. But my"—that pause again—"girlfriend, she likes old movies. Obscure ones."

"Clearly. But as for mailing the movies back, all I can give you is a very flabby maybe. I'd have to ask the owner. We take a credit card for all accounts, you lose a movie, we charge your card, but I've never had anyone ask if they could mail it back. I know this much—if it got lost in the mail, that would be your problem."

"As you said, you don't even have it in stock. But if you find it, yeah, I'd like to know." He takes out his Visa card, fills out the paperwork. Bob can't help noticing he lists his home address as Baltimore, which has its own Video Americain.

As he's finishing up, he asks: "What about *She*?"

"Who?"

"*She*. The movie. Do you have that?"

"Oh, Christopher Lee, Peter Cushing, Ursula Andress. That might be in."

He finds it in general horror, which strikes him as sloppy. They should have a Christopher Lee shelf.

"Another kind of bonfire movie," he says. "Your girlfriend have a thing for fires?"

The guy's smile flickers, slow, like neon blinking before it reaches full tilt. "You know, I should probably wait to check this out until I find out what it's going to cost me to mail these back overnight. I work almost every day."

"Who doesn't?" Bob asks agreeably.

"Is there, like, a vintage store nearby? With household items?"

"Household items?"

"I'm looking for an old sprinkler bottle, the kind women used to use to wet down clothes when they ironed. My girlfriend talks about how much she wishes she had one."

"She likes to iron *and* watch old movies. Dude, you have hit the jackpot. Does she have a sister?"

"I have no idea."

35

Polly pulls two drafts for Max and Ernest. The High-Ho is quiet tonight. It's quiet almost every night now. The youngish couples in town might come in on Fridays and Saturdays, but weeknights are slow. Adam has been making old-fashioned comfort food—brisket and chicken pot pies and what locals call Maryland stew—but it is, as he keeps pointing out, a small town. That's why they need to make the restaurant a destination unto itself. She has been reading up on a restaurant-hotel in Virginia, the Inn at Little Washington. It opened in a garage in 1978 and, in less than ten years, became the first restaurant to earn five diamonds from AAA. They could do that here if they had some cash. You don't have to have water views to have a successful inn if the restaurant is good enough.

Meanwhile, Mr. C seems to be getting whiter and whiter with each passing day. Adam is careful with the budget, and the kitchen doesn't cost that much more to run than it did when it was all hamburgers and chili and frozen french fries. But the biggest line item is Adam. Mr. C doesn't want to go back to cooking, and if he does, it won't be like Adam's cooking. Whatever reputation the High-Ho has earned over the past few months will be lost. Maybe the townies won't complain and, come summer, the tourists won't know it ever took a downturn. But Polly can almost see the wheels turning behind Mr. C's ghostly white face: Can he get Adam back if he turns him loose? What happens to Polly if Adam leaves?

Yes, what happens to Polly? She stayed here for Adam, gave up Reno and her quickie divorce. Will he stay here for her?

Max and Ernest like the bar in its near-deserted state. They were unhappy when the restaurant section was filled with noisy diners, out of towners who said things like *Does the television have to be on?* And *Is the corn Silver Queen?* They mocked the specialty drinks the nonlocals ordered, things that Polly had never heard of, like a cocktail made with vodka, Cointreau, cranberry juice, and lime. Polly never minded learning how to make a new drink, but Max and Ernest resented these requests. It was *their* bar, Polly was *their* bartender. Now they have the bar and Polly back, all to themselves. Hip hip hooray.

And they still don't tip her well. They seem to think their company is compensation enough. It's not, especially given their obsession with politics, a topic that bores Polly silly. The last few days, all they want to talk about is Delaware's attempt to encroach on the New Hampshire primary in February. The plan has backfired, and politicians are now falling in line with New Hampshire's demand that candidates skip the Delaware primary or rue the day. Dole, the Republican front-runner, has pulled out of Delaware. Max and Ernest are outraged on behalf of Delaware, which they note is officially the *first* state, the first to ratify the U.S. Constitution. Why shouldn't they have the first primary?

"Why is everyone kowtowing to the Granite State?" Ernest says. "What's so great about New Hampshire?"

"I like its state motto," Polly says. "Live Free or Die."

They pay her no heed. She's not supposed to insert herself into their *serious* discussions, only indulge their jokes. She knows that. But she feels ornery tonight.

"If you ask me, small states are like small men. Big chips on their shoulders. Something to prove. Also—wasn't New Hampshire's claim to fame that every president first won his party's primary there?"

"Not Bill Clinton," Max says.

Oh, right. Hillary Clinton on *60 Minutes,* eating humble pie because she dared to say she wouldn't bake cookies and stand by her man. Polly had watched that with Gregg, whose only comment was: "I wouldn't fuck her."

"Slick Willie," Ernest mutters darkly. "I wonder if we'll be stuck with him for another four years."

"Clinton," Max says. "A sweet talker. How I hate a sweet talker."

"They're all alike," Polly says. They assume she means politicians, so they nod.

––––––––––

Mr. C comes in just after the kitchen closes, most unusual. Sure enough, he summons Adam and Polly to the office.

"I'm bleeding money here," he says. "I never kept a cook past Labor Day before, I always did the cooking myself through the cold months. We just don't do enough business. Adam, it's not personal—"

"I know it's not," Adam says.

He looks almost relieved, Polly thinks. *He* wants *to go.*

"What about me?" she asks. The question could be for either man. Mr. C is the one who answers.

"I still need you, but I'll understand if you want to leave. I know how thin the tips have been."

"Yes," she said. "The tips are getting thin."

She and Adam don't say a word on the drive home. Adam and Eve, on a raft, but where is the raft taking them? What happens when only Adam gets kicked out of Eden, but Eve gets to stay despite being the one that everyone has pegged a sinner?

In the weeks since Cath died, Polly has straightened out her name issues, opened accounts. On paper, she is still technically Pauline Hansen. It's easier that way for now. When the divorce comes through, she'll go to Social Security, reclaim her maiden name. And it's simple enough to tell people that Polly is a nickname for Pauline. Simple, because it has the virtue of being true. She has a checking account with her new address on Lilac Way. She has put down roots, shallow as they are.

And now they're being ripped up.

"What are you going to do?" she asks Adam. *You*, not us. She wonders if he notices. But Adam notices everything. Not much gets by him. Not much gets by her, either.

"I'm not going to find anything else here," he says.

"Not as a cook. But aren't there other things you can do? What were you doing when we met?"

"Oh, I had just finished sailing a boat up from Florida to Rehoboth and was driving back to Maryland."

"I can't remember—how did you end up in Belleville?"

"Car trouble. My truck threw a rod. Look, what about Annapolis?" he asks.

"What about it?"

"There's always work for—someone like me. I can find some kind of job to carry us through the winter. You can, too. The legisla-

223

ture will be in session, the local restaurants will be slammed. We'll be together. Isn't that what matters?"

"Is it?"

"It is to me."

"I like it here." Her voice is petulant and she knows it, hates herself for it. She doesn't do petulant. Petulant is for weak women, dependent women. She doesn't need him, even if he's been helping her carry the rent on this place.

She wants him, though. Adam is the first man, the first thing she has ever chosen for her own pleasure and delight. That's hard to give up.

"I'll look," Adam says. "But without a paycheck for me and your tips as small as they are—"

Nothing left to do but try to save the evening with a joke. "Hey, there's nothing wrong with my *tips*."

He laughs. Adam is probably a good man, all things considered. She wants to make a life with him. But she had been hoping to make a life here, too. Which will she choose? Is the choice even hers?

And maybe Belleville isn't the answer. Maybe she likes it because it felt like a kind of cockeyed destiny. She reminds herself that the plan, back in June, was to find a job, build up a nice little nest egg, then head to Reno. But after Cath died, she feared that leaving would make Adam even more suspicious of her. She should be almost divorced now, her prize within reach. She stayed in Belleville for Adam. Why won't he do the same for her?

"I love you," she says to Adam.

"I love you, too."

"That should be enough."

Should, should, should.

The next day, he sits down with the *PennySaver* and the *News-Journal*. "I could commute," he says. "If that's what it takes. Work in Baltimore during the week, be here on weekends."

"But then you'll have the cost of another place."

"Don't worry. I'll still help with the rent here."

"I'm not worried."

She wonders if he is as exhausted by all the lying as she is.

36

When Adam crosses his own threshold for the first time in months, he finds himself thinking of a few lines from Kipling that his father taught him long ago.

> *Down to Gehenna or up to the Throne*
> *He travels the fastest who travels alone.*

Only "The Winners" is not really an homage to traveling solo, as Adam learned in college, but a case for selfishness. Kipling's "heretical ode" urges us to make use of others' labor, then leave them behind.

Is that what he's done? Or is he the one being left behind? He's baffled by Polly's refusal to come with him. It's not a bad place, this apartment, a one-bedroom in a high-rise with partial views of a deep park known as Stony Run. But it's sterile, charmless. The apartment, so long neglected, doesn't even seem to register his presence. It goes on without him, like the automated house in that Ray Bradbury story, postapocalypse.

And that's fine. He has never wanted to be rooted to any one place and this address is exactly that, an address, nothing more, a concession to a world that demands a place to send bills and the annual auto registration. The lease is month by month. The furniture is rented; even the plates and glassware are rentals. Things weigh you down.

Things and people.

There is no mail, not even junk. When it became clear that he was going to be stuck in Belleville for a while, Adam got a P.O. Box in Denton, had everything forwarded there. "Everything" was his utility bills, his credit card bill, his monthly bank statements, and the occasional missive from Irving, who was so cheap he preferred a stamp to a phone call. A postcard stamp at that, usually a bland souvenir card with terse questions and demands. "Anything?" "Call me." The last one arrived September fifth and had a bushel of blue crabs on the front. On the back, Irving had written in large block letters: CONTRACT TERMINATED. It was postmarked Sept. 3, the very day that Adam called Irving and told him he was quitting. But he let Irving have the last word, let him pretend that the postcard was sent before Adam called him.

Adam's answering machine is also empty because he checked it remotely once a week. In the beginning, there had been calls, inquiries about work. The past couple of weeks, it has been mostly wrong numbers. At least, he assumed that the hang-up calls were wrong numbers. Who else would keep calling a machine and hanging up?

Now he has to work the phone like some rookie telemarketer, checking his traps, trying to rebuild his business. Adam has always marketed himself as the king of surveillance, the guy who can get fast results where others would let the minutes pile up. He begins

227

dialing the various lawyers, insurance brokers, people who have used him from time to time, people who might know people who know people in need of a private detective. Not Irving, of course. Adam knows he burned that bridge by coming up empty after so many weeks on Irving's payroll. Doesn't worry him. Irving was a small-timer on his roster, usually used Adam to check out the occasional slip-and-fall case at his strip center.

Cold-calling is a pain, but it yields results. Adam's business thrives on misfortune and distrust, two things that know no season. He picks up a few small jobs—surveillance on a divorce case, some financial investigation for a prenup. The bride is willing to sign, but she thinks the groom is hiding assets, maybe in a dummy family foundation registered with the state. Isn't love grand? But, good, he'll start earning again. When he ended his relationship with Irving, things got thin, pretty fast, living off what Mr. C was paying. Adam had to dip into his savings the last few weeks, especially as he began to cover more of the bills for Polly. Adam never touches his savings. His parents, like him, cared nothing for possessions or money. But they believed that one should live within one's means. Savings were sacrosanct. They lived so carefully that there was a nice inheritance for him once both were gone. Out of respect for them, he keeps that money separate and uses it for his trips and adventures. It's a choice they would respect. His parents wouldn't want their only son to settle for Belleville, not even for love.

He sits at his dining room table, which has a view of the high-rise next door, which makes it cheaper than the apartments that have only the expansive southern exposures. People pay so much for views and then, within a few weeks, don't even notice them. Art is better than views, his mother always said, especially if you paint your own. She could and did, huge, vivid abstracts. He has two of her canvases, but he has never bothered to hang them. He's saving them for a day when he might put down roots.

What if his mom were alive? What would she think of Polly? His mother was a trusting, openhearted person who saw the good in almost everyone. The only person she never liked was Adam's wife. But she was right. Lainey—she always said it was short for Elaine, Adam always pointed out it was the same length, letter-wise and syllable-wise—wasn't for him. She couldn't indulge his wanderlust. What wife would? Could Polly?

This forced separation will give them a chance to see, he reasons. *Rationalizes.* Not much bullshit gets by him, not even his own. Maybe if you never marry a woman, she never becomes a wife. Polly says she never wants to marry again. Yet there she is with the weekly *PennySaver,* looking longingly at houses in Belleville. Could anyone dream smaller? The tiny scale of her desires—Adam, a house, a bed-and-breakfast—makes her achingly precious to him. He just needs to bring her up to his level, take her hand and lead her to a peak where she can see the world spread out at her feet, imagine something bigger. Even a partial view of a park called Stony Run would be a step up for Polly.

But where there's smoke, there's fire. He thinks of Polly's face when they stood next to the dying bonfire the Friday before Halloween. She was happy that night, and it wasn't the feverish glee of a firebug. Right? She just likes bonfires. And movies about fires. True, she also was married to an arson investigator, but she didn't like him. Everything can be explained.

He drinks a beer, watches the news. Polly is a quiet woman, but a solitary silence is different from one shared by another person. He misses her silence.

He drives to Annapolis the next day to see if there's any kind of nonprofit set up in the family name of the suspect groom. Unlikely, but it's a basic thing to check and he likes having a reason to go to Annapolis, a smallish town that doesn't feel like a small town. When he's finished checking the state office for nonprofit filings, he buys a sandwich and eats it at the foot of Main Street, looking out on the bay. Where is Polly this time of day, what is she doing? Probably reading the goddamn *PennySaver* or taking a walk. He liked how Polly would get up in the morning and go out, letting him sleep, then slipping back into bed before he awoke. Not many women would do that.

And not many women would kill someone and blow up their own apartment to cover it up.

He finds he can't finish his sandwich, so he feeds the leftovers to the gulls. Six months ago, when Irving came to him with this job, Adam thought it would be a few weeks of work, enough money to allow him to take off about now. Instead, he's rooting around in one soon-to-be-married couple's finances. And tomorrow, he'll be watching a woman whose husband believes her to be having an affair. *Quite a life you've made for yourself, Adam, my boy.*

He drives back, straight into the sunset. It's different from the sunset he remembers from Belleville, the slow flattening of an orange disk over the endless fields. It was so flat there. Flat in every sense. Dull, every day the same, only the rotating specials at the restaurant helping him distinguish between Wednesday ("spaghetti" night, although it was homemade fettuccine, rolled out and cut without even a basic pasta maker, then tossed in a deep, rich lamb ragu) and Friday (roast chicken). He's looking forward to watching *Monday Night Football,* drinking a beer, in his own home.

Only it's not home, he realizes, as he watches the Browns lose to the Steelers. It can never be home, even if he bought his own furniture, signed a longer lease, hung his mother's paintings.

Home is wherever Polly is. For better or worse.

37

Polly is depressed as the holidays approach, although she denies it, even to herself, embarrassed by the cliché of her feelings. Not that anyone notices her mood, or seems to care. And it's not as if she has great holiday memories unless she reaches all the way back to childhood. The orange Schwinn parked in front of the Christmas tree, its basket filled with Nancy Drew books. The tiny brass monkey in her Christmas stocking when she was eleven.

Ditmars freaking out over how dry the tree was and knocking it over, breaking half the ornaments. Ditmars throwing a plate at her head when the Thanksgiving turkey was overcooked and she made the mistake of not serving his mother's oyster dressing.

Her life is a series of holding patterns. With Adam, who drives over almost every weekend, but never talks about the future. With Gregg, who has not answered her open-ended inquiries about moving forward with the divorce. With Max and Ernest, her own private hell. She likes to tell Adam: "They have only two topics. One of them is the weather and the other one isn't."

She decides November feels dreary because she remembers

where she was a year ago, the giddy high of planning her escape. She had just hired Barry Forshaw to sue the hospital and while he was properly cautious about keeping expectations low, she knew they would do okay, even with a settlement. On Thanksgiving Day, Polly made the smallest turkey possible—it was only the four of them, Gregg, Savannah, Jani, and her—and didn't trouble herself too much, taking any shortcut that modern convenience could bestow, buying the sauerkraut instead of preparing it herself, a sacrilege in her mother's book. (Polly's mother was old Baltimore. Polly should make Adam sour beef one day, and cabbage rolls.) Thanksgiving a year ago, when it was time for the blessing, Polly-still-Pauline bent her head over a plate of white meat and ready-made cranberry sauce and bakery-bought Parker House rolls and gave thanks for what she had decided would be three million dollars, give or take. *Take,* it turned out, because Forshaw was getting 40 percent, plus whatever interest her money generated while it waited for her. She was not a big believer in signs or portents, but the number three had been swimming in her head for days and she believed it was more than superstition. Let other people play El Gordo, the big state lottery with a ten-million-dollar jackpot. She was playing her own game.

Four weeks later, the hospital, perhaps keen to close the fiscal books on 1994, had offered $3.3 million. Barry took $1.5—more than 40 percent, by the way, but he nickeled-and-dimed her for almost every paper clip along the way. That left her with $1.8 million. Still, not bad. Twelve years ago, her father's lungs, wrecked with mesothelioma, had earned him only $250,000 and he was too far gone to enjoy a penny of it. When her mother had died in Florida while Polly was in prison, she left what little she had to her nieces and nephews. Polly's aunt, who still lived in Dundalk, came to see

Polly in prison and said, "Well, what can you expect? You broke her heart."

Polly took her aunt off her visitors' list, which left exactly no one. She had no family. She had lost whatever family she had when she was convicted and the state, at her behest, took custody of Joy.

Polly knew the night Joy was born that something had gone wrong, that the doctor had dithered in failing to order a C-section. But Joy's condition wasn't immediately apparent and Polly decided she was just a nervous Nellie. For a few weeks, she was a normal new mother. Exhausted and terrified, but all first-time mothers are exhausted and terrified. There were even unexpected fringe benefits. Ditmars treated the mother of his child quite differently from the way he had treated his bride.

Until it turned out that the child was disabled.

The day they learned how severe Joy's cerebral palsy was, Ditmars went out drinking with his work buddies, leaving Polly home alone to weep and wonder at what she had done, what she hadn't done, saying good-bye to every small dream she had held for her child, even dreams she never realized she had. In the final weeks of her pregnancy, she had been in Marshalls and seen a pair of Mary Janes, a child's size 5, and even though she knew it would be years before her child could wear them—and, even though she didn't know her unborn child's gender, at Ditmars's insistence—she had to buy those shoes. They were $65 marked down to $7. How she had marveled at that original price, wondering what it would be like to be the kind of person who could spend $65 on shoes that a little girl might wear three, four times before growing out of them.

Five months later, the night of the diagnosis, she held those shoes to her face and wept. Maybe Joy would wear them one day, but she would never walk, not a single step. She would probably not speak, doctors said. Her body, as Polly understood it, would look the way Polly felt—twisted, stunted, useless.

When Ditmars came home and found Polly asleep at the kitchen table, that box of shoes nearby, he focused on the original price, even though the Marshalls price and the final reduction were visible. He began hitting her with the shoes, calling her a whore, saying it was her fault, that she hadn't taken proper care of herself, that she was probably sneaking coffee and beer and God knows what else during her pregnancy. They were flimsy little leather shoes, but they hurt as he slapped her face with them. They left welts and Polly, who had long learned to hold her head high no matter the bruises or the welts or the cuts, hated those half-moon shapes on her cheeks.

Now, almost fifteen years later, that $3.3 million doesn't seem like enough, but it wasn't the doctor's fault that Polly married Ditmars. That was her choice, her mistake, and she shouldered it, almost without complaint. She had tried complaining to her mother in the early years, only hinting at how badly Ditmars treated her, but her mother said, "Marriage is hard." Now that her mother is dead, Polly feels more generously toward her—so funny how that works—and she can see her side of things. Her mother probably felt bad that she couldn't help Polly. Just because she moved to Florida, it didn't mean she didn't love Polly.

Three point three million. Okay, 1.8 million. It sits, one hundred miles to the west, waiting for her in a money market account in Barry Forshaw's name. Monday through Friday, Adam is about the same distance to the west, doing whatever it is he does. He says he has found a short-term gig as a claims adjuster. Polly can't be bothered to ask the questions that would expose his lies. Eventually— *when, why are things taking so long, why does everything she need have to take so long?*—he will know he should have trusted her.

She hears Adam's pickup truck rolling up the driveway. It's not a bad trip, not on a Friday night in November, especially as he doesn't leave until well after rush hour. *I come to Belleville for you, I don't want to sit around waiting for you to get off.* He brings her cash, every week, to help pay the rent. She doesn't want to take it, but she needs it. Things are so slow, her tips so small. How had Cath made it, during the winter months? Polly suspects she was skimming receipts. She wonders if she should float that idea with Mr. C as a way of making a case for a raise, but it seems mean, tainting a dead woman's reputation.

"Hey," Adam says, coming through the door.

"Hey."

He picks her up, carries her to their bed. She thinks, as she often does, of the quilt, the iron bed, the kimono, back in the apartment she loved. *I was happy then.* She notices the tense, the wistfulness she feels toward the summer, particularly the day of the auction, when all was anticipation. Things are so complicated now. It wasn't supposed to be this complicated. There wasn't supposed to be an Adam. But he planted himself in her path and she can't shake him, even though she knows she should. Eventually, he will trust her, come to see that he was wrong to doubt her.

But how can she trust him?

rving seldom attends synagogue, even during the High Holidays. He doesn't like the way people look at him. It has been twenty-plus years since he was in the news for being a slumlord, and although he knows he should be grateful that he wasn't promoted to murderer, he still bridles at the unfairness of the term. He didn't make his properties slums. That was on the tenants. He remembers the place where he and Birdy started out, thirty-five years ago, that terrible little apartment over near Pimlico. It was worse than anything he ever rented out, but Birdy somehow made it clean. Down on her hands and knees with Pine-Sol, every day, on those splintery floors, that curling linoleum. If they had had marble steps, she would have scrubbed those, too. The people he rented to, they didn't have it in them to clean like that. And don't get him started about lead paint. His first son, Eric, was born in that terrible apartment, probably licked the walls, and he went to Wharton.

But it is officially a year since Birdy's death, so he goes to synagogue to light a yahrzeit candle, say kaddish. The rabbi smiles, hopeful.

"So maybe we'll be seeing you here more often?" the rabbi asks. But it's Irving's wallet he likes, not Irving.

"Sure," Irving says. What does it cost, a kind, assuring word? Almost nothing.

He doesn't drive directly home after leaving shul, decides to take a trip down his own memory lane, starting with that wretched apartment near Pimlico, not far from that psychic, the neighborhood's one constant. Then he heads north on Park Heights Avenue, as so many of his people did, first to Pikesville, then Owings Mills, then Reisterstown. Reisterstown Road—how changed it is. So many memories. He was a good husband to Birdy—an excellent provider who never loved another, although he enjoyed what he considered an essential release with the occasional woman. He and Birdy had three accomplished children, eight grandchildren. She was a firecracker, full of energy to the end. If one of the two of them was destined to have a heart attack in the middle of the night, there's not a bookie in town who wouldn't have said Irving was the odds-on favorite. But it was Birdy. A lot of people thought the nickname was Bertie because her name was Beatrice, but how did that make sense? She was "Birdy" because she had that aspect to her—a round, plump body, which was mostly breast, propped up on tiny stick legs. Her voice was like a bird's, too, sweet and high.

How he loved Birdy. He cheated on her no more than three or four times, always one-offs, opportunities not to be disdained, sort of like having a slice of cake when you weren't that hungry, but your mother-in-law kept pushing, pushing, pushing. Birdy never knew. At least, he doesn't think she ever knew. Surely, she wouldn't have stayed if she suspected an indiscretion on his part. She was a confident woman, sure of her worth, happy every day. The night she died, he swears he heard her giggling at her dreams.

Then—gone. And only fifty-five. Just one of those things, the doctor said.

It was about a week before she died that Irving ran into Barry Forshaw, flush with success, thanking him for the referral. How close he had come to saying, *What referral?* He hadn't sent anyone to Forshaw, never would.

Was that the slip-and-fall?

No, the medical malpractice case. That's where the dollars are. She's an odd duck, your friend. An enigma. She could have—well, obviously, I can't say more.

An enigma. Irving's mind ran rapidly through the women he knew who might hire a personal injury attorney. He didn't have many female friends, so that made it easy, and fewer still would have heard the name "Barry Forshaw" from his lips. He used to complain about him to Ditmars. Forshaw had been a genius at going after landlords with nuisance suits. Irving had sat in the Ditmars kitchen, grousing about Forshaw, thinking it was empty chatter, nothing more.

Pauline, he realized. That bitch. She must have sued over the daughter's disability, and, given Forshaw's glee, done quite well. But the state had custody of the daughter, so how could she be entitled to money? If she was entitled, he was, too. Even her evil lummox of a husband always gave Irving his share. She still owed him for that life insurance policy.

And in the numb shock that followed Birdy's death, Irving's rage sustained him, gave him purpose. He had to find out how Pauline Ditmars had gotten yet more money, and where that money was. Once he did, he would blackmail her, her with her new life. If she didn't give him a cut, he would reveal her past to the new husband, tell the state she was double-dipping. He had her coming and going.

Until she went, stood up on a beach one day, walked away from that new family with barely a backward glance. He should have realized she'd make mincemeat out of Adam Bosk soon enough. It's what she does. He remembers a song that his daughter played on her stereo maybe fifteen years ago, about a man-eater. Funny to think that Sheila is now the mother of three and God knows what those kids play on their stereos.

He pulls into his driveway. It's a nice house, a brick Colonial. But it was already too big when it was just the two of them, and it's way too big for a man living alone. He needs to unload the place. He's been putting it off only because the kids are sentimental, but he's ready to downsize. For their thirty-five years together, Irving and Birdy's life had been a series of upgrades. That terrible first apartment, then their first house, then to a house that was big enough for each child to have a bedroom, and finally this place. He's not old, not really, but he sees where he's headed, a process of diminution. Everything will get smaller, except his belly and his bank account. And then one day, he will die, and his money will be split among the children and the grandchildren, so his money will end up smaller, too. He loves his kids, but they're wasteful.

He notices a patrol car parked across the street, unusual for this neighborhood. Maybe a burglary? He waves at the police. Even when he was up to his neck in all sorts of shady business, he never had a moment of guilt when he walked by a police officer. In his heart, he never did anything wrong, not on purpose. He made a mistake, starting that trash fire, that was all, and he was forced to pay for it. Even then, all he did was paperwork. The victims were not his, he knew them not, he wished them no ill. He was a good man surrounded by bad people. Left to his own devices, he would have never broken the law.

Even now, as he sees two dark-suited men get out of another car on the street, calling his name as he stands on his doorstep, he feels nothing more than an idle curiosity.

"Irving Lowenstein?"

"Yes," he says. Mormons? They look too old to be going door-to-door to convert people.

"We have a warrant for your arrest. For murder."

"Whose?" he says, honestly baffled.

Then he hears Pauline's voice, back in his office. *The fire on Eutaw. Paca,* he had corrected. He had been smart enough not to give her Coupay's name when she fished for it, but the street would have been enough. Easy to pin down a fatal fire, once you had the address and general time it happened. Easy to find out who had owned the building, who had carried the insurance, who had brokered the policy. They will subpoena his records, if they haven't already. Serve a warrant on Susie, start going through his files.

He is on the doorstep of his house. The house he has just disowned in his thoughts, replacing it, in his imagination, with a condo downtown. Or maybe even Florida. He has enough money, he could retire. And do what? Marry again. He's a catch, or would be in Florida. Naples, he thinks, somewhere on the Gulf side. That's always been his preference. He doesn't play golf, but maybe cards. His children would visit, on their way to or from Disney World. Five seconds ago, this was a reasonable dream for his future.

Now he doesn't know if he will ever walk through his own front door again.

"When we get downtown," he says to the detective, "I'd like to call my lawyer."

"Oh, you don't want to do that right away," the detective says. "You know how it goes." The game is afoot. They're going to try to persuade him it's better if he talks, just a little, that once lawyers get involved, they have no choice but to charge him.

It's going to be a long night.

The cops take him to the car, not bothering with cuffs. They're not worried about him trying to run or attack. But the detective, perhaps out of force of habit, still puts his hand on Irving's head as he gets in the back seat of the patrol car. People are watching, although it's no one Irving recognizes. He's grateful for that. Grateful, too, that his children live far enough away that their newspapers will carry no photos of him. And maybe there will be no photos, no charges, no attention. If this is all the cops have—but, no, Pauline has talked to them, told them what she knows. Ditmars told her everything, over the years. He bragged about it, how scared she was to cross him because she knew the things he had done. And Paca is probably enough, on its own. That poor girl and her baby, the house was supposed to be empty. The trash can fire, the one he set, the one that brought Ditmars into his life—it was supposed to leave that family homeless, nothing more. He's not a bad man, he's a good man who made some bad decisions. It's an important distinction.

"Amazing," he mutters to himself. He threw a cigar into a trash can thirteen, fourteen years ago and now his life turns to ash.

39

Adam has decided to take a long weekend and go hunting, although he told Polly that he's on a *job* in western Maryland. Why did he lie to her? Why does he feel obligated to justify taking a weekend for himself? He never promised to come to Belleville *every* weekend. Polly doesn't hold him accountable in any way. She doesn't even expect him to call on a regular schedule.

Yet he feels guilty the entire time he's in the woods. Two days running, he takes his position in a tree just before sunrise, bow in hand. The old pleasures—the silence, the time alone, the stillness—no longer deliver. The forest is as silent as ever, but the loud thoughts echoing through his head ruin everything.

He doesn't even get an opportunity to take aim. The only animal he sees is a bear, in the distance thankfully, lumbering past as if rushing to catch a bus. Adam had hoped to have venison to freeze for the winter, maybe make a stew. Two days, sitting in a tree, and nothing to show for it. He gives up on Saturday afternoon and heads home. He could make Belleville by evening, if he wanted to. But does he want to? Polly is not much for surprises.

All the more reason to surprise her now and then.

Of course, as soon as his journey becomes urgent to him, he finds himself in an inexplicable clog of traffic on I-70. He flips to WBAL, hoping to find out what's going on, not that there's an alternate route. He just misses the traffic report—of course—and hits the news on the top of the hour. He'll have to wait another five, ten minutes to find out if it's a notable backup.

"Police have arrested a sixty-three-year-old insurance broker from northwest Baltimore and charged him in a 1986 arson that killed a young woman and her child. Irving Lowenstein—"

No. He wants to talk back to the radio, argue with the dulcet-voiced reader. But he also needs to hear what she's saying.

"Lowenstein is alleged to have secured a range of policies for a third party, from buildings to people, pocketing a share of the claims. His participation came to light when a fire similar to the 1986 blaze and explosion was set in Belleville, Delaware, targeting the ex-wife of one of his coconspirators. Police believe Lowenstein attempted to have Pauline Hansen killed because she was the only person who knew about his crimes."

No, Adam repeats to himself. Irving Lowenstein is not a killer. Money is what motivates Irving. Blow up Polly and you never find the pot of gold you're seeking. Irving's never even been in Belleville.

Although he knew where Polly lived, of course.

He knew because it was in one of the weekly reports that Adam sent west this summer, when Polly was still nothing more than a job. "Subject has moved to an apartment on Main Street in Belleville."

Get to know her, Irving had said. *Ingratiate yourself with the husband. Find out everything about what she does, how she spends her days, if she's spending money.*

Maybe all Irving ever wanted was enough information to figure out a way to have her killed that would look like an accident, or a random crime. And killing her makes so much more sense, if she knows his role in these long-ago deaths. Hire one guy to watch her, then another guy to kill her. Irving, sitting a hundred miles away, didn't even have to worry about an alibi.

So this is the strain Polly has been living with since Labor Day—this chronic fear and Adam's impossible-to-conceal doubts about her. Someone tried to kill her and she was terrified to confide in him because she didn't think she'd be believed. Her mysterious errands, those extra miles on the truck—she's probably been talking to Baltimore police for weeks, helping them build this case.

He'd drive straight to Delaware right now if he didn't have two days of hunting funk on him. As it is, he's back in the car, showered and shaved, thirty minutes after stopping at his apartment. Hits the fancy market in Annapolis to buy steaks and wine only to find himself in another traffic jam on the Bay Bridge, but he doesn't mind. He can't imagine minding anything, ever again. He has come so close to losing her. Once, when Irving tried to kill her and now because of his own doubts and skepticism.

Years ago, in a clog of traffic just like this, Adam's car was rear-ended. It wasn't bad, one of the last links in a chain reaction of fender benders. His was the penultimate car hit, and he barely tapped the bumper of the car in front of him. Then Adam had gotten out of his car, a sporty little Nissan, and looked back, seen the eighteen-wheeler that had started it all, steaming on the median where it had finally stopped, car bodies strewn like corpses. A Corolla opened on one side like a can of tuna, a Volvo's trunk accordioned, a Mercedes that seemed almost V-shaped after the impact. Yet, best Adam could tell, no one had been seriously injured. He started to shake from the knowledge of what might have been, how many people might be dead right now if the truck driver, coming over the ridge into a traffic jam, had applied his brakes even five seconds later. Nothing makes you feel more alive than almost dying.

The steaks aren't as good as they should be—it's hard, making a perfect steak in an electric broiler, not that Adam can blame Polly for wanting no part of a gas stove these days—but the wine is wonderful, worth the cost. They curl up on the couch, his arms so tight around her that she has to break the seal when she wants to reach for her glass, take a sip.

"Why did he want to—why did he—" It's a hard question to ask.

"Let's not talk about it," she says. "I'm safe. We're safe."

"I'm going to move back here," he says. "As soon as I can. I'll figure out a way to make ends meet. I'll—"

She shakes her head. When Polly says she doesn't want to talk, she means it. Here, with her in his arms, Adam feels the peace that eluded him while deer hunting. He will move to Belleville. He will be the man she wants him to be, the man she believed him to be until his doubts caused her to lose faith in him. There will be time enough to travel, to coax her from this tiny town, this provincial life. If she wants something and he can give it to her, he will.

He thinks again about how close he came to getting her killed, the lies that Irving told him to throw him off the scent of his real aims. It makes sense now, that postcard sent before Adam quit, Irving's decision to terminate Adam's employment. He wanted her dead because of what she knew about him. He hired someone to kill her and the guy—it had to be a guy—screwed up, plain and simple. Poor Cath. But Adam can't lie. If someone had to die, better

246

Cath than Polly. Cath didn't deserve to die, no one really does, but no one deserves a shot at a normal life more than Polly.

She has fallen asleep in his arms, her cheek pressed against his chest, her hair tickling his chin. Her hair smells of the High-Ho—grease and beer and french fries. The roots are slightly darker than the rest of her hair. She thinks he doesn't know that she uses a henna rinse to amp up the red, but of course he does. He knows everything about her.

The hard part has been keeping track of what he's supposed to know and what she has yet to tell him. But those days are over. No more secrets.

40

Christmas is coming
The goose is getting fat
Please put a penny in the old man's hat
If you haven't got a penny,
A ha'penny will do
And if you haven't got a ha'penny, then God bless you.

Polly doesn't have much more than a ha'penny this Christmas season, but she feels blessed. Belleville does the holiday right. The shops and empty storefronts on Main Street are hung with white lights, which Polly's mother always believed more tasteful than varicolored bulbs. There is a manger outside the Lutheran Church at the far end of Main Street. And there is one house—there is always one house—that goes over the top with its yard—a rocking sleigh with a Santa reciting in a mechanized voice: Ho-Ho-Ho. Ho-Ho-Ho. People drive twenty, thirty miles just to see this place.

The only Dundalk tradition Polly misses is the Christmas

Garden at the Wise Avenue fire department, where they re-created Baltimore in miniature with a train set, right down to the DOMINO SUGARS sign. Maybe one day she'll make her own Christmas garden.

A year ago, she was running around, trying to give Gregg his version of a perfect Christmas. Jani, not even three at the time, would have been happy with anything Polly did. Not Gregg. The Hansens had definite ideas about Christmas. Savannah Hansen brought over her ornaments, showed Polly the angel for the treetop, the stockings she had made, garish, tacky things of red felt with glitter glue names. "Here's the one I made for Gregg and now Jani."

There was no stocking for her daughter-in-law.

The Costellos had traditions, too. Not the seven fishes, although her dad's family was pretty Italian. Her dad, unlike Gregg, didn't think a husband's family had to swamp the wife's when it came to rituals. Then again, to be fair to Gregg—*Wow, where did that thought come from?*—he knew her as Pauline Smith, a woman with no family, no history. It probably never occurred to him that she had a distinctive past with its own traditions, such as turkey and sauerkraut, or a Christmas garden in the basement. Even in the getting-to-know-you phase, the phase where men pretend great interest in women, he never asked her a single question.

Adam didn't, either. But that's different, of course.

Adam. Polly is, with the help of Mr. C's wife, knitting him a sweater. She tries to tell herself that it will be more meaningful than any store-bought gift. And if a better knitter was working on it, this would be true. The fact is, even the wool, a sky blue that matches his eyes, strains her pocketbook. She's beginning to think she will never have any money, that it was all a dream. Everything, her entire life, is a dream. There was never a girl in a yellow two-piece. She didn't marry Burton Ditmars. There is no Joy, no Jani. There are no fires, no schemes, no Cath. She is not in Belleville. She never met Adam.

But her imagination snags; she cannot imagine life without Adam. For better or worse, this is her life. Lately, it's all for the better.

She wonders what Adam will give her for Christmas. She tries to catalog the gifts she received from Ditmars and Gregg, making it a memory game.

She remembers:

A nightgown. The first Christmas with Ditmars. There was still hope.

A vacuum. The third Christmas with Ditmars.

A sweater. Not cashmere, but something almost as soft. Christmas number two?

Earrings. Amber, dangly. He liked dangly earrings. That was Christmas number two, the sweater was number three, the vacuum cleaner number four.

A Sony Walkman. Gregg, their first year. He wanted one, so he assumed she wanted one.

A pear tree. "Partridge not included," Gregg joked upon presenting her with it on Christmas Eve. Bizarre, but she had liked him better for it. It hinted at some version of her that he had in his head, something funny and quirky. The kind of gift that a woman in a romantic comedy might get from a would-be suitor.

He probably saw it at some Christmas tree lot near a liquor store, while he was buying El Gordo lottery tickets.

She cannot, try as she might, needles clicking faster and faster as if to keep pace with her whirring memory, remember what Ditmars gave her their last Christmas together. She has heard somewhere that when it comes to a list of seven or more, whether it's the dwarfs or the nine Supreme Court justices, the memory always comes up one short. But then, she also has heard that it was possible to memorize seven-digit phone numbers in a way that we can never remember the new ten-digit ones. The ten-digit numbers aren't truly new, but they became common while she was in prison, and she thinks of the world that way, as if the years between her two selves, her two marriages, aren't real. Those years are like scar tissue, the purplish, rubbery damage done by burns, thick and marbled.

Polly has a burn like that, high on her thigh, so high that a modest, skirted swimsuit can conceal it. By the time a man sees it, he doesn't know how to ask about it. How does one get a burn there, beneath the curve of the right ass cheek? How does something hot touch that almost hidden place? How long would it have to be held there to do that kind of damage?

No one wants to hear the real answers to questions like that. No one. She has to assume as much, because Gregg never asked. Adam never asks. The scar might as well be a tattoo: *If you can see this, you are too close.*

She's going too fast, and she's dropped a stitch. Mrs. C showed her the fix for that, but it doesn't come naturally to Polly. She wants to think that Adam won't notice, but she's kidding herself. He notices everything.

He's certainly going to notice when she's suddenly rich, but she already has a story picked out for when that day comes. Which will be soon, she's pretty sure. It better be soon.

41

Adam can't figure out how to make his move to Belleville plausible. There's work enough, up in Wilmington, for someone who knows how to investigate insurance fraud, but how does he convince Polly that he fell into that line of work. She'll see through him, she'll figure out that he came into her life as a PI, murder riding his coattails. Will there ever be a right time, a right way, to come clean?

He distracts himself by deciding to drop a bundle on her Christmas gift, going into the once sacrosanct account, the money his mother left him. He can almost hear his mother whispering to him when he transfers $5,000 from his inheritance account to his regular checking. *You don't need to spend a lot of money to impress someone who truly loves you.*

Of course, he doesn't have to spend the whole amount. Money can always be transferred back.

But he does spend it all, and then some. He goes to Washington, D.C., one of those old-line jewelers who buzzes you in, assuming you don't look like trouble, and Adam, with his blue eyes, always makes the cut. Adam knows Polly likes old stuff, vintage, but he's helpless when the guy starts throwing terms at him. *Art deco, art nouveau.* He shrugs, wishing it wasn't the owner himself waiting on him. He'd feel better confessing his ignorance to a woman, someone young and romantic who would be charmed by a man's good intentions toward his girlfriend.

His eye is drawn to a diamond solitaire in an old-fashioned setting, really simple. It's a whopper by his standards, almost two carats and, of course, the guy has to blah-blah-blah about purity and cut and resale value, how unusual good canary diamonds are. Adam has done enough divorce work to know that the resale value of gems is almost always overstated.

But he likes that this ring is simple. No pavé diamonds surrounding the stone, a slender platinum band. He's not sure if it's to her taste, but it looks like her, clear and bold and beautiful, with a flicker of light at the center.

It's also $6,000. He dickers with the guy, gets him down to $5,200, barters his time. He probably could make Polly just as happy with a cheaper version of this ring, something from one of the mall stores. God knows, if she finds out what he spent, she'll probably be angry at him. Five thousand dollars in their current circumstances could carry them to next summer, to a time when the High-Ho is thronged once more. She's talking about the bed-and-breakfast business again, which strikes him as crazy. Escoffier reincarnated could open a restaurant in Belleville and it wouldn't do enough business to go year-round.

He's glad, watching the guy pack up the ring, that he came to this kind of shop. You can fool a woman with a ring, if it's pretty and shiny enough. But you can't fake the box, the presentation. This velvet box is a deep, deep blue, and when he looks at the inside, he wishes they made beds for people as soft and billowy as the white satin on which this ring sits.

He'll wrap the velvet box inside something bigger, surrounding it with tissue, maybe even weighted things, to maintain the illusion. Maybe he'll get a box for a hand mixer or a Dustbuster. He imagines her taking it from under whatever kind of tree they put up. Christmas Eve, not Christmas morning. The best gifts are the ones you open on Christmas Eve, whether you're a kid allowed to open just one present before Santa arrives or, well, an almost forty-year-old guy who's going to go down on one knee, say words he never thought he'd say again to anyone.

Or maybe, he thinks that evening, nursing a beer, waiting for her to finish up at the High-Ho, the blue velvet box like a tiny happy bomb in the pocket of his leather jacket, he'll propose to her *here*. That's it. He'll reenact the night they met, then slide the box to her, cool as cool. What did she say that night? It was funny, he remembers that. He'd been trying to mock his own pretensions, called himself an asshole and she had one-upped him. Then later, she had made a joke about being a Pink Lady apple.

It's so hard now to remember being dispassionate about her. Maybe he never was.

"Ready to go?" she says at closing time.

"Sure thing," he says.

Mr. C comes out of his office, a letter in his hand. "I almost forgot, Polly, but this came for you today. Registered, certified, whichever one you have to sign for."

Polly slides it into her pocketbook but not before Adam, expert in reading upside down, notes the address—Kentucky Avenue, Baltimore, MD. *Her ex,* he thinks.

Her not-yet-ex, he remembers. It's easy to forget about him. She never speaks of him, or their little girl. It's as if neither one has ever existed. Polly gave the first kid to the state and she's giving this kid to her dad, with nary a backward glance.

Unnatural, Irving Lowenstein had said. Irving Lowenstein, who had wanted her dead.

Still, that doesn't make him wrong.

Maybe it's too early for anyone to be giving anyone a ring. He'll wait until Christmas Eve, after all.

42

Polly waits until she gets to the Royal Farms to open the letter. With Adam gone most of the time, she no longer has to spend her mornings at the Royal Farms, not on weekdays, but she retains much affection for the place she considered her summer office. A place where she reads and thinks, even writes from time to time.

A letter from Gregg. Finally, he is ready to move forward. They could be divorced by next June, not even six months from now.

Dear Ms. Smith, it begins.

Oh, interesting, he's using what he thinks of as her maiden name, the legal one she bestowed on herself after prison. He has already taken his first "asset," his name. Excellent.

The letter is crafted by a lawyer, which probably cost Gregg $500 right there. Dumb, Gregg was always dumb about money. That's because he's always had just enough to waste a little. No cutting coupons for him, no living on a budget, finding ways to shake out a few dollars until you have enough to pay for a life insurance policy. When Gregg hit a rough patch, he called his mother for a loan.

Even with its lawyerisms, the letter is clear in its demands.

Gregg wants both cars, all his savings, and any equity there might be in the house. All their furniture, all their wedding presents. Fine, fine, fine. Oh, she'll pretend to want more, but all she really desires is her freedom.

She gets change, feeds it into the outside pay phone until she has enough for three minutes. When Gregg answers, she tries to sound unsure of herself.

"Hi, it's Pauline. I got your letter, but I'm at a pay phone. Would you call me back?"

"I'm at work," he says, as if she didn't know what number she dialed.

"So am I," she lies. It's a strange, small lie and one easily spotted if he remembers where she works, which he clearly does as he used that address to send this letter. But her pride demands it. *Pride.* That's what gets her in trouble every time. Pride and fear. She can't imagine how rich she'd have to be to afford those two things.

He hangs up on her with a grunt. She decides it sounds like agreement, so she stays where she is, resting her forehead against the rectangular shield around the phone. Mild as this December has been, it's too cold and raw for her. She's prone to chills, always was, even when she was carrying more weight. She likes summer, the abundance of light. What will next summer bring? Where will she be?

Who will be with her?

Minutes tick by. She doesn't wear a watch anymore, so she counts the seconds as she was taught as a child. *1-Mississippi, 2-Mississippi.*

She's counted off almost six hundred Mississippis when the phone finally rings.

"I had to take a whiz," he says. Good, he's offering explanations. That means he still feels some sense of obligation.

"So, how do you want to do this?" Clever, she thinks, to put it on him to let him feel he's calling the shots.

"Didn't my lawyer's letter make things pretty clear?"

"We don't need lawyers," she says.

"Don't tell me what I need."

She's trying to indicate that it's going to be easy, that he's going to get his way, but he's too insecure to register the information. *Don't be stupid, Gregg.* She might as well ask water not to be wet.

"I want to sell the house. We won't make any money back, but I can move to a place closer to my mother, a rental for now."

Always was a mama's boy. So far, so good. She no longer has any affection for the house on Kentucky Avenue. Imagine, thinking a built-in breakfront was somehow going to change your life.

"I also want you to waive your share of my 401(k)."

She has to protest at least one of his demands or he'll be suspicious. "I don't know, I stayed home, I took care of our child, it seems to me I should get *something*."

"Not a cent, Pauline. You're getting nada, nothing, zilch."

"I guess that makes it easier in some ways." She still needs to put up a little more fight. "But about my car—"

"I'm selling the Toyota. You don't need it. Besides you wrecked the other one and took the insurance, so we're even on that."

Of course she'll need a car, she thinks, especially if she stays in Belleville. And he's the one who wrecked the other car. But, okay, soon enough, she can buy her own. The Toyota's no good, anyway.

"Gee, Gregg—"

"My way or the highway," he says. She yearns to say, *I'm the one who decided, okay? I took the actual highway. I ran away from you with a suitcase and nothing more.*

Instead she makes her voice small and defeated.

"All right. When do you think we can finalize all this? Seeing as we agree."

"By year's end," he says, and it's all she can do not to jump up and down. "Better for taxes if we have all this straightened out. I know we can't get divorced that fast, but we should have everything figured out by January 1. And I guess we've covered it, right? House, car, 401(k)."

"What about child support?"

"I'm not going to ask for any, for now."

It takes a moment for his words to sink in. She did not see *that* coming. She thought five months as a single parent would have Gregg begging for joint custody at best.

"So you're asking for—"

"I'm not asking for anything, Pauline. I'm *telling* you, okay? You left your daughter. I've done just fine. You probably didn't think I could, but it turns out, it's not as hard as you always made it out to be. I don't know, maybe you're just not cut out to be a mother."

She needs him to spell it out, wants him to say exactly what he wants.

"But if I decided I wanted visitation—"

"If you want it. But it's been five months, and you haven't visited once."

But she has, in her own way. She has sneaked into Baltimore every chance she has using Adam's truck or taking the Peter Pan Bus.

"I don't have a car. And now you're selling the one I do have."

"See, that's all you can think about, the car. You have a kid, Pauline. You left her."

This is indisputable. But there are, as Gregg's lawyer would undoubtedly write, mitigating factors.

"The postcards—did she get my postcards?" She has sent one

every week since Gregg found her at the High-Ho. True, they were only scrawled hearts and "I love yous," but it's not like a three-year-old can read.

A pause. She knows that pause. It's the pause that always followed certain questions, questions that Gregg found inconvenient. *Where were you last night? Did you remember to get the things I needed from the store on your way home?* First a pause, then a lie.

"No," he says. "I thought it would confuse her."

It has the ring of truth, which throws her off more than anything else in this conversation.

"She's only three," he continues. "She can't read. She didn't want postcards. She wanted you. And you never came."

No argument there.

She says, "I know I'm the one who said 'no lawyers,' but if you insist on full custody, then—"

"Don't, Pauline." His voice is infuriatingly kind. "I'm not going to pay you for the privilege of keeping our kid. You've got your freedom, which is clearly what you wanted. I'm not going to give you money on top of it."

"You think that's how I am?"

"I know, okay? I know everything, Pauline."

It feels as if her heart rises up her throat, all the way to her teeth. If he's found out about the settlement, then everything—everything—she's done is for nothing. She's been told he has no legal rights, but she doesn't want to spend a penny fighting to keep what's hers, and Gregg will fight for money. "Know what?"

"It came out in the papers over here. You're a killer, who's already lost custody of one kid, then got a second chance. Well, you had it. Maybe the third time will be the charm for you. This, us—we're over."

Close to being over, she thinks. *So close.* But then, every time she thinks she's close to the end, something else happens, another bump in the road.

"Okay," she says. Now she knows exactly what he wants. Wasn't that Barry Forshaw's advice? Trick Gregg into revealing what he wants, and then you'll have true leverage. Gregg wants Jani. He's probably bluffing, but maybe he thinks that's the only way he gets the other stuff. He's expecting her to counter. She wins by not doing what he expects.

Still, she can't help allowing herself one little zinger.

"You can't rely on your mother for child care forever, you know."

"Who said I was?"

"I just assumed that's what you were doing."

"Fact is, I found a really good day-care center near the office last week."

Interesting. Gregg always said day care wasn't right, that it was for welfare mothers or people who didn't really love their kids.

"Are you dating?" she asks.

"Pauline." Kind, beseeching, as if he thinks the information could hurt her.

"You're entitled," she adds.

"There's a woman at work. But she's more of a friend. She has a little boy about Jani's age."

Gregg has never had a female friend. Gregg doesn't believe in female friends. They specifically had that argument after watching *When Harry Met Sally* on video one night, with him maintaining that "real" men didn't have female friends.

"That's nice for you." She tries to think of what a normal woman would say in this situation, a woman who's not trying not to conceal how much she wants a man out of her life, how much she loathes him. "Do the kids like each other?"

"Pretty well. Look, Pauline—"

"Yes?"

"Whatever happens, we'll make it work," Gregg says. She wonders who the "we" is—Gregg and her? Gregg and his mother? Gregg and Jani? Gregg and his *friend*? But that's secondary. He has established his terms. She knows what he wants, what he's willing to give.

"Could I get this in writing?" she asks. "The financial stuff. Have your lawyer draw up something based on what we talked about today, about the property, and I'll sign it. Have it notarized if that's what it takes. But then we'll be on our way. Just the financial stuff, though."

Polly also knows what she wants and what she's willing to do to get it. She swallows hard, dials Barry Forshaw collect, and tells him what she needs. He asks a lot of pesky questions, complains that it's not really his kind of thing, but in the end, he's happy to do what she wants. For a price. When you help a man make more than a million dollars with very little effort, he tends to be kindly inclined toward you. Paper trail commenced, now she has to mark another kind of trail. Lead the horse to water. Make him drink.

That night, when she goes to work, she checks to see if Mr. C really does keep a gun in his desk.

43

Adam's possessions, the ones he plans to take with him to Belleville, require exactly eleven boxes, eight of them for books. He could probably live without the books if it comes to that. But they're easy to box and they are the only objects, along with his mother's paintings, about which he allows himself to be sentimental. Half the books belonged to his parents—his mother's art and photography books, the old man's biographies and histories. He will build a shelf for them in Polly's place. Not some college-kid thing made out of plywood and cinder blocks, and not some prefab IKEA shelf. He will build a real one, borrowing tools from Mr. C or someone else in town.

His life in Baltimore is almost as neatly packed away as his possessions. The lease on his apartment will end February 1, phone and utilities will be turned off then, too. On Christmas Eve, he's going to drop to one knee and ask Polly to marry him. So why not cancel his apartment by December 31?

Because I'm not sure what she's going to say.

When he's in his soon-not-his apartment, he checks two, three times a day to make sure that the blue velvet box is safe in its hiding place. He goes to look at it again now, nestled inside a box of tampons that some woman left behind, he's not even sure who. Someone gambling that she was going to be spending more time with him than she ever did, that's for sure. Since Adam's marriage ended, he's never come close to living with anyone. A month, maybe two, was the most time he put in with a woman.

Then Irving Lowenstein hires him to follow Pauline Hansen and the next thing he knows is that he's in love with Polly Costello. A woman who killed one man, walked out on another. But he's the one who almost got her killed. He can't forget that.

Maybe he shouldn't ask her to marry him until he's man enough to tell her that.

Irving's lawyer keeps calling Adam, asking him to come see him in the city lockup, where he's being held without bail. The lawyer leaves a message every three days or so. "Irving Lowenstein would like to see you." "Checking back to see if you'd like to visit Mr. Lowenstein." "I've identified you as a contractor for my firm, so you don't have to worry about filling out a visitor's application. You'll be treated as an employee of the firm."

Adam has nothing to say to that snake. He owes him nothing. Sure, he felt guilty last summer when he fell in love with Polly, but he still did right by Irving. Irving Lowenstein, teller of tall tales, pretending that a vulnerable woman ripped him off, preyed on kids, when he's the one who was trying to kill her all along.

It is December 21, a Thursday. That means Christmas falls on a Monday this year, a nice three-day weekend for regular folks who won't even notice how many other people still have to work December 25. Cops, firefighters, waiters at Chinese restaurants. And there's not even Chinese food in Belleville. Adam bets the only thing open December 25 will be the Royal Farms near the soon-to-be bypass. Belleville is beautiful at Christmas—and he has never found it more cloying. It has a real *It's a Wonderful Life* vibe, and *It's a Wonderful Life* is only the most depressing movie ever made. Work your whole life, be good, and maybe your friends will save you. Except they probably won't, and every small town is Pottersville in the end.

He decides he won't take his books to Belleville on this trip, or his other boxes. It will look presumptuous, even if he and Polly did live together for part of the fall. Going forward, things between them will be stated, out in the open. He will tell her that he was hired as a private investigator to follow her, that he never knew Irving was trying to harm her. If she forgives him, he'll ask her to marry him.

That said, there's no law he has to wait until Christmas Eve to propose. She'll be looking for something then. Why not do it—*tonight?* No one expects a proposal on December 21. Polly doesn't even expect him to be there. When he'd first told her he didn't think he could get away until Saturday afternoon, at the earliest, they both agreed that it might be better for him to drive over Sunday morning as the roads would be wretched that afternoon. But he's been to the bank, deposited his checks for his last two gigs and there's not a lot of work this time of year. His last job, in fact, was so awful it made him want to quit PI work forever. Some poor woman with five kids, shopping at the Dollar Tree, was hit by a car, all her cheap little presents scattering in the wind. No one was at fault—it was dark, she stepped off a curb—and the tortured good citizen behind the wheel immediately established a fund in her name. But the sister who stepped up to take donations on the kids' behalf turned out to be completely shifty. The driver called Adam, and Adam sussed it out in less than two days. The woman, under a slightly different name, had several penny-ante convictions—bad checks, stealing some stuff from a roommate. Real *People's Court* shit. There was no way she should be overseeing that fund.

But the part that soured Adam on his job was the happy client giving him a bonus for scaring the shit out of the shady sister. It was as if her misdeeds cleared the slate for the poor mope, made him feel less guilty about the accident. True, she'd probably skimmed some money off the donations that came in, but there was still almost $5,000 for the five kids, which will help. It won't send them to college, but it will buy groceries, keep the heat on. Five thousand dollars is a lot of money.

It's almost enough to buy a canary yellow engagement ring.

Shit, he's approaching the bridge and he's left the ring behind. Should he take that as a sign? Maybe he should wait until the new year. Maybe he should wait until she's legally divorced. That letter—why didn't she read it in front of him? He knows Maryland law and he realizes she can't initiate the divorce, not for a while. If her husband doesn't file, she has to wait two years for a no-fault.

Two years. June 1997. Where will they be? Who will they be?

He takes the last exit before the bridge and heads back. It will cost him almost ninety minutes, but he can't stop thinking about it.

———

It is almost nine Thursday night when Adam reaches the High-Ho, but the bar is packed. Business picks up during the holidays. People get giddy from all the socializing, want to keep going, and the High-Ho is one of the few places open after eight. Mr. C has put up decorations that appear to be fifty years old, right out of that *Christmas Story* movie. Strands of multicolored lights, an illuminated wreath in one window. The air inside the bar feels overheated and smoky after even a few seconds of the cold, crisp air in the parking lot. Adam's eyes need a moment to adjust.

Mr. C is tending bar.

"Where's Polly?"

"She wasn't expecting you tonight, Adam."

"I wanted to surprise her."

"Oh, I think we have a gift of the magic here," says Mr. C, mangling the name of the old O. Henry story. "Polly asked for today off, for a mystery errand. I assume it's for you. The—the thing she was making for you, it's not coming out so good. She said there was something she needed to pick up in Baltimore and she took the bus. But you weren't supposed to be here until early Sunday, I thought."

"I was trying to surprise *her*," Adam mutters, taking a stool. Might as well have a beer or two.

"Like I said, gift of the magic."

He doesn't have the heart to correct Mr. C's repeated malapropism, explain that the story is correctly called "The Gift of the Magi," and that it's more than two people trying to surprise each other. It's the catch-22 of gift-giving. It's also another one of those Christmas stories that everyone thinks is so nice when it's depressing as hell. Two desperately poor people try to do something nice for each other as Christmas approaches, sacrificing their most cherished possessions. The woman's hair may grow back, but it will never be quite the same. Women's hair never is after they cut it. And what do you do with a watch fob when you don't have a watch?

What do you do with an engagement ring when you don't have your girl?

"When did she say she was coming back?" Adam asks.

"She didn't. Doesn't matter, because she asked for today and tomorrow off and we're closed Christmas Eve and Christmas."

"She didn't tell me she was off."

Mr. C clapped a hand to his mouth. "Maybe that's part of the secret."

Adam goes to her garage apartment, soon to be theirs. Senseless to expect her as no buses run this late, but he keeps hoping she'll slide in next to him. But she doesn't come home that night.

Or the next day.

Or that night.

When Saturday, December 23, dawns, and there's still no sign of her, Adam can't stop lying to himself. Something is wrong, terribly wrong, and there's only one person who can assure him that Polly is okay.

44

"Merry Christmas," Irving says to Adam over the low partition at city jail.

"Don't be funny," Adam says.

"What a sad world this is when even a polite greeting is suspect. I'm glad to see you, if surprised by the timing. I guess it's a good thing that my lawyer listed you as one of the firm's employees. Can't have been easy, getting in here on the Saturday before Christmas."

"A friendly judge made it happen. Your lawyer's very well connected."

"I would hope so," Irving says. "My legal affairs are not a place to cut corners. I always hire the best. Or try."

Lowenstein looks terrible, at least ten years older than he did when Adam last saw him face-to-face, which was in June. The orange jumpsuit is unkind to most complexions, but Irving looks particularly haggard. The blood vessels in his face are more prominent, his eyes rheumy like an old dog's. He has a cold, but no handkerchief, and keeps honking into the crook of his elbow. His cough is syrupy, almost a gurgle.

"You've been trying to talk to me since you were arrested. Why?"

"I had information that I thought you should have."

"About Polly? Is someone still after Polly? Are you still trying to kill her?"

Irving needs a beat. "It's funny, I still think of her as Pauline. But then, in my head, she still has short blond hair and is a little overweight. *Zaftig* is the better word. It's Yiddish, it means—"

"I know what zaftig means."

"They say almost no one can maintain a significant weight loss. But she has, hasn't she? Still skinny almost five years out. Maybe prison can be a kind of spa, if you treat it right. I can look forward to that at least. If I'm convicted."

"You'll be convicted."

Adam waits for Irving to contradict him. Does the case against Irving rely on Polly's testimony? It occurs to Adam that he hasn't really thought too much about the evidence against Irving, what the cops have. If Polly is the key witness and Polly is missing—

"Where is she?"

"Pauline? I'm sure I don't know."

"You tried to kill her before."

"Really? You may have noticed I'm not charged with that particular crime. They can't even put me at the scene—I flew to Toledo that morning to visit my daughter. In fact, I've never been to Belleville, Delaware."

Adam had assumed that Delaware charges would follow after Maryland was through with Lowenstein. But of course Lowenstein has never been to Belleville.

"You never do your own dirty work. You hired me to keep tabs on her, then you hired another guy to use the information I had gathered, tried to make the death look like an accident. When they find him, it will be a race to see who flips on who first."

"They're never going to find him," Irving says. "Because he doesn't exist."

"You wanted her dead."

"I do now."

The simple words chill him. "What have you done, Irving? Where is she?"

He shakes his head, his face serious but without malice. The graveness of his expression worries Adam even more. He would feel better if he sneered or laughed mirthlessly, like some cartoon villain.

"I hold no brief for her. But I never tried to kill her. What, you think I'm some criminal mastermind, orchestrating things from city jail? I'm a grandfather, near retirement. The case against me is based on Pauline's say-so and a collection of, let's say, inconveniently coincidental policies I helped to broker, years ago. Yes, if she doesn't testify, I have a better chance at acquittal. But I've never arranged a hit on anyone." He seems to lose himself in a memory before he repeats, more firmly: "I never tried to kill anyone."

"And yet people ended up dead because of you. How many? And what would one more mean?"

"I know you're here as a contractual hire of my lawyer," Lowenstein says. "But I'm not going to presume confidentiality. I put my trust in you once. I won't make that mistake again."

"You put your trust in me? You lied to me, again and again. Claiming she had money, that she had ripped you off, that she had stolen from one kid and she would do it again. You were biding your time, waiting for the perfect moment to try to kill her."

"I knew where she was before I hired you, sonny. The point was to figure out if she had money, if she was spending it. Now it's six months later, you're just a poor schmendrick who fell in love with her. Is it possible you know even less about her than you did when you started? Oh, you know the names, the sad history, her crime. You know she had a daughter with Ditmars. Do you know what happened to her?"

"I assume some relative took her in."

"No one wanted that kid. Joy Ditmars has a severe form of cerebral palsy—can't walk, can't speak—and is institutionalized at Mount Washington Pediatric Hospital. It's on Rogers Avenue. Sound familiar?"

Two taxis on a hot summer day. One turns on Rogers Avenue. Adam made the decision not to follow, reasoning that she would spot him on that suburban road. But he told Irving what he saw, where they went. Turns out Irving knew all along what was on Rogers Avenue.

"And here's how canny she is. The life insurance from her first husband, the policy that almost ruined me, got me investigated— that was in her daughter's name, in a trust administered by Pauline. Insurance company wouldn't have to pay if it were for Pauline, but they couldn't keep the money from the daughter. It pays for her care there. Pauline then surrendered her parental rights—voluntarily, she couldn't get rid of that kid fast enough. But Pauline wasn't done, oh no. She likes to play the innocent, but she picked up some tricks from that husband of hers. Last year, she settled out of court with the hospital where the kid was born, blaming them for her condition. Deprivation of oxygen at birth, probably. I'm not sure why the hospital didn't do due diligence about custody—they were probably so excited to settle that they didn't get very far into the investigation—but if the state has the kid, she's not entitled to the damages. I figured she could cut me in for a share, or I'd tell the hospital they'd been taken. But I needed to figure out why she was keeping it a secret. Now I realize it's an asset she's hiding from her next ex-husband. She's a shark, that one, always moving forward."

She's the opposite, Adam wants to say. *She's been swimming lazy circles in Belleville all these months.*

"I'm telling you, she doesn't have any money. She can barely make rent some months."

"And you help her with that, don't you?" Irving does smile now, but it is an infuriatingly kind one, almost pitying. "She has her charms. I know, believe me. There's something about her—a stillness, a capacity for quiet. Maybe she always had that quality, but sometimes, I think it was from living with Ditmars. She learned to freeze, like a deer, or a child playing that game. Freeze tag? And she gave a man a sense that he was a hero, that he could save her. If she made me feel that way, I can't imagine what it's been like for you."

"You had associates, other people who were involved in the things you did—" Adam is grasping and he knows it. But there has to be an explanation for Polly's disappearance. Would he really rather her be dead than duplicitous, playing him for a sucker all these months?

Yes, yes, he would.

"Adam, here's one thing you can take to the bank, one thing you already know, if you would just let yourself: I've never killed anyone, not directly. Do I know of deaths? Sure. But I was caught between two vultures, nothing more than a paper pusher. I've never shoved a knife in a man's heart. She has. And she probably killed that girl, too, the one who died in the explosion. You should know these things."

"So you've been calling me out of concern with my welfare these past few weeks?"

"No, but there is something I think you should know. Something that will change everything you think you know about your relationship with this woman."

It's a mind fuck, Adam tells himself. He's a bitter old man and Adam did do him dirty in a sense. If he hadn't fallen in love with Polly, probably none of this would have happened. Cath's death, Irving's arrest. It's not his fault that Irving sent someone inept to kill Polly.

Someone inept—that's the real threat. Irving doesn't have to ask the guy who killed Cath to kill Polly. He'll know to do it on his own. If she's dead, the charges against Irving go away and no one has to flip on anyone.

"I can't believe anything you have to say."

"Be that way. I'm still going to give you a little stocking stuffer, something small to occupy your thoughts." But instead of leaning forward as most men do when sharing a confidence, he leans back and presses his arm on the table in front of him, almost like someone bracing for an accident. "She knows about you. Has for months."

"Knows what?"

"Knows that you're a private detective and that I hired you. She was pretty slick, I have to admit. Called up, pretending to be a housewife with a cheating husband, checking your references. But you know and I know that I wouldn't have been giving you a very good reference as of August, right? I told my mystery caller that, per the law on confidential personnel information, I would confirm only the dates of your employment with me. And I did. Can you think of anyone else who would have been thinking of hiring you last summer?"

Adam hasn't lost his ability to think on his feet. "That's not news to me," he tells Irving. "Polly and I came clean with each other a long time ago. About everything."

"Oh, so you knew what I told you today. About the daughter. And the money."

"Right. All that money is for the daughter, she's never touched it and she's never going to." He lies for himself, not Irving, and finds the lie credible. That explains everything. There is no money, she is not dishonorable. She found out he had a secret and kept her own, tit for tat. He'll tell her everything and she'll tell him everything. If he finds her, when he finds her, assuming she can be found.

"Well then, Merry Christmas," Irving says. "And a Happy New Year. I don't know about you, but I feel cautiously optimistic for 1996."

45

Polly waits.

She sits in the High-Ho Saturday evening, which closed early today and will not open again until Tuesday. She has left the car she's using, a bright red Toyota with Maryland tags, in the lot. From where she's sitting—behind the bar, but to the side, so she has a view through the window—she can see the light on in room 3 at the Valley View. She decided to leave the door unlocked, which is a little risky, but the manager knows where she is if anything happens, says he'll keep an ear out.

But for the first time in almost a year, Polly can admit to herself that she has no idea what's going to happen. Which is not to say that all her careful plans have proceeded as she hoped over the past year. Quite the opposite. She did not foresee how long things would take, that's for sure. She was not prepared for Gregg's reactions— the macho posturing of last summer, the sudden dedicated daddy game he's playing now.

She did not plan for Adam, for love. No one plans for love, much less decides to love a man she cannot trust. But maybe that will be okay. She can work out the Adam problem later. First, she needs to get through the next few hours. She has left her trail of bread crumbs and all she can do is wait and see who comes through the door.

The door at which she is aiming Mr. C's gun.

The crunch of gravel, the rattle of a doorknob. A man's shape fills the door, backlit by the neon of the Valley View sign. Even in silhouette, she knows him instantly. The shoulders are broad, the posture perfect.

Adam.

Fuck, she's wrong again.

46

"Polly?"

"Hi, Adam."

"What are you doing?"

"Working a little overtime."

She puts the gun down on the bar. Adam walks over to her. It is nine o'clock, the eve before Christmas Eve, Christmas Eve's Eve. Was it really only forty-eight hours ago that he thought he would be down on one knee in this spot, asking a woman to marry him? This woman, standing vigil with a handgun she probably doesn't even know how to use.

"Whose car is that out front?"

"Mine. Or used to be. But I would think you would know that. I assumed it was in your dossier on me."

"My dossier?"

"Isn't that what private detectives call their reports? Remember I didn't go to Oberlin, only community college. But you knew that, too. You know where I went to high school and the dates of my marriages, all that stuff. It must have gotten confusing at times, trying to remember what you were supposed to know and what I hadn't told you yet."

He wants to hold her. But there is the bar between them. The bar and the gun.

"I'm sorry," he says. "There never seemed to be a right time to tell you. Once we were in love—did it really matter?"

"I don't know," she says. "I don't have the luxury of thinking about things like that. There are more pressing matters."

Adam looks at the gun on the bar. He remembers thunder, an explosion. Which came first?

"Polly, did you kill Cath?" he asks.

"What do you think?"

"I don't know what to think anymore."

"That's honest, at least."

She still hasn't answered his question.

"Where did you go, Polly? Where have you been?"

"I went to Baltimore. Gregg told me earlier this month that he's going to pursue full custody of Jani. That he might even expect child support from *me,* down the road, although he's waiving it for now. Isn't that rich? Of course, he doesn't know that I have money coming to me. That was the whole point, to get out of that marriage before Gregg found out about the settlement. I'm guessing you know about that, too? I assume that's why Irving hired you. He heard I had money, he wanted it. And not because he needed it, just to make things hard on me."

"I get why you don't want your ex to have your money, but if you're not going to raise your kid, would it be the worst thing in the world to pay support if you can?"

"You don't get anything." Her tone is weary, impatient. "Come with me."

She leads him out of the bar, across the street, to room 3. As she opens the unlocked door, he's saying, "I don't think this is the time to—" Although part of him thinks maybe it's exactly the time, maybe it's the only thing to do now. Maybe if they make love, he'll remember why he loves her.

But the bed already has someone in it—a little girl with high color in her cheeks and dark, tight curls. It's only seeing the girl, close up, that Adam registers how much she looks like her father—and how much she looks like Adam. He couldn't see that before, but he and Gregg bear a strong resemblance to each other.

"Jani," Polly says. "But, again, you know that. You've seen us together, right?"

He nods. "At the beach. Before you left her."

"I figured I was only going to be gone for a few months, tops. I didn't realize how long things would take. I thought I could get to Reno, get a divorce in six weeks. Belleville wasn't part of the plan. Neither were you. I had so many lovely plans. I sure didn't expect her father to fight me for custody. I assumed he'd be going crazy after a few months alone with her, would beg me to take her off his hands."

"You kidnapped her."

"She's mine. There's no custody order, no law broken. I took a bus to Baltimore Thursday afternoon. Spent the night in the bus station, which was interesting. On Friday, while Gregg was at work, I went to the old house, packed up a bag for her, put it in the trunk of the Toyota. I still had my keys, after all. Then all I had to do was let myself in about eleven, when the house was dark, and pick her up. She wasn't even that surprised to find me carrying her. I think she always knew I would come for her. I drove straight to the Valley View, checked in about one A.M."

"Why did you bring her to the motel instead of our place?"

"I didn't want to involve you." It's the first thing she's said that doesn't ring true. After all, she was sitting across the street, in the dark, with a gun.

"Involve me? Like you said, there's nothing illegal about a mom having her kid. He could call you in for auto theft, I guess, although if your name is on the title—"

"It is."

"Then I don't think the cops can get involved. But your ex must be going crazy."

"He shouldn't be. I left a note that I was taking her for Christmas and would bring her back next week. He had her for all other holidays this year. It's only fair."

Adam has never had a kid, but he's pretty sure that sneaking into your estranged husband's house and taking your daughter two days before Christmas is guaranteed to make a man crazy. And he's pretty sure that Polly knows that, too.

The girl stirs in her sleep. "Let's go back to the High-Ho," Polly says. "She's a light sleeper."

"Is that safe, leaving her here?"

"Safe enough. I told the desk clerk to keep an ear out for her, that I had to do some inventory for overtime pay, but that my daughter was sleeping." Her voice positively caresses those last few words.

"What about the gun?"

"I heard someone pulling up and I got a little scared."

But Mr. C keeps his gun in his desk. And you don't do inventory in the dark.

They cross the highway, head into the still-dark bar. Now they are on the stools, just as he imagined it. Where is the velvet box? Back at their apartment, still hidden in that little grove of tampons.

Maybe that's for the best. This isn't the time for a romantic proposal. Instead of a blue velvet box between them on the bar, there's a gun.

"Polly, what are you really up to?"

"I'm going to run, Adam. Possession is nine-tenths of the law. I'm going to disappear with her, make him divorce me in absentia. Once we're divorced, I'll be okay to use my money. With money, I can fight for her."

"He has rights, Polly."

"Don't talk to me about his rights. There's already a new woman, with her own kid. I know Gregg. He'll marry her. She'll favor her kid. Then they'll probably have a kid together and Gregg will favor *that* kid. Jani's a strong little girl. That's why I could risk being away from her for a few months. But she's not strong enough to rely on Gregg. No one is that strong."

"Polly, did you kill Cath?"

"Did you really think I was the kind of woman who would abandon her kid? Because if you believe that of me, you might as well blame me for Cath and anything else. If you already think I'm a monster, I'm not going to persuade you otherwise."

There's a flaw in her logic, but Adam is too overwhelmed to nail it. And, once again, she has sidestepped the question about Cath.

He goes over to the jukebox, tries to remember the selection he pressed not that long ago, when they danced here together. Why is it so hard to find this time? Ah, Double A, Double 1. He presses it. Spanky and Our Gang start to sing, but the notes can't cover the sound of crunching gravel, the bar door being slammed open hard enough so it almost bounces off the wall.

"You bitch," Gregg says from the door, running toward Polly like a linebacker. "You crazy sick bitch. Where's my daughter?"

Polly dives for the gun, bobbling it a bit, and Adam realizes his fears were well placed: she has no idea how to use a gun. It doesn't matter, because before she can do anything, Gregg is on her, dragging her to the floor, while she tries to hold on to the weapon with both hands, kicking and flailing, even biting him.

The fight between them seems almost intimate, filled with the passion and bitterness that only two former spouses can manage. She never loved Gregg, Adam is sure of that, but she definitely hates him now. It's as if Gregg is every man who ever hurt her or disappointed her. And Gregg, who has no compunction about hitting a woman, fights her on her terms, slapping and scratching and pulling hair.

Adam attempts to pull Gregg off Polly, succeeds only in loosening one of her hands from the gun. She yanks Gregg's hair with her free hand, but no matter how hard she tears at his hair and face, he won't let go, they are tangled together as if they may never part. Gregg has closed his hand over hers, Adam needs to step in to grab the gun, who has the gun, where is the gun—

Polly studies the tomatoes at the farmers' market. It's not even summer officially, which makes these lumpy heirlooms quite suspect. "Tomatoes this early?" she asks the farmer, an older man. Then she realizes he's probably about her age, late fifties. She never remembers how old she is.

"Hothouse," he admits. "But just as good."

She's dubious, still she sorts through them, looking for two that are ripe and ready. She has Nueske's bacon at home, some American cheese. She needs only to pick up a loaf of good bread from the organic baker, a head of Boston lettuce. Jani specifically requested "your famous grilled cheese sandwich" for lunch today and Polly seldom says no to either of her daughters. Besides, Jani has just graduated from law school, UB, near the top of her class. How can Polly deny her a grilled cheese sandwich? She asks for so little, this second child, has accepted with unfailing good grace that family life has to center on Joy's needs. Jani hasn't found a job yet, but only because she's choosy. No Wall Street, no white-shoe firm for passionate Jani. She plans to represent people like her sister, although through a nonprofit, not a money-churning personal injury firm. How Jani loves to sneer at the cheesy commercials for such lawyers, the refrigerator magnets they send out with the Yellow Pages.

Polly doesn't have the heart to tell her that it was just such a lawyer who made their life—their little jewel of a house, Joy's ability to live with them—possible. It's not important.

Should she get a good cheddar? Adam always said that nothing melts like American cheese. Maybe a mix of the two, though, so you get the best of both worlds—a perfect melt and more flavor.

Polly just hopes Jani won't start harping on her new favorite topic: Polly dating. While Jani seemed to appreciate having Polly's attention focused on her and Joy all these years, she is suddenly intent on pairing Polly up with someone, anyone. She talks about Match.com and eHarmony and the lonesome law professor who looks a little bit like Ichabod Crane, but is *so funny*. Polly doesn't even bother to tell Jani that she has no idea who Ichabod Crane is. She says only: "I'm happy, honey. I can't be any happier. I had a true love, once upon a time and that's more than most people can say."

Jani assumes that true love was her father, Gregg. Why wouldn't she? Stories are like dough. Did Adam tell Polly that? No, but it sounds like something he would have said. Put your hands in your stories, work them, but don't *overwork* them. Polly has always told Jani that the summer of 1995 was a "rough patch." She ran away, she took a job in a small Delaware town, took up with another man. "I never expected things to end the way they did."

Who can contradict her story? Fourteen years ago, when Jani was only eleven, her father was executed for the murder of Adam Bosk. Gregg always insisted it was an accident, that Polly was the one who grabbed the gun, fired the fatal shot. But there was the convenient fact of that restraining order she had started to pursue, via Barry Forshaw, only two weeks earlier, the belated police report on Gregg's attempt to stalk her back in July. Polly feared Gregg. He was dangerous. The record showed that.

But, Adam—Adam wasn't supposed to be there. He wasn't due until Christmas Eve. Twenty-two years ago, when almost no one had a cell phone or e-mail, there were gaps and mysteries in communication. He'd said he wouldn't be in Belleville until Sunday morning. She had no reason to doubt that.

And the fact is, Gregg probably wouldn't have been found guilty of a capital crime if he had shot Polly instead of Adam. When a husband kills his estranged wife, it's just love gone wrong. When he kills the handsome bystander who's trying to break up the fight—that's when things get serious.

A month later, Polly, looking for a tampon, found the jewelry box that Adam had hidden. When she had the ring appraised, she was tempted to sell it, but she couldn't bear to part with it. She has never worn it. She keeps it in a safe-deposit box for the day when Jani falls in love. She hopes against hope that Jani will pick a good man.

For her part, Jani insists she'll never marry. Jani says she has to be responsible for Joy's care when Polly is gone. But neither Polly nor Joy wants Jani to live that way, to see her sister as a burden that requires swearing off earthly pleasures. Joy is a joy, everybody's favorite, the heart of the family, a truly old soul. Now thirty-six, she communicates with an iPad, and it amazes Polly how funny she can be, her gift for wordplay and poetry. It makes no sense, but Joy, whose movement is limited in every sense of the word, reminds Polly of footloose Adam. She is just so very present, day to day. And it was proven long ago that Joy doesn't need Polly. It's Polly who needs Joy.

Besides, Polly can't imagine being gone. She will live forever. That's her curse. She's indestructible. She is *She,* she is the Leech Woman.

Only, unlike the Leech Woman, Polly killed another woman, and lived.

She was going to confess to Adam about Cath. Eventually. She believed he would understand, once he had all the facts. And she would have left Irving out of the whole mess if Cath's brother-in-law could have stopped sniffing around. It was just another story that Polly had to work without overworking. She knew things about Irving (true). He had hired a private detective to follow her (true). The fire in her apartment was exactly like one Ditmars had set, years ago (true). A fire she had heard them plotting. (Not so true, but she was willing to perjure herself on that one detail.) There was no injustice in locking up Irving Lowenstein for a crime from which he did profit. But it never came to that. Irving Lowenstein had a fatal heart attack a few weeks before his much-delayed trial.

Everyone is dead. Except Polly.

She had yearned to tell Adam everything, if only to test his love for her. But to do that, she would have been forced to share the worst parts about her marriage to Ditmars, the most shaming details. How she knew of his crimes, the people he had killed, but did nothing until she came to believe he would harm her and Joy. How he liked to take her curling iron and hold it against her flesh, demanding that she not scream, teaching her resilience until she learned to stay silent even when he gave her a third-degree burn on her thigh. How, with increasing frequency toward the end, he would choke her during sex.

And she liked it.

Not because being deprived of oxygen heightened her pleasure, as Ditmars claimed it would, but because, for a few moments, she allowed herself the fantasy of dying. It beckoned, her only real hope of escape.

Then she would think about Joy, remember that she was not allowed to die, not yet, and she would scratch and cough her way back to life, Ditmars laughing all the while.

She had managed to forget that, almost. The curling iron, the choking, what it was like to lie beneath a man, sex and death mingling, until it was impossible to identify which release you wanted more.

It all came back to her when Cath, enraged by a simple retort, leaped at Polly, knocking her to the ground. When Cath tried to put her hands around Polly's throat, Polly felt no confusion. She knew in that moment she wanted to live by any means necessary.

They rolled and grappled on the kitchen floor, equal matches. But at some point, Cath got on top and reached for her throat again. People say they see red when angry, but in Polly's memory, the room began to turn green, more of a greenish-gray yellow, the color of the sky before a late-summer storm. Dots floated in front of her eyes. Unlike Ditmars, Cath wasn't going to stop in time. She wasn't even pretending to be interested in Polly's pleasure.

Polly squirmed across the floor, inch by inch, until they were under her metal table. Once in the table's shadow—knowing she would have one chance, it was like holding that knife over Ditmars's chest as it rose and fell with his snores—she bucked as hard she could, driving Cath's head into the underside of the metal table again and again. Her only thought was to dislodge her, to make her let go.

But once again, Polly's aim was true, her strength superhuman. Cath's skull cracked on the third or fourth blow. She collapsed on Polly, heavier than the weight of any man she had ever known.

Polly's first instinct was to run. She could take Cath's keys, steal her car, drive to a bus station or train station, disappear. But she would have to run forever, sacrificing her dream of a life with Joy and Jani. And it was an accident, self-defense, not her fault. Only who would believe her? How many times is a woman allowed to defend herself? In Polly's experience, not even once.

She had time. Not much, but enough to calm down, make a plan. She took a shower, not worrying about the clothes she was leaving behind, the blood on the dress she'd been wearing. If her plan worked, it would take all evidence with it. If it didn't—she refused to consider that possibility. She put on her favorite dress, chose her sandals, despite knowing they were her least practical shoes. They were too pretty to lose. She fastened her rose necklace from the thrift store around her neck, only on a velvet ribbon, the better to hide the marks left by Cath's fingers. She turned on the pilot, closed the windows, left candles burning near the curtains, made sure the pink scarf on her bedside lamp was touching the bulb. If enough gas built up before the fire got going, nothing would be left standing.

And nothing was. Except Polly.

She should have gone to Reno, after all. Might have cost her Adam, but it would have saved his life. She shouldn't have wound Gregg up like a top, knowing he would come spinning right at her. She never planned to shoot him. Or did she? She wanted only to provoke him into crossing some line, proving that he was the unfit parent. It's hard to remember all her beautiful plans, which ones worked, which ones didn't. She saved herself. She saved her daughters. Everyone else was—what was that word that Adam liked to use? *Lagniappe*.

She is paying for her tomatoes when she hears a band at the far end of the parking lot start a familiar song. The man next to her—cute, probably ten years younger than she is, his graying hair gathered in a short, thick ponytail—begins to croon, almost under his breath. When he sees her head jerk up in recognition, he talk-sings the words to her: "I'd like to get to know you."

She sees the dim interior of the High-Ho, the jukebox's tubes glowing pink and green. The sun setting and rising over the cornfields, bigger than any other sun she has ever known. An iron bed, a quilt folded over the footboard. A silk dressing gown. A metal-top table. Room 3 at the Valley View. A slip of green paper, the scrawled order for poached eggs and rye toast carrying an erotic charge unlike any she had ever known, or would ever know again. The summer of 1995 feels like a century ago. Last August, she took Joy and Jani to Rehoboth, ignoring the Belleville bypass and choosing the old main road, the one that goes past the High-Ho. It's a Mexican restaurant now, advertising Margarita Mondays and Two-fer Taco Tuesdays. The Valley View? Razed, leaving only a view of the nonvalley. Mr. C died in 2002, and it's doubtful that Max and Ernest are alive, much less showing up for Margarita Mondays in a bar that's been repainted with red, white, and green stripes, the better to resemble the Mexican flag.

Everybody's dead. Except Polly.

Ponytail smiles at her, pulls out his cell phone and offers its blank text screen to Polly. *Give him your digits,* Jani would say if she were here. *What could it hurt?*

Oh, honey, if only you knew.

"I really would like to get to know you," he says with the confidence born of never being turned down.

Polly shakes her head, glad for the dark glasses that hide her eyes.

"Trust me, you wouldn't."

Polly drives home, to the perfect house with the two perfect daughters—yes, *both* perfect; anyone who doesn't see their individual perfection is dead to her—who will never know, must never know, what their mother did to provide them with their happy lives. The summer sky is a cloudless blue that seems hundreds of miles away, a towering ceiling, out of reach, higher than any bird or plane could fly.

You could even say it arches.

AUTHOR'S NOTE

Where to start? I owe a daisy chain of thanks. To the usual suspects: Carrie Feron, Vicky Bijur, Sharyn Rosenblum, their staffs, and everyone at William Morrow. To Angus Cargill, Sophie Portas, and everyone at Faber and Faber. To Lizzie Skurnick, who didn't mock my commas. To the FL's, who cheerfully mock everything about me. To the social media tribe, with a particular shout-out to Ilana Bersagel for giving me a word that led to a chapter. To Michael Ruhlman, who agreed to vet that chapter, along with all my cooking/restaurant details, for nothing more than the promise of a dinner out. To Ann Hood, who introduced me to Michael, and if I'm going to thank Ann, I might as well thank the entire faculty at Eckerd College, with a particular shout-out to my favorite Frisbee/biking pal, Henry Hays-Wehle. And to Dennis Lehane, Sterling Watson, and Les Standiford, for organizing that merry band of writers who have become a family of sorts for one week every January. To Molli Simonsen, Sara Kiehne, and Reena Rexrode. To Lauren Milne Henderson, who helped me crack this plot on a glorious July day in her garden. To Marjorie Tucker, for a key detail about insurance. To Todd Bauer, for helping me combat the sedentary writing life. To Anne Tyler and James M. Cain, for inspiring me. To David, Ethan, and Georgia Rae Simon, who tolerate those "lost" weeks when our household goes to hell as I ponder deep thoughts about insurance, grilled cheese sandwiches, and arson. To all the places where I worked on this book—St. Petersburg, Florida; New Orleans, Louisiana; New York, New York; Fenwick Island, Delaware; Havana, Cuba; Barcelona, Spain; London, England; Spannocchia, Italy; and, of course, Baltimore, Maryland. It is a deeply wonderful life.

Also by Laura Lippman

Wilde Lake

Luisa 'Lu' Brant is the newly elected state's attorney representing suburban Maryland – including Wilde Lake, the famous planned community, a utopia of racial and economic equality. Prosecuting her first murder case, Lu is determined to prove herself.

But her preparation for the trial unexpectedly dredges up painful recollections of another crime, back in the 1980s when her brother, AJ, saved his best friend at the cost of another man's life. Only eighteen at the time, AJ was cleared by a grand jury. Justice was done. Or was it?

In an acclaimed modern twist on *To Kill a Mockingbird*, Lu is plunged deeper into the past as she is forced to face a troubling reality – what if, for the first time, she doesn't want to know the truth?

'*Wilde Lake* is a knockout. You should get right on that.' Stephen King

'Excellent . . . Subtle, moving and intriguing.' *Guardian*

ff

Hush Hush

Laura Lippman returns with private detective Tess Monaghan, in an absorbing mystery that plunges the new parent into a disturbing case involving Melissa Harris Dawes, a manipulative mother whose arrival back in Baltimore reopens a notorious chapter in the city's past.

'One of Lippman's finest novels.' *Chicago Tribune*

'*Hush Hush* is cleverly told . . . Dawes and Monaghan are poles apart, but Lippman unites them to make salient points about the invidious labelling of women as good or bad mothers.' *Guardian*

'As absorbing as any story to come from the pen of former journalist Lippman whose consummate writing skills, innate sensitivity and inside knowledge of the media, the law and crime investigation procedures have made her award-winning books almost instant bestsellers.' *Lancashire Evening Post*

ff

After I'm Gone

Twenty-six years after Julie Saxony went missing, her remains are found in a secluded Baltimore forest. When Roberto 'Sandy' Sanchez, a retired detective working cold cases, picks up the investigation for extra cash, he quickly discovers a tangled web of bitterness, jealousy and greed stretching over five decades and connecting five intriguing women. At its centre is the man who, though long gone, has never been forgotten by the women who loved him: the enigmatic Felix Brewer . . .

'Lippman's finest novel, it meshes a compelling family drama with a tragic crime story.' Jeff Abbott

'A compelling mystery.' *Sunday Times*

'Thoughtful, persuasive and well worth reading.' John O'Connell, *Guardian*

ff

A *New York Times* Bestseller

And When She Was Good

Heloise: single mum, runs her own business, avoids attention, keeps her private life to herself.

But Heloise's life is also a precarious one – because her business is one that takes place in discreet hotel rooms and, for the right money, she could be the woman of your dreams.

Now her carefully constructed world is under threat – her once-oblivious accountant is asking loaded questions; her long-time protector is hinting at new, mysterious dangers; and, in the next county over, another so-called suburban madam has been found dead in her car.

With nothing quite as it seems, Heloise faces a midlife crisis which threatens the safety of both her and her son.

'Mesmerizing. Lippman writes with clarity and power.' Stephen King

'Laura Lippman is not just the author of top-notch psychological thrillers, she is one of the finest writers in America. Simple as that.' Mark Billingham